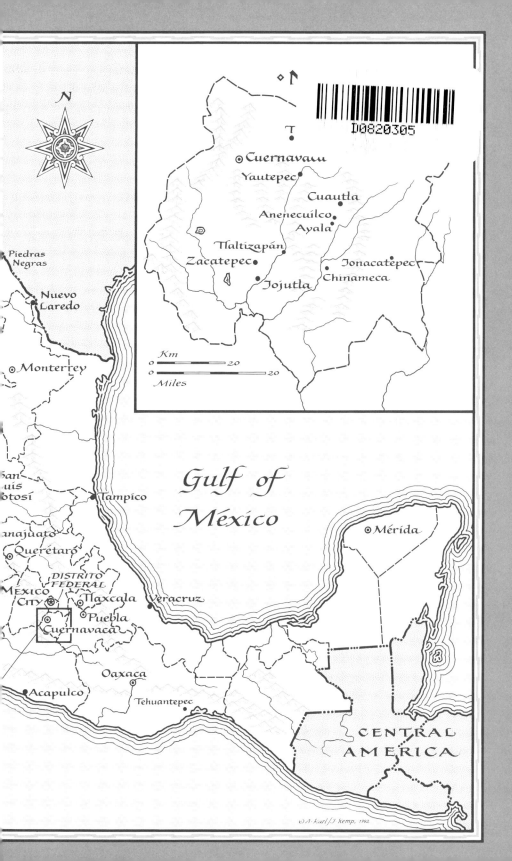

N

Cuernavaca
Yautepec
Cuautla
Anenecuilco
Ayala
Tlaltizapán
Zacatepec
Jojutla
Jonacatepec
Chinameca

Km
0   20
0   20
Miles

Piedras
Negras

Nuevo
Laredo

Monterrey

San
Luis
Potosí

Tampico

Gulf of
México

Mérida

Guanajuato

Querétaro

DISTRITO
FEDERAL
MEXICO
CITY   Tlaxcala   Veracruz
              Puebla
Cuernavaca

Oaxaca

Acapulco

Tehuantepec

CENTRAL
AMERICA

© A. Karl / J. Kemp, 1992.

for rhetoric or surprises, who don't need gestures, without even looking at one another.

What had it all been about, I asked Eufemio when the siesta ended and the men parted. "Just the things men talk about when they become serious and get down to the important matters," he answered.

And what were these things?

"Oh, coño, *you* know," Eufemio said. "Soil, and crops and horses, and guns, and a little about women."

This, I thought, was the kind of conversation we anarchists wanted more than anything else, not only for the masses but for ourselves as well — men talking to men, simply, with no complications, no abstractions. Precisely the kind of conversation we'll never have. And only seldom will the others, the Villas and Zapatas, ever have them, either. Because we're all caught in this stupid *danse macabre* of nations and governments. I know there's no way out of the dance, especially in Mexico, and we all must die violently before it's over, Villa and Emiliano and Eufemio and I. Maybe the best that men like us can have is a little moment now and then, when we can rest together and talk of the important things. Or they can talk, and I can watch them.

Enough for today. My eyes are blurring out already, and before the guard comes to take away my pen and paper I still have to write Weinberger, my lawyer, and Lilly Sarnoff, the nice, smitten little anarquista gringa in New England who sends me not only erotic words of encouragement but also toothpaste and toilet paper. (Vulnerable reader: why should I add this last little note if not to make you feel just a little sorry for me — who would surely reject your pity if you offered it?)

The clown wants to go to bed.

Notebook 2

October 29, 1922

There's time enough now for writing: no prison duties — who needs a librarian who can't see? — and no more seminars in the exercise yard, because they tell me I am too dangerous to be allowed from my cell. Next door to me is Ralph Chaplin, my Wobbly friend, and from time to time he gets word to me: that Harry Weinberger has appealed to the attorney general for my release on grounds of health, to no avail; that the Mexican government, my own beloved worst enemy, has instructed its Washington embassy to intervene on my behalf, to no avail.

In the wing opposite mine is the cell of little Librado Rivera, almost the last of the true ones, and from time to time I imagine that I can see his burr-head bobbing up and down in his window, as he jumps up to try to get a peek at me. Librado tells Chaplin that María Talavera is well and working with Enrique and Teresa in Los Angeles. She's a good, brave woman, who's stuck with me since I met her in 1905; I wish I could have loved her more.

Chaplin has smuggled a copy of *Freedom* to me, with a piece on Mexican anarchism by William Owen, who now and then wrote the English-language page of *Regeneración* for us. He says that I "was one of the most powerful writers the revolutionary movement has produced" (Why the past tense, I wonder? Has the Movement decided it's time for obituaries?); and that "Except when he allowed himself to be allured into deplorable polemics, he did not waste himself on minor details. He struck invariably the major chords, and with extraordinary firmness." That's good of Owen, I suppose; but since I've always been a polemicist, does he mean I've always been a bad one? If by "deplorable" he means "extreme" or even "bloodthirsty," then he's right, of course: I never, ever argued on the side of moderation. I never called for nonviolent resistance. I was never one of those parlor anarchists who saw the lion lying down with the lamb.

Last month in *Mother Earth* someone was admiring my "eloquent, florid style." I never thought a style could be both of those things at the same time, but I am not my best critic. Perhaps I have always been a spare writer trying to get out of a fat style. Maybe my public style is florid, and this one, this purely private one in which I write for you in the haste of days, bourgeois reader with enough time to spare for the notebooks of the moribund, is the true voice of Ricardo Flores Magón, no public man but a plump little fellow from Oaxaca snatched up and dragged through history and finally deposited, breathless and ruined, in Leavenworth, Kansas. I've lived on rhetoric; now, at the last, I want to write the way Zapata fought in the early days, con puro fusil, with just a rifle. And I'll try not to make up too many English words, even good ones like *intermeddle, candorous,* or *ephemerous,* for which my critics have often mocked me.

When I started these notebooks three days ago, I didn't mean to commit an autobiography, except incidentally. I wanted to write of what It, the Revolution, the Whole Thing, was really like. And I knew before I started that It was too complicated for any one man, even I who leapt and capered

through much of the center of It, to encompass. So I resolved to tell you of what for me, for *me*, was the heart of
It: me, and the Zapata brothers, and Amparo Urdiales — one
soon I think to die, two already dead, and one disappeared,
gone into the hills of Morelos or Guerrero, or maybe the
mistress of one of the new-rich Liberals in Mexico City, or
maybe (my fondest hope) just a schoolteacher, uncomplicated and with no aura of greatness about her, in some dusty
pueblecito in northern Oaxaca, where she could tell her pupils all the wonderful things about our people that she only
began to tell me, before our erotic little quadrille blew itself
away in a corral one July night in 1917.

I know you will want to hear that the roots of the Revolution are deep in the Mexican earth, tellurian, mystical,
and beautifully simple. Shall I write out for you "The Advice
of the Old Aztec Wise Men," which Amparo translated from
the Nahuatl and taught me? It ought to set the theme for
how we are supposed to feel about the earth:

> Now that you see with your eyes,
> take notice.
> See how it is here: there is no joy;
> there is no happiness.
>
> Here on earth is the place of many tears,
> the place where breath gives up
> and where are known so well
> depression and bitterness.
>
> An obsidian wind blows and sweeps
> over us.
> The earth is the place of painful joy,
> of joy that pricks.

> But even though it were thus
> though it were true that suffering is all,
> even if things were thus on the earth,
> must we always go with fear?
> Must we forever tremble?
> Must we live forever weeping?

Do you want to hear of how, in my pueblo, the placenta of the newly born is buried among flowers, so that the child may live? And that, so love may live, lovers bury their knotted hair?

Do you want to know that, in the town of Anenecuilco, when the ancestors of Emiliano and Eufemio Zapata were given images of Christ and the Virgin by the Dominican friars who had come to save their souls, they buried those images in the earth so these new gods would fertilize their fields of corn, nopales, and beans, and then were burned at the stake by those friars for blasphemy and desecration?

Do you want to know, in short, that behind the Revolution there is a beauty of great and terrible simplicity, a knowledge that the earth is what one must love and hold to above all, and that religions and governments and armies and haciendas and, yes, revolutions, are nothing more than foolish man-made obstructions between man and the land and his freedom to work it?

Well, I can tell you all that, and mean it too, now, innocent of rhetoric (yet still aware that I am making a pretty appeal to your emotions as I do so). It will all sound to your Anglo ears like some sort of primitive romanticism; and, God knows, enough stupidity has already been written about "mystical Mexico, garden of the gods" — some of it even by Mexicans. But my father knew what was true about us, in his simple, declarative way; and so, more subtly, did Amparo. And so did I know it, even if all these years I've tried to hide it behind the official rhetoric of the classical anarchists.

Or shall I tell you of the simple, natural Indian communism out of which the doctrines of our Revolution grew? I can do this, too. Listen:

If biographers ever come after me, they will note that I was born on September 6, 1873, in the municipality of Teotitlán del Camino, in the southern state of Oaxaca. They will probably miss that my actual birthplace was in a tiny part of that municipality, on something called a pueblo comunero, which is an Indian community whose existence goes back before the time of the Conquest, and in which everyone (except for women, naturally) possesses everything equally. The community is governed by a group of elected elders, the calpulli.

My father, Teodoro Flores, was a Zapotec (with Aztec blood, too, he claimed). He spoke only Nahuatl until he was fifteen. He was a natural warrior: he led the men of the pueblo first against the gringos in 1847, then fought with Benito Juárez in the War of Reform, and finally helped to oust Maximiliano, that man of good heart and silly mind. My first memory of my fierce little father (and I have been told this story so many times that it may not be my actual memory at all, but something history has grafted onto it) is of his taking me and my two brothers, Jesús the elder and Enrique the younger, out into a field in Teotitlán, and drilling us.

"All belongs to all," he would say. "Repeat that!"

"All belongs to all," we three little chamacos, kids, would say.

"Land, water, woods, houses, oxen, harvests. To all. Repeat that!" And we would. He never let up. If we asked him to tell us about the Sierra de Juárez that wrapped itself around

Teotitlán, he would tell us first about how people lived in Teotitlán. How those who could work did so and everyone got what he needed. How no one was allowed to take more than he needed, and if he did this it was a serious crime, punished in the more primitive sierra by silence, scorn, or expulsion. How there were no jails until the government brought them to us.

And at the end of every lecture: "What God created and what man creates, all belongs to all. Repeat that!" And we would, until he let us go to bed. I want to believe that this anecdote is true, if only because it helps account for much of the way I have behaved ever since those early days.

The trouble with simple truths is that they are so . . . simple. They are learned so easily, and are almost never forgotten — elaborated, expanded, warped, maybe; but not forgotten. "All belongs to all." Can the whole business be this easy? Mustn't we find complicated minds who will make it sound more complicated for us? Is it always necessary that the first, simple utterance must become a slogan, then a battle cry, then a manifesto, then a constitution — until it means all things, and thus means nothing at all? In any case, my heart learned my father's words, even as my mind leapt beyond them into the intricate ideological languages of men who live by words, not things.

The fact is that my father was a fanatic, maybe even a bit of a bore to us kids, and to a lot of other people, too — as I was, for most of my life, knowing it all the while.

My mother, Margarita Magón, was no mere bashful campesina, either. She was half Spanish and half Zapotecan, had fought beside my father in two of his campaigns; and she had ambitions for us. One day when I was five years old she announced that the family was moving to the Capital so we three boys could become lawyers. She had never seen one of these, but knew that they had to be able to read and write, and that the only other people who could do that were schoolteachers, who were of course women.

So in 1878 we packed up what we had, left the fields we had worked, and moved up to Mexico City, to the old ex-convento de San Antonio, near the Plaza de San Juan, to live in a pair of the damp, unheated cells the nuns had used in the days when the Church still had power. I had seen the last of the South that I was to see until I returned in November 1914, when I sneaked back into Mexico to make contact with Emiliano Zapata.

And so I became a city boy, and have remained one. As you have already learned, I can't ride, which is a dreadful thing for a Oaxaqueñan to admit. (Come to think of it, I've never met *any* Mexican, from Francisco I. Madero to the old blind man who hands out towels in the brothel in San Luis Potosí, who did not claim to be a master horseman.) I can't tell you about nature. The only tree I know the name of is the cazahuate tree, the stupid tree, because if you sit under one and it drips its sap on you, you become stupid — and I don't know what one looks like, or what its sap feels like, though I am sure I ought to. Aside from what little I can tell you of my parents, the only childhood memories of Oaxaca I carry are like memories of vivid but long-past dreams, or bright and simple illustrations in some geographical primer I might once have studied. Indeed, except for the vast and arid northern states, gray sand and black-rock sierra from horizon to horizon, this is all my mind sees when someone says "Mexico." This, and the equally magical fields and hills of Morelos I saw years later, more through the lovely brown eyes of Amparo than through my own blurred and bespectacled ones.

Once or twice at night, after the prison quiets down, I

have lain with my eyes closed and tried to re-create any scene, any scene at all, from my early childhood. All I could come up with was what must be the remains of a trip down to the city of Oaxaca for a day at the great Saturday market; and the best I can do there is a flower-covered gazebo with a military band playing within it, and crowds of people wearing the white blouses and baggy calzones of Zapotecan campesinos, with here and there a cluster of great and haughty women up for the day from Tehuantepec, terrifying to me in their majesty and their thick, long robes. These Tehuanas were the only people not chattering as we all wound time after time around the zócalo. Once one of them, who I was sure must be a queen, dressed as she was all in purple and half again as tall as anyone else, stopped us as we passed her, looked us up and down, ignored my father completely, and asked my mother what was wrong with her, that she could produce only sons. I have never understood this encounter, and have often wondered what life must be like for the men of Tehuantepec.

That's it for the Indian roots of Ricardo Flores Magón — unless you choose to get into all that earth-worship mystical business I wrote about a few minutes ago, which has never done more than distract and annoy me in my vocation as the Voice of Anarchism in Mexico. Or did, until Amparo and the Zapatas got to work on me. Corrupted me, or brought me to life (to make a distinction I perhaps should not make) so that now, at what I presume must be the end, after all the trials and jails I had come to accept as the norm for a man of my profession, I find for the first time that prison is intolerable. I, who have used up a life writing and speaking for freedom, was talking about *political* or *economic* freedom, which is nothing compared with the freedom of the body and mind to roam, to find one's land and people and to live with them.

I horrify myself: do I really believe what I have just written? If so, I am no martyr, but only a fool who has thrown a life away for some abstraction. It doesn't really matter: only you and I, hypothetical reader, shall ever know that I know. Allow me a little snigger, here.

No, stop it, Ricardo. No snigger: what your father and, later, Amparo described for you was a vision of life of such clear beauty, so empty of greed and duplicity, so austere in its privileges and its few laws, that you never ceased looking for it all those years, never really ceased believing in it. Early on, you came to believe that in ideological and economic theory — oh, hell, let's just call it *politics* — lay the paths to that simple goal. I never forgot my father's lessons, as one never forgets his lullabies and folktales, but I put them behind me in order to become what I am today: a professional obscurantist.

My father never let up on us in Mexico City. He would take us out on cold and blustery winter nights, stand us under the tenuous candlelight of a streetlamp, and point out the passersby.

"Look at the miserable state of the workers here in the city!" he would shout (he always shouted). "They work twelve hours a day or more in a dirty factory. And what do they earn? Twenty-five centavos a day! And the peón on the hacienda? He works from sunup until sundown or more. They give him twelve centavos a day! A little corn and a fistful of beans . . . and a good lashing from the overseer if he feels like it!" We all stood wide-eyed and aghast, afraid to look at the workers, afraid to look at our ferocious father, waving his arms in rage and indignation. And when we returned to the ex-convento, my mother cried and pounded her hands on the table when he told her what he had shown us.

I thought for years, and so did Jesús and Enrique, that

my mother's distress at these times was caused by the anger she shared with my father. But now the demon whispering in my ear as I write these notebooks says to me: Stop, think. In Teotitlán your father owned (though he hated to admit it) three neat little haciendas given him as a reward by Benito Juárez, with rich land around them. When we moved to the Capital he could have sold all this, or mortgaged it, or rented it; and we would not have been so poor in the city all those years that followed. But he insisted that the land belonged not to him, but to the tribe, as part of the "tierras comunales"; and he explained to anyone who raised the subject that the land belongs to the people who work it, and that he, who lived in the city now, worked no land and should therefore benefit from nothing.

The demon asks me to consider that the reason my father had so much time for egalitarian lecturing in Mexico City was that he did no work of any kind at all, and that we were all of us supported by my mother, who put in two shifts a day as a laundress at the Gran Hotel de la Ciudad de Mexico. It is my father we all remembered best, because he had so much time to spend with us. I think my mother had many reasons for crying and pounding her fists on the table that had nothing at all to do with her revolutionary fervor — which was, don't mistake me, very real.

But such heresies had no part in my life for many years; and anarchists have no time for subtleties and reservations of a nonideological nature. I shall tell you now, as fast as I can, how one becomes the public figure, the small monument-to-be called Ricardo Flores Magón. I shall in fact move with such epileptic haste, in such jerks and leaps, that you will think you are in a theater watching what you call moving pictures, or cinemas.

In 1892, when I was eighteen and Jesús twenty and we

were both students at the Escuela Nacional Preparatoria, we joined a students' protest march against the regime of Porfirio Díaz, who had just put himself up for election for the fourth time. With 15,000 others we crowded into the Great Zócalo and up against the walls of the Palacio Nacional, where we "made rude noises and shouted inflammatory slogans," in the words of a Porfirista journalist. Unnoticed at first, a squadron of mounted police rode silently out from behind the cathedral, drew up in line abreast facing the crowd, and raised their rifles simultaneously. We, of course, took this as just a threatening gesture intended to disperse us.

As we stood staring wonderingly at them, smoke puffed from those rifles and we heard the impact of bullets tearing into the crowd. For the first time in my life, I knew panic. I heard screams, felt myself crushed against the others trying to flee, tripped over those who had fallen, heard myself screaming too, in a voice I never heard before. The police shot maybe a hundred of us, and would have shot more if we had not been protected from them by mobs of angry citizens who poured into the zócalo out of nowhere, men and women, like most of Mexico's masses, spoiling for a fight against the Porfiriato. Finally the police herded a dozen or so of us, including me and Jesús, inside the gates of the Palacio, piled us into waiting horse-drawn vans, and hauled us six blocks west to Belén Prison, where we spent the next three months on a charge of sedition.

If you are going to make a career of prisons, as I was, then Belén is the place to start. For one thing, in the days of the Porfiriato, to have been in Belén carried a certain cachet: it was *the* place for unlucky journalists, pamphleteers, dissidents. It was where you went to become known among those who counted in the growing movement against Díaz. (And also, unfortunately, it was where you became known to the Porfiristas, where they started a file on you that would grow larger every day of your life.) One learned to joke about how many times he'd been tossed into Belén.

The trouble was that actually being in the place was no joke. Belén was vile and pestilential. We sat on wooden benches in our dark, unventilated cells, trying to keep our feet off the dirt floors, which were covered with inches of mud and excrement, joking to keep our spirits up as we watched and listened and felt for rats, scorpions, spiders, and lice. The cells were large, big enough to hold fourteen prisoners in each, with walls twelve feet high. Near the ceiling was a small barred window. Above our heads hung monstrous festoons of spiderwebs, swaying in the slight breeze that came from the window. During the days we could talk, laugh, even read when enough sunlight came through the window. These were the times we could be tough, and brag about what a joke Belén was to us. But I shudder as I sit here now, so many years later, and remember the nights when I lay on my damp, thin petate, waiting with terror for the soft *plop!* that meant another spider had fallen from its web onto the soggy blanket I'd pulled over my head.

I know American prisons well, and I have never seen anything to compare with the awfulness of Belén or its sister, San Juan de Ulúa in the Veracruz harbor. I could stand neither now, so spoiled as I am by these "penal universities" (as I once unwisely described them) they try to frighten us Mexicans with in the United States. But in 1892 Jesús and I were anxious to display what I would now describe as political machismo; so after our five months in Belén we swaggered out, went home for a bath and change of clothes, and were back on the streets looking for trouble the same evening. (When I told the Zapatas about Belén, Eufemio only laughed, and I knew that he probably would have thrived in the place; but Emiliano sat silently for a minute, then nodded slowly and said very flatly, "I would have died." And I believe he would have.)

For a few weeks Jesús and I strutted around the city, dos cojudos a la vela, two studs under full sail, as we say, looking for ways in which we personally could bring down Don Porfirio Díaz. We were innocent of revolutionary theory, knew little of history, and were, in short, primitives, a pair of earnest rubes who had learned to read and write. Of the present state of Mexico we knew, from the teachings of our father and the jovial cynics we had met in Belén, that Porfirio Díaz had, in his greedy and vain old age, sold the country to whichever foreigners would pay the most for it; that he had reduced the mass of Mexicans into peonage and even de facto slavery; that all elections were rigged and all officials corrupt; that there was no such thing as a free press; that the police and the army were either impressed campesinos or lazy battalions of mercenary murderers; that the Church, while pretending to divest itself of worldly power, was as venal and autocratic as ever — in short, that the condition of the nation was desperate, and that nothing could be done for it until Porfirio Díaz and his regime were brought down.

What else did we need to know? We had gone out on the broad, frenchified Paseo de la Reforma, where the poor in general and Indians in particular were never allowed on weekends, and seen the great Don Porfirio (himself almost pure Mixtec Indian) riding by in his Paris-made coach, solemn and splendid in top hat and black frock coat ablaze with medals from every nation, seated beside his child bride who was, we heard, trying to teach him to eat with a knife and fork. What else did we need to know about the state of our government?

I shan't give you statistics on what life in Mexico City was like, except for one: each decade the Capital killed off the equivalent of one-third of its inhabitants, whether through disease, infant mortality, famine, or political homicide. I shall, however, call up for you my memory of how most of the poor, all the campesinos and what I would learn to call the lumpenproletariat, slept. Because they were not allowed to spend the night on the street or in the parks, one-sixth of the population of the city was herded each evening into mesones, or flophouses, where they bedded down side by side, head to toe, men, women, and children, most of them strangers to one another, on sour clumps of straw.

First with our father, and then the three of us boys alone, we used to walk past these mesones in the mornings on our way to Chapultepec Park, almost the only place in the city where we could walk on grass, look up at trees. We would stand in the doorways (there were no windows to peek into) and watch as the keeper of the mesón walked through his rooms, waking his lodgers. Without fail, every morning he would find four or five dying, usually of typhus, and at least a couple of corpses, already cold and stiff, in each tiny room. Belén smelled better than these mesones. And the barrio of the mesones began only four blocks behind the Paseo de la Reforma where Don Porfirio rode each day, and where visitors from foreign countries delighted him by comparing Mexico City favorably with Paris and London.

We were grown men by 1893 (or almost: Enrique was still sixteen, but by country standards that was as good as grown). We did not much look like Indians any longer, dressed as we were like good bourgeois, in dark jackets, fedoras, and loosely gathered cravats. We had begun to take on a certain dignified portliness (definitely *not* porcine: just a little . . . *stout*); we drank cognac and smoked cigars; we even knew something of women. Well, not much, actually: there were a few progressive and scrawny bluestockings in our classes at the Escuela Nacional de Jurisprudencia, from which we were shortly to be graduated; but, I ought to be ashamed to say, we did not take them seriously. The ones we liked (all right, lusted after with all our hearts) were the bonny little rich girls who went to the convent school a block down from the Escuela.

Jesús and I walked past the entrance to the school at least four times a day if we could, because its courtyard and entryway were always thronged with these marvelous little biscuits of girls, in their blue pleated skirts and starched white blouses, hiding their little cigarettes and pretending not to notice us and talking faster than any humans we had ever known. Of course there was no trying to understand what they were saying, sounding as they did like a flock of canaries perched hysterically along a naked branch. They seemed never to have to go inside to class, so that we began referring to their school as Our Lady of Perpetual Recess.

There was, of course, no way in the world to get to know them, short of leaping the railings of the courtyard and running amok through them, tearing off their blouses and pulling those pleated skirts over their heads and roaring our eternal love into their blushing ears. (Eufemio Zapata asked me in all earnestness why we had not done this.) We had our own tiny flat, then; and Jesús and I spent hours fantasizing about what we would do to how many of these devout little tortas if we could entice them up the five flights of stairs to that flat. So, as I say, we knew something of women, or at least of lust and fantasy, by then. All around, we lacked only a little in the way of sophistication.

We were not so bashful about our vocation: we knew from our time in Belén that the best way to aid the coming Revolution would be to become not lawyers (for lawyers could work only for the regime) but journalists. In February 1893, we joined the staff of the opposition newspaper, *El Demó-crata*, with Jesús and I as editors and Enrique as handyman. I have been a journalist ever since.

I don't remember what we wrote, but someone must have read it: three months after we took over, the offices of *El Demócrata* (which is to say, our flat) were surrounded by the police, everyone inside was arrested (except for clever Ricardo, who escaped out a first-floor window), and *El Demócrata* ceased to exist. I hid out with friends for another three months, during which time our father died, and I could not go to his funeral. Our mother told me later that he had died proud of his sons, and that she shared his pride. They were glad we were turning out so well.

I must stop for today. I'll try another letter to "Ellen White," as Lilly Sarnoff for some reason wants to be known. The American anarchists are a little romantic, I think. I write my most flowery prose for her (shall I call it my "Floresiana"?), and she seems to love it — almost as much as she loves it when I write in my martyr voice.

I'll add only one final thought before I stop. Somewhere in the process of growing up and becoming educated, I lost my way — the way my father had set me upon. At some point between those visits to the barrio of the mesones and joining the staff of *El Demócrata*, something went wrong: I stopped thinking like a campesino and began assuming the role of "activist" — which is to say, bourgeois poseur. To put it another way, I contracted the disease of consciousness. I became the sort of man romantic young American girls would be thrilled to correspond with.

October 30, 1922

I am supposed to have spent the next five years in revolutionary reading. I regret to say that I did nothing of the kind. I continued in law school, and was admitted to the bar in 1895, before graduating. My days were not filled with *pro bono* work for the poor, as I should like to claim. I did the occasional will, wrote the occasional threatening letter to a landlord, but worked only enough to pay my rent and lead Mexico City's version of *la vie de bohéme*. What I did to occupy my days was to sit in cafés along the Alameda, drinking coffee and smoking and disputing with other out-of-work journalists, professional students, angry little clerks and druggists, desperate middle-aged maestros who made a poor living teaching the children of the gente decente to speak English and French — in short, bourgeois, all of us. What was I, the son of a man who thought of himself as an authentic Aztec, a man with a serious mission, doing among such sad debris?

Hiding from my destiny of a harsh life and ultimate martyrdom, I might try to say. No? Well, *waiting* for my destiny, then. Waiting for the moment when fate should tap me on the shoulder and take me into history? I suppose you might say that. You might even compare me with St. Francis, who had his libertine years before God set him to licking lepers' sores. Or you might just say I was a fat Mexican señorito with time on his hands, who liked to hang about in cafés and drink and smoke cigars because it beat working.

It occurs to me now that, while I was so busy learning to be a petty bourgeois so that I could become a revolutionary, my haunches stuck into the rattan chairs of the cafés, the young Zapata boys were romping around down in Morelos, riding in charreadas, showing off in makeshift corridas, spending maybe a night here and there in some local calabozo, full of tequila and guilty of nothing more than shooting out a window or two. That was *their* preparation for careers as revolutionaries. Why do I persist in thinking that their way was superior to mine? My way was surely harder, demanding thought, study, prison, an almost priestly self-abnegation. I never went to a dance or got stumbling drunk. By the age of forty I had made love to two women (and one of them, Emma Goldman, only once, and that only, as she often reminded me, for three minutes). I was never the libertine my enemies claimed I was — though I would have liked to be, and dreamed always of nights of debauchery and drunkenness, as I suppose priests must do. Surely my way was harder than that of the Zapatas. Why can't I believe that?

Because I am no fool, and know that my suffering, though physically real enough, was ultimately false because it was self-imposed. And because I was suffering for no one but myself. Any silly little priest mortifies his flesh for something greater than himself (that thing he calls God); but I was mortifying myself for — myself. Or because of some cause I only dimly understood.

I never got my law degree. My biographers will say that I was tossed out of school for my political activities; but I was dropped from school for nonpayment of tuition and failure to show up for the final exams. Jesús, for some reason, had done better: he was practicing law, had married a good, hardworking shopgirl, and still managed to remain politically active. He never spoke a disapproving word to me; nor did he to Enrique, who by now had become my shadow: it was clear that, whatever I was to become, Enrique was to become another of the same. Except handsomer, by far, as all agreed. In Mexico each man has his nickname, and everyone knows it and uses it — but almost never to the face of the man it belongs to, who must pretend not to know what everyone calls him behind his back. Well, I was "Ranón," the Big Frog — and that says all you need to know, or at any rate all I'm going to tell you, about my appearance. Let's just leave it that Enrique was always the handsomer of us two.

Finally, with the turn of the new century, fate grabbed us all up and began to shake us hard, and I became almost overnight the man I was to become. Jesús and his partner, Andrés Horcasitas, began a review called, that's right, *Regeneración*, which was supposed to report irregularities in legal proceedings and other matters of interest to lawyers. Because of course the whole judicial system was totally dominated by the Díaz government, the new review quickly became a political organ; and, since I was not only an out-of-work journalist but the most political person they knew, Jesús and his partner made me the editor. I took over in November 1900, master of a third-floor flat containing a small hand-press, two typewriters, a carton of cheap paper, and a two-liter bottle of ink. On December 31 I announced at the top of my first editorial column that *Regeneración* was henceforth to become "an independent journal of combat," which would be "opposed to centralism and autocracy."

At this stage, I was like every other dissident: all I had in mind was the overthrow of the Porfiriato and restitution of the old Juarista constitution which Díaz had been trampling on for so many years. My first editorials were very simple: all I did was compile a list of the promises Díaz had made at the beginning of every term, and alongside it an answering list of what had become of those promises. Jesús applauded me, as did the steadily growing anti-Porfirista community. A better grade of dissident sat with me in the cafés. From time to time I would be invited by older, more prosperous editors to a meal at the solid, serious Restaurant Danubio on Calle Uruguay, just a few blocks south of the zócalo where our big protest had taken place.

Things might have gone on in this smoothly progressive and enlightened way, with Díaz and his people annoyed but not too outraged at what I was printing about them. I had a good, solid reputation as a liberal (an ugly, weak word I should have repudiated sooner than I did), and might have ridden quickly to the forefront of Mexico's faintly daring dissidents. But I became the real thing instead: a radical of the purest sort, an anarchist, one who repudiated the very concept of government.

I would like to believe that my conversion to anarchism was in some vital way connected to the radically simple Indian communism of my father, whose words had stuck in my mind through all my years of education, resisting all the European revolutionary ideologies crossing the Atlantic at this time. For my father, there was no ultimate authority but the calpulli, the council of elders. The people's rights to their land were written in Nahuatl, in their fueros, old manuscripts carefully hidden and preserved by a sabio, the town's wise man. A campesino belonged to one barrio or another of his pueblo; and it was understood that he would donate some of his work to the barrio, and some to its crops.

My father's thoughts extended beyond his pueblo, of

course: he knew he was a citizen of Oaxaca, and of Mexico, and that he might be called upon to fight the enemies of this Mexico. For him, though, the real enemies were not so much the yanquis or the franceses, but all the hacendados and politicos and oficiales: men who took his land and then tried to tax him for the land they had stolen — which they then tried to make him farm as if it were still his own. Against foreigners he fought not because he was angry, but because fighting is what a man is called upon to do every now and then. But against the owners and bureaucrats he would fight with wild, implacable ferocity.

You must understand, my reader, that in Spanish *pueblo* means not only "village," but the people of the village as well. My father's loyalty went to his town, its people, and its fields. The first two of these he loved; the third he venerated with religious fervor. Everyone in the pueblo shared everything with every other citizen of the pueblo. To behave otherwise brought shame and ostracism.

Although I would love at this hour to say that my turning to anarchism was solely the result of my father's teachings, I am afraid that around the turn of the century the theories of Bakunin and Kropotkin were the most daring and faddish of the ideologies available to young Mexicans anxious to make a name for themselves as thinkers. And so I, intellectual dandy that I was becoming, abandoned my father's crudely innocent anarchism, and took up the more glamorous European Anarchism, with a capital A.

Ironically, this change in ideology started to take place when I was most my father's disciple. In February 1901 there was a Congress of Mexico's Liberal Clubs, held in the Teatro de la Paz in San Luis Potosí. As the editor of *Regeneración*, I was of course invited. There must have been a thousand delegates there, from all over Mexico, with their only avowed purpose to speak out against undue influence of the Church in the affairs of government. But when my turn to speak came, and I was led to the center of the big stage of the Teatro de la Paz and saw all those thousand ardent young faces looking up at me, I never thought of the Church.

I spoke to them in my father's voice, of the workers and how they lived. I said all the things my father had said. I hollered at them, "All belongs to all. Repeat that!" And they repeated it. I had them on their feet, hollering back at me. I must have harangued them for half an hour, and I ended finally by leaning out over them and hoarsely whispering to them, but whispering so my voice would carry across all the faces, "Don't talk to *me* about the Díaz government: They're all a den of thieves!" Una madriguera de bandidos. Tumult.

I spoke my father's words that day, but more important to my anarchistic education was my encounter that night with the leaders of the Congress, two young men, Librado Rivera (yes, the same Librado who lives opposite me today in Leavenworth Prison) and Juan Sarabia, whose loyalty was to be something less than Librado's. They were history teachers at the Escuela Normal in San Luis Potosí, and their rooms (where they asked me to stay) were full of the writings of men whose names meant nothing to me: Bakunin, Kropotkin, Grave, Malatesta; in English or French translations which I could scarcely read.

I suspect that my new friends were a little horrified that this big-city politico should know nothing of radical ideology; but they were polite. (They *always* were polite, even after one of them became my enemy. *All* my friends seem to be my friends for life, even after they have turned against me and reviled me in the press — even Antonio Villarreal, who was to write in 1911 that I was a "blackmailer, swindler, coward, and a drunken pervert and scoundrel who shared his mistresses with all men of bad taste." Antonio, in fact, sent me a copy of the journal in which he had written this, along with a warm note of apology, acknowledging that not one word of what he had written was true — as indeed it was not. Ah, how fortunate to have had such friends.)

Librado and Juan were not only polite, they were generous: they loaned me all their books to take back to the Capital at the end of the Congress. At which time I was a hero, especially in my own mind.

I left San Luis Potosí the next morning with a satchelful of heretical books, a reputation that would carry me quickly into the terrible convolutions of victory and failure that involve the true revolutionary, and a small following of men and women it would not be imprecise to call disciples. I walked to the train surrounded by an honor guard of students and delegates, because my hosts were afraid the dictator's agents would try to arrest or kidnap me.

Two weeks later the police came to the offices of *Regeneración*, arrested me and poor innocent Jesús, and flung us into Belén for a year, for "insulting the president." This was the worst mistake the Porfiristas could have made: it gave me time to read and absorb all those books I had brought back with me from San Luis Potosí, to confirm myself in my new role, and to grow in my hatred of *all* authority, not just Don Porfirio's. By the end of that year I knew who I was, and who I must become. I was on the track that would lead me, with an inexorability that still amazes me, to sit here now in Kansas, dying in prison at forty-nine, writing coy and flirtatious letters to a dilettante lady anarchist in New York, and a few scrawled notebooks to you, hypothetical reader I grow tired of insulting. In fact, I may come to count you among my many friends.

Notebook 3

November 3, 1922

But perhaps not. For one thing, you probably suppose I am writing my notebooks in English because I intend for you to be my audience. Why would I want this? I've spent all of my last nineteen years in your country, the majority of that time in your jails and prisons. Most of my troubles, and most of my poor Mexico's troubles, have come from you. Why do I write for a people who despise me, and whom I must despise?

Because my political education has been in English. Because most of the books I have read since I was twenty-two have been in English. Because poor old Bakunin and Kropotkin had to speak English when they came to your country, and were laughed at because they did it so badly. Because great men and women like Alexander Berkman and Emma Goldman came to America and fought so hard to help your victims of your own ignorance and venality — and did so in the clumsy English of immigrants, again to be laughed at. And reviled, and jailed, and finally expelled from what I once truly thought of as the land of the free and the home of the brave. ("Vámonos," I said to Enrique in 1903, "a la patria de los libres y la tierra de los bravos.")

And I write in English because, God damn you, I have

spent so long in the United States of America that English, not Spanish, is the language at the top of my head. I use your language not because I want you as my reader, nor because I have an ironic desire to write in the language of my jailers and killers-to-be, nor for any other reason you may imagine, but because I must. Your language owns my mind, the way your money owns my Mexico.

This morning, clean from my escorted trip to the shower room, still trembling just a little from the shame of having to bathe before the incurious eyes of my guard, and dressed in a fresh woolen jacket and trousers, slippers on my dead-white, numb diabetic's feet, I intend to calm down, cease berating you (I have no time to waste on anger, and there is always my reputation as a gentle, saintly man to consider), and jump you back again to that strange time in the late fall of 1914, when the Revolution still seemed possible to all, even a little bit to me. Let me efface myself for a while, so that you may look on people more palpably heroic than I. I shall tell you what happened to us in the days following the famous meeting of the two rebel generals; and I shall try to introduce my new Zapatista allies to you, both as I saw them then and as I recall them now, from prison.

After the big parade of the massed troops of the Army of the North and the Liberator Army of the South, after Pancho Villa and Emiliano Zapata had lain about in Xochimilco making their mutual assurances and promises to each other, Pancho gathered up his Dorados, his gilded thugs, and rode back to his railroad car in the suburb of Tacuba, ready to raise hell, though not necessarily quite yet with the forces of Venustiano Carranza that were moving against him in the north and northwest. Pancho had not so far made his presence felt in Mexico City, but in the weeks that followed

Xochimilco he made everyone in the Capital know who he was and what he proposed to do there.

He was delayed in this for almost a month by the necessity of rushing off to recapture Guadalajara. (One of the curious characteristics of this war was that cities never stayed captured: one always had to retake them again every couple of months.) But within a week after his return, Villa moved himself and his entourage into the center of the Capital, into a grand estate on Calle Liverpool, where, ignoring the fact that Eulalio Gutiérrez had been chosen by the Convention of Aguascalientes as temporary President, and was therefore still at least nominally in command of the country, he began to rule like the most capricious of feudal barons.

Unless Pancho said so, no train entered or left the city; without his permission, no telegram went out — and every one that came in was read to him. He went every night to the Teatro Colón, to holler propositions at the leading lady, María Conesa, as she strutted her way through *The Lady of the Kisses*. He went to the corrida every Sunday and screamed death threats at matador and bull alike. He tried to seduce the pretty cashier at the Hotel Palacio; and when the Frenchwoman who owned the hotel hid the girl (to save her, presumably, from yet another of Villa's marriages), Pancho grabbed the Frenchwoman and locked her up in one of her own suites, promising to come back that night to rape her. The French government made formal protest at this, which prompted Pancho to lock the doors of their embassy for a week, letting no one in or out. ("How can a sober man have so much fun?" Eufemio Zapata asked me, his voice full of admiration.)

When all these capers began to pall on Pancho, the killings began. He sent his executioner, Rodolfo Fierro, to get rid of poor little Paulino Martínez, as Emiliano Zapata had promised Pancho he could do. In return Emiliano had Guillermo García Aragón shot, as Pancho had promised Emiliano he could do. Soon after this a group of Villista generals dined well at the San Angel Inn, and refused to pay their bill. A young Conventionist colonel named Berlanga very conspicuously paid it for them. Villa sent Fierro after Berlanga, who surrendered graciously, lit a cigar, and followed Fierro to the San Cosme barracks. Berlanga stood with his back to the wall, smoking his cigar so calmly and steadily that its ash did not fall. Finally, when it was clear to all that Berlanga was far cooler than Fierro, the young gallant tossed the cigar aside, spread his arms, and told Fierro to be a man and kill him well. Villa laughed when he heard this tale, and said that if he'd been there, he would have shot Fierro and promoted Berlanga. As it was, no one ever got to shoot Fierro: he died a few months later up near Casas Grandes when he and his horse sank into a bed of quicksand, going under fast because of all the stolen gold in his saddlebags. I would have wished a less pleasant death for him.

Then Juan Banderas, one of Emiliano's most brutal officers, shot a fellow general in an argument over an auto that neither knew how to drive. The killings spread, and with them, kidnappings. After two weeks of Villa's Mexico City vacation, more than 150 men had died or disappeared. He was clearly in danger of wearing out his welcome, and President Gutiérrez sent around a circular asking the various generals to control themselves and their men.

Villa called a press conference for foreign correspondents and issued a statement which read: "My only mission is to restore order in Mexico without resorting to personal vengeance. In this task I will not function as a coarse soldier but as a respectful servant of the government created by the

Aguascalientes Convention. I will scrupulously respect property, both national and foreign, and I will not intervene in
anything except in the interest of order and justice." The
next day he ordered Gutiérrez's new Secretary of Education,
that good man José Vasconcelos, to leave town or be executed. Gutiérrez complained, and Villa responded by taking
two thousand of his cavalrymen to surround the Braniff
mansion where Gutiérrez lived. He burst into Gutiérrez's office, Colt revolver in hand, his face purple with rage, his
eyes two amber beads, and began screaming at the president. "You're betraying me," he said. "What the fuck are
you trying to do?"

"I'll tell you, General," said Gutiérrez calmly, tossing back
a cognac. "I'm getting out of town."

"The fuck you are, you little pendejo. I won't let your
fucking train out of the city."

"In that case, I'll take a burro, General," said Gutiérrez,
pouring himself another cognac.

Villa was perhaps not one's idea of a gentleman, but he
never failed to show his respect for courage, especially when
it came from someone polite. I think it genuinely puzzled
him that it was possible to be calmly brave. He nodded, sa-
luted Gutiérrez, and withdrew himself and his troops. Felipe
Angeles, Villa's artillery commander and Emiliano's old ad-
versary in the early days of fighting against Porfirio Díaz,
told me of this encounter. Since Angeles was an honorable
man, and one of the few Villistas I would judge to be human,
I believe him.

Gutiérrez must have thought he had used up either his
courage or his luck or both, because as soon as Villa left
he wired his brother in Saltillo and Antonio Villarreal in
Monterrey, asking for help in controlling the Centaur of
the North. "Tell him to get up north where he belongs,"

Gutiérrez pleaded, "and get into a big battle, if possible a fatal one."

As for himself, Gutiérrez intended to clear out of the city immediately, and maybe out of the country. And in the second week in January, the poor man issued a decree removing both Villa and Zapata from their commands and appealing to the Mexican people to repudiate all their other revolutionary leaders and continue allowing him to govern Mexico — from San Luis Potosí, to which he promptly removed himself, along with his ministers and 10,453,473 pesos from the National Treasury. (I don't know why he needed to sack the Treasury: he had already made himself a millionaire in the few short months he had served as provisional president.) He also wrote a letter of encouragement to Álvaro Obregón, who was marching up toward Puebla from Veracruz, telling him that he was withholding supplies from the Zapatistas, who were hoping to defend Puebla against Obregón's Carrancista forces, and urging him on to take the Capital.

Meanwhile Villa had departed from Mexico City himself, leaving the fighting in the north to Felipe Angeles while he slipped up to El Paso to celebrate life with his gringo army friends. We, his allies who had stayed in the south, never received any of the supplies he had promised Zapata in Xochimilco; nor did we ever see him again. So much for the grand union of the Revolutionary Armies of the North and South: another moment when we might have prevailed, but failed to do so. Without Villa hurling his troops against the Carrancistas in the big states above us, it was only a matter of time until Obregón should take the Capital from us, and look south toward Morelos, where we would have to fight him alone, without allies.

You will have noticed, careful reader, that I have begun using words like *we* and *us* when I speak of the Zapatistas.

The reason for this is not only that I had remained, out of simple idleness, in Xochimilco with Emiliano and his friends while Villa played his games in the center of the city during this Christmas season. There was ample reason to stay out of the center, God knows, aside from Villa's presence: for one thing, food was scarcer even than it normally was; for another, the season was a particularly cold one, and charcoal was as scarce as food. And if deprivation of one kind or another didn't get you, you stood a good chance of being run down in the streets by drunken generals learning to drive stolen automobiles. Finally, if *they* didn't get you, the typhoid epidemic might. It was a good time to stay down in Xochimilco, among the floating gardens and fresh breezes from the two great volcanoes to the east. But these, as you can guess, were none of the reasons I chose to stay away from what was, after all, my hometown.

I stayed, of course, because I had business with no one but Emiliano Zapata. And I stayed because I could scarcely take my eyes off Amparo Urdiales.

Today I find myself considering the possibility that I am at my most Mexican in believing that history must be seen as a series of *tableaux vivantes* (cuadros vivos, we'd call them): everyone arranged, singly and in groups, in attitudes appropriate to our notions of them — the proud sneering, the humble simpering, the sensuous leering, and so on. Perhaps a better term for what I have in mind would be *tableaux hubristiques* (cuadros orgullosos, maybe?), in which we see all the heroes and their hangers-on as they were just before they fell, betrayed or betraying. Later on I shall have to show them lying dead, or propped up, swollen and bloody, in their makeshift coffins, stared at by the morbidly pious who cluster around them. But for now I want to give them to you as they were that Christmas of 1914 in Xochimilco, at what they did not know was the apex of their power — at the moment just before that power began to evaporate (or when it had already begun to evaporate, but only I had noticed).

But I find I cannot do this unless I imagine them all as though they were being photographed by the wizard Agustín Casasola, that faceless little man who was everywhere in those years, popping up with his clumsy wooden camera in the midst of battles, conferences, boudoirs (almost), and executions, making the Revolution stop and pose for him. Casasola, or one of his brothers (he had several, all of them photographers) must have taken dozens of photographs of Pancho Villa and Emiliano, the Bully and the Dandy, both of whom would happily stop whatever they were doing if he asked them to hold still for one of his thirty-second exposures; but he had just as easy a time with enraged warriors, or men about to be shot or hanged, or drunken generals on the point of disappearing up a flight of stairs with a convoy of prostitutes. Let me show you my dramatis personae, then, as it were through the lens of Casasola, in grainy black and white.

The prints will be, let's say, eight-by-ten enlargements of slightly dusty negatives. The paper is cheap, curling already at the edges. The contrast is high: the blacks are too black, the whites too bleached. The features are sharp enough, but there is little subtlety or shadow. Especially if Casasola is firing his flash powder at them, his subjects look a little startled, dazed. Even those who want their pictures taken (and by no means all do) trust neither Casasola nor his mahogany box on its spindly tripod. Perhaps they will try to hide how they truly feel (who does not, always?), by assuming a mask of indifference, or of sanctity, or of ferocity. You will have to trust me, poor Ricardo Flores Magón, who has spent his life doing everything but learning about people, to reveal their authentic selves to you.

Right, then, let's frame General Emiliano Zapata Salazar as he stands, raised by a small mound of bare earth above the others, rolling a cigarette but looking at Casasola's lens with his large black, almost tearful eyes, which are barely visible in the shadow of his wide black sombrero. His cavalryman's mustache is thick and carefully groomed. His skin is dark, his full mouth slightly downturned, his expression almost lugubrious. He is a splendid example of what we call "indio triste": his air of melancholy has nothing to do with feeling sad, but is merely the way his culture has taught him to compose his face when he wishes to convey nothing at all.

General Zapata (or 'Miliano, as everyone but me calls him) would seem of only average height to gringo eyes, but he is tall enough when he stands among the Tlahuican Indians and mestizos who are his people: perhaps 5'8" or 5'9" and 130 pounds, on a taut, wiry frame. From his clothes — another charro outfit, with short jacket, loose cotton tie, tight riding breeches and high-heeled black boots — and his carefully relaxed but somehow soldierly posture (casually haughty, maybe even a little arrogant?), you might think "caballero" or "hidalgo." But you'd be wrong. 'Miliano is no poseur. He looks like what he is: a confident, propertied peasant, a leader of peasants, who are pleased that their chief should dress in a manner appropriate to a caudillo, a man of substance and authority. If he is a dandy, he is *their* idea of a dandy, and they are well pleased with him. "Nuestro Plateado," they call him: Our Silver One, perhaps not realizing that they are inserting their chief into the old legends of the silvery bandits, los Plateados, who roamed the sierras in the last century, who took from the rich and gave to the poor, flinging romantic corridos and ballads at fainting señoritas as they galloped by on the way to their picturesque hideouts in mountain caves. Zapata, of course, did nothing to pop this harmless mythic bubble.

If he sees me studying him, standing as I am behind Casasola as he hunches over his camera with its canvas hood thrown over his head, 'Miliano will study me back, briefly. Then he will say, quietly and in a voice that is, surprisingly, a little high, even almost shrill, "Well, Don Ricardo, have you come to teach me how to throw bombs today, or shall we just stand here together in the warm sunlight?" (The "Don" is friendly mockery: he knows I am no more gentleman than he; but he recognizes that I, too, have my little affectations — and know that he has his.) Since I have nothing to contribute at the moment but my scrutiny, he will drop his eyes from me and let me go, courteously but definitely; and continue to stand on his mound, moving nothing but the hands that form his cigarette. His Winchester carbine, its butt in the sand, rests as always against his leg.

At this moment in the late fall of 1914, as he poses for Casasola, 'Miliano is the master of an area three hundred miles long and two hundred miles wide: all of the state of Morelos, and sizable pieces of Guerrero, Puebla, and Oaxaca as well — the richest land in Mexico. He commands an army of twenty thousand men and women, and governs a people who (I use the word in its precise, religious sense) adore him.

Twelve feet away, behind and a bit to one side, stands Amparo. She too looks at me, though I sense that most of her attention is focused on 'Miliano. She is not at all what you, gringo, would call "Indian," especially if you have seen the tough little soldaderas who run with the army, barefoot and braided, bandoliers and pistol belts wrapped around their cotton skirts and dusty petticoats. Nor is Amparo like the pallid Hiawatha that the more literary of you have in mind — a slightly tawny version of the delicate Anglo princess you all secretly long for, while settling for your loud, strident, *competent* American women.

Amparo (*my* Amparo) is as tall as 'Miliano, with broad, straight shoulders. Her breasts and buttocks are too small for your taste. Her neck is a little too strong. It is not at all swanlike. Her legs are far too long for her compact torso. Her hands and feet are too large, her ankles a little thicker than they might be. (I blush at having to describe her to you, share her with you.) Her nose is too long and sharp for you, a true hawk's nose. Her hair is black and thick and straight, and falls over her shoulders and down to her small breasts. Her eyes are as large and dark as 'Miliano's, but they are not, like his, soft and liquid. They are, in fact, hawk's eyes, raptor's eyes, eyes to strike terror into the heart of any gringo. As she stands twelve feet from 'Miliano (a distance she has chosen precisely and for no reason anyone else could determine), she is, to me, quite the most perfect of her kind.

This is as much of Amparo as I can bear to show you just now. You do not deserve yet to hear her voice, or watch her as she moves about the encampment in Xochimilco, seeing everything but never taking much of her attention away from the figure of 'Miliano as he stands almost motionless among his people. You may perhaps learn more later.

Casasola twists a knob on his tripod and shifts his camera to the left, to focus now on a group of four clumsy men standing close together, looking like any campesino's idea of "intellectuals afield." This is exactly what they are, and I do not mean to treat them slightingly, simply because they look out of place and awkward. One of them is already a traitor, soon to be found out; another, innocent, would be executed for treason four years hence; and the third and fourth would survive (at least they would survive *me*) to try to keep intact the ideals of the Revolution long after 'Miliano and Villa and Carranza and most of the others were gone.

Bakunin made no secret of his contempt for the intelligentsia, and marked them all for extermination after they had been exploited by true revolutionaries; but, being what passes here for an intellectual myself, I have much compassion, even love, for three of these men. The eldest and simplest is the doomed one, the schoolteacher from Ayala called Otilio Montaño. In this group, on this day, he appears ridiculous, pobrecito. He is doing his best to look like a warrior, in his white pajamas and crossed bandoliers, with pistol strapped to his belt and Mauser at his side. But he is short, even by the standards of Ayala, and fatter than a Flores Magón, and conspicuously bowlegged in an army of bowlegged men. He tries to make himself appear taller by combing his hair up into a great, greasy pompadour; but it doesn't work, poor Otilio. How his pupils must have laughed at him; how they laugh at him here, even 'Miliano, who loves him more than anyone else does.

As well he should love him: Otilio has been with him from the first days. It was he who rode from Anenecuilco to Mexico City in 1909, to tell the town's troubles to those prominent liberals, Paulino Martínez and my own digno brother, Jesús Flores Magón, in the vain hope that they would speak for the town in its struggle against the hacendados. It was Otilio who wrote the famous Plan de Ayala in the Sierra de Ayoxustla in November 1911, and gave it to Emiliano Zapata to sign as his own. You will imagine that a village schoolmaster can be no very authentic intellectual; but it is a fact that Otilio Montaño spoon-fed Molina Enríquez's *Los grandes problemas nacionales* to 'Miliano, who learned in

1909 from this book that there could be no land distribution without violence; and that, when a Spanish translation of Kropotkin's *The Conquest of Bread* reached Morelos in 1910 (I had commissioned the translation in 1902, but books travel slowly in Mexico, even inflammatory ones), Otilio read this to 'Miliano, too.

Otilio knew what scholars apparently do not: that leaders do not read, whether or not they are literate. They need a few ideas on which to hang their actions, but there must be someone to hand those ideas to them; for they are too busy, too impatient, to sit down with a book. But they will *pretend* that they have read a great deal, just as they will pretend that they are really simple men, anxious to end the fighting so that they might take up their books (or their easels, or their fishing rods, or their lechery) and fade once and for all from public view. In this they fool only scholars.

Otilio was no scholar, but he was naive in several important ways. He did not know, for instance, that his benign kind of reformist zeal ("primitive Indian socialism," we advanced revoltosos called it) would be out of style in no time, as we more sophisticated, better-educated intellectuals came along, convinced that we could insert Russian and French ideas into Mexican minds. I wish now that I had listened to Otilio more, and paid less attention to my more sophisticated friends.

You can see on Otilio's face, and in his uneasy posture, though, his awareness that he was no longer of much use to the Liberator Army of the South; that he was becoming, in fact, an embarrassment. My arrival in Xochimilco must have been the last straw for him. In three years his fellow intellectuals would bring charges against him, and invent fatal evidence; and 'Miliano, tears running down his ashamed face, would order the shooting of Otilio Montaño, another victim of history. Now, as he sees me looking his way, Otilio smiles, twitches his broad behind in a little dance step, and sings the last couplet of "Valentina," his crow's voice empty of irony:

Si me han de matar mañana,
Que me maten de una vez.

If they're going to kill me tomorrow,
They might as well kill me right now.

About to edge in front of Montaño is a tiny, spidery man, no more than five feet tall, with a head so large, and the sombrero over it so huge, that one feels assailed by disproportion. Surely, one thinks, this must be the court dwarf, kept around by the Zapatistas to provide amusement and uncomfortable truths. Neither assumption would be correct: Manuel Palafox is not funny, and he has nothing to do with any truth at all. To me, to everyone except (for now) 'Miliano, he represents a kind of deceit incarnate. This Palafox is here to lie — to us, to our enemies, and perhaps even to himself. There is more than one villain in these notebooks, but I'll tell you right now that Manuel Palafox is among the very worst.

I paid no attention to him during my first days in Xochimilco. His pockmarked face and expressionless almond eyes told me nothing; and I suppose he did not think me important enough to notice. I became aware of him only as the center of an ugly little fracas that popped up in the midst of our relative tranquillity, a piece of nastiness that I learned was typical of what happened whenever Palafox was around.

The decamping Eulalio Gutiérrez had been quickly replaced as acting president by the very young, very inexperienced Roque González Garza, who tried manfully to control the increasingly fractious Villistas and Zapatistas left in the

Capital. With no money in his treasury, and a police force that had for the most part dissolved into Veracruz with General Obregón, González Garza was soon reduced to presiding over petty wrangling among drunken soldiers. Two weeks before the Zapatistas' vacation in Xochimilco, when my imaginary photography session takes place, he had been confronted by Manuel Palafox, whom Zapata had ordered installed as Minister of Agriculture — a post from which he could preside over the distribution of land among the campesinos, and therefore a key position in the eyes of the Zapatistas. But this Palafox, like so many others, was mainly bent on enriching himself: he put the mordida, the bite, on González Garza for a lot of old uniforms he claimed the Liberator Army of the South had worn and paid for themselves. Since the army never had any uniforms at all, old or new, this claim was more blatantly meretricious than most; and González Garza refused it.

Palafox said nothing. But two days after his request was refused, his sponsor, General Zapata, sent a note to González Garza that he was about to fling his troops back into Mexico City to avenge the slight Palafox had suffered. The brave temporary president (now *there's* a redundancy for you! Presidents were nothing if not temporary in Mexico those days) rode out to meet Zapata, taking with him only a pair of secretaries as escort. Zapata, at the head of a squadron of cavalry, was drunk and surly. He drew his pistol and threatened González Garza with it: Palafox must be kept in his important post, and apologies must be made to him. González Garza refused, and Zapata rode with him back to the Palacio Nacional, where he continued his drunken abuse of the man.

Finally, after hours of this, Zapata stomped out of the palace, rode his horse onto a platform car belonging to the tramlines, and rattled back to Xochimilco. There he bellowed angrily until little Palafox came out from wherever he'd been hiding. I was there to see the dwarf scuttle over the floor of the hacienda's corral toward Zapata's horse, and fairly throw himself into the arms of his general, his rat's face full of injured innocence and devotion.

I think you will agree that this vignette reflects little credit on Emiliano Zapata, whom I have so far given you as a model of rustic aristocracy. Well, you're not children, or you wouldn't be reading a felon's notebooks; so you ought to be able to understand how a man like Zapata might drink (which he did from time to time, but seldom so clumsily as this) — just as you might come to understand how he might have a wife, and love her; and still have other women (rather a lot, in fact), and love them, too. We are, after all, only dealing with Mexicans here, and peones at that, right? It's not as though I were trying to tell you about a gathering of righteous gringos, Protestant and steadfast. Right?

What I want you to notice here is not just 'Miliano's dubious conduct: I want you to ask yourselves how he could be brought to behave as he did by a man like Manuel Palafox. Villa, you will remember, kept Mariano Azuela as *his* court dwarf, without making a fool of himself over it. But Azuela, whatever I say about him, was a man of substance and probity. (As I write, he's living in a Mexico City slum, giving medical care to the poor.) For Zapata to have behaved badly on behalf of someone like Palafox means, among other things, that he not only respected the dwarf, but loved him, too. How could one love a Palafox, a man we all came to call "the Ulcer of the South"?

I asked Otilio Montaño just this, soon after the event I have described. "Look, señor Anarchist," the plump schoolteacher said, "do you suppose that great warriors must also be great judges of character?"

"Well, no, of course not," I answered. "But I don't expect them to clasp knaves to their bosoms, and make fools of themselves on their account, either. What kind of spell has this odious little toad cast over Zapata?"

"Don't talk of magic, Don Ricardo. Palafox came to us two years ago, just a little engineering student from Puebla, full of zeal and humility, anxious to serve 'Miliano any way he could. Before long, anytime anyone said the word *loyalty*, there was Palafox. Say *devotion*, and there he was. Or other words, like *sacrifice* or, a little later, *courage*; or slogans, any ones you'd care to name. If we had a flag, he'd be wrapped in it; mention the Virgin of Guadalupe, and he's got a picture of her slapped on his ass for you. The man became our symbol, Don Ricardo; and you've got to love your symbols."

From this I learned not only how Palafox had insinuated himself into his master's affections, but also how it became necessary for Palafox to bring about the betrayal and execution of Otilio Montaño four years later. If these notebooks are to continue, you'll learn more of Manual Palafox, of his disloyalties and, yes, even of his sexual perversions; but for now, let me cleanse my palate, and turn to the other two men standing in the group of "intellectuals afield."

Gildardo Magaña and Antonio Díaz Soto y Gama are better men than I. I have no doubt about this, and can say so at a time when false modesty would look foolish. (These notebooks are neither a final atonement nor a last attempt at self-inflation; neither are they mere *amusettes* for a man close to his death. I am trying to get something straight here.) This is what I mean: both men are true revolutionaries, totally different in their practices and approaches to problems, and indeed in their personalities; but absolutely united in their desire to bring social and economic justice to the people of Mexico. (I know how stilted that sounds; believe me, it's hard to write well about virtuous men, or about such hollow things as causes. Try reading Kropotkin or Marx, why don't you? Next to theirs, my rhetoric fairly sings.)

In appearance they are almost polar opposites. Gildardo is large and plump and amiable, un verdadero hijo de papá, a true daddy's boy. He looks comfortable, in his three-piece woolen suit, his sturdy jodhpur boots, and his gray felt fedora. He looks as though he *belongs* somewhere, with a family, a business, a pretty little wife and a pack of fat, happy children. What business could a good young man like this have with a bunch of thugs and misfits like us?

Antonio Díaz Soto y Gama, on the other hand, looks like the kind of madman who accosts you on the street, shrieks at your wife that she is the whore of Babylon, and then collapses weeping on your shoulder. He looks more like the man who drives the pulque wagon in Tlalpan than like anyone's idea of a committed revolutionary. He is tall and cadaverous, with great eyes that seem to look upon doom, and I think that he has almost never smiled. But he is the real thing, the genuine anarchist article, a saint of social destruction. He makes me proud to be his leader.

He and Gildardo are inseparable, which says something good about both of them.

Gildardo came as a gift to the Zapatistas from Mexico City in 1911, when he and his two brothers had to flee from police that General Huerta had set on them. The Magañas were members of a group called the Tacubayans, who were somewhere vaguely to the left of Madero (who was vaguely anywhere at all you wanted him to be). When Huerta broke them up, the Tacubayans took off in all directions, and

Zapata was fortunate that the Magaña brothers wound up in Morelos, looking for him. The eldest, Octavio, came to serve as Zapata's conduit to Madero; the second, Rodolfo, brought 12,000 pesos of Tacubayan money to the Zapatistas, as well as a gift for smuggling quinine out of the city to the malaria-ridden guerrilleros; and the youngest, Gildardo, came to be Zapata's most accomplished diplomat.

On his first trip for Zapata, in June 1912, Gildardo was captured in the Capital by Huerta, who threw him into the military prison of Santiago Tlaltelolco, where his cellmate was none other than Pancho Villa, temporarily down on his luck. (Huerta had arrested Pancho after his victory up in Parral, over something to do with a missing horse. He had almost succeeded in putting Villa before a firing squad, but Madero had intervened at the last moment and ordered that Villa be brought back to Mexico City.) When Gildardo moved across the cell to introduce himself, Villa stopped him, looked him over, and said, "You look like a smart son of a bitch. I'll bet you can even read and write."

"Yes, my general, I can do those things," said Gildardo, thinking (he told me) that he had never before been accosted by anyone who could manage to combine respect and contempt so completely.

"All right, then, Gordito. We have maybe two weeks until they either shoot me or let me go. Teach me, and don't fuck up, you piece of meat with eyes. What have you got that I can read, Professor Hijo de Puta?"

Gildardo, who was much bigger even than Villa, but who was quaking with terror throughout this exchange, rummaged around in the rucksack they had let him bring with him into the prison. He came up with two books: *Don Quixote* and *The Three Musketeers*. He and Villa sat down side by side on Villa's bunk, and Gildardo began to read to the general, tracing his path along the words with his finger, telling of a knight from La Mancha being written about by a soldier in prison.

Villa was delighted, commenting favorably on the narrative skill of this Spaniard, Cervantes. He grinned at Gildardo like a child at a magician, his yellow-brown eyes squinting almost shut, hugging himself in glee. "Tú y yo," he exclaimed, "somos algo nuevo!" "You and I, we're something new!" He and Gildardo, between them, were making this old gachupín, Cervantes, come to life to tell his ridiculous story of another crazy gachupín, Quixote, who was after all no crazier than other Spaniards. (Villa might have killed Mexicans in great numbers, but he reserved his special hatred for Chinamen and Spaniards.)

Gildardo said they read Cervantes for two weeks and never got to Dumas, and that Villa never learned to read a word beyond "In a village of La Mancha," but they both had a great time in prison. Villa even bought a typewriter from another prisoner, thinking that if he owned one, and knew how to put paper into it, he would automatically know how to write. At the end of the two weeks he was freed, to go back north to resume command of his army, convinced that he was now not only a literate man, but a literary critic as well. Gildardo said that it had all been like two weeks spent tossing marzipan cookies to a crocodile.

For the rest of it, Gildardo Magaña worked as Zapata's go-between, his conciliator, his calm intelligence in a storm of confusion, deceit, ignorance. The war in the South had degenerated into long periods of silent waiting, of sitting in the shadows of boulders and deep in arroyos and tlacololes (the sandy, arid little indentations in the sides of hills where the hacendados expected the campesinos to grow their corn), interspersed from time to time with wild outbursts of noise and violence, as haciendas were torched and trains blown away from their trestles, and Zapata's peasant army went spontaneously and unpredictably mad — only to subside moments or hours later back into its customary torpor. In the midst of all this there were a few men like Gildardo who tried to give some shape, some control to things; that is, to make the Revolution rational.

Gildardo, and the few men like him on both sides, were finally only good socialists, wanting a good government over good men, in a place and time when good government was impossible and good men impotent. (Does the word *good* begin to bore you? It does me.) I loved Gildardo, but ideologically speaking he was my enemy — even when, as did happen, he tried to save my life.

Antonio Díaz Soto y Gama, on the other hand, was virtuous, but not good. Like most of Zapata's intelligentsia, he was middle-class and northern — another of those thinkers from San Luis Potosí who were at the heart of the Liberal movement against Porfirio Díaz in 1901, at the time I had spoken out against the Porfiriato and gone back to Belén Prison for a year. Antonio had written me often during that year, helping me to organize my thoughts, telling me what to read, preparing me for that time when I should emerge as Mexico's chief revolutionary thinker — teaching me, that is, to be his leader. Historians of the Revolution are already describing him as a "petty bourgeois, low-status intellectual," and so he was (and so were we all, out-of-work journalists, lawyers without clients, cavalry officers without horses, libertines without enough pesos for liquor or women); but he was miles ahead of me as a radical, and shrewder by far. It was he who wrote me, as early as 1902, that we must not yet begin to speak of "anarchism," or even "socialism," but must announce ourselves in our writings and speeches as "liberals," if we hoped to get the masses behind us. The masses, Antonio knew, had not begun to think beyond pulling down Porfirio Díaz; it had not yet occurred to them that he would have to be replaced by something quite different, quite new — so for the time being, we would have to masquerade as "liberals."

Antonio was a volatile, even explosive man. I do not know how he managed to remain invisible for so many years in the underground; but, except for a spell of editing *El Hijo del Ahuizote*, our satiric journal, while I was in prison in 1901, no one noticed him until 1911, when he turned up in Mexico City to announce that our new little president, Francisco I. Madero, was nothing more than a vapid "liberal," a naïf who wanted, after overthrowing Díaz, to effect his tepid reforms with the same, corrupt old parliament and army that had belonged to Díaz. "Tear it all down!" Antonio shrieked at anyone who would listen. "Give it all to the people! The land is theirs! Death to the owners!" Suddenly his voice, the voice of a mad crow, was all over Mexico.

And it was I, Ricardo Flores Magón, imprisoned then on an island in the Pacific off Washington State, who was signalling instructions to this crazy Antonio Díaz Soto y Gama, telling him what to say and where to say it. And the louder he yelled, the deeper I dug myself into prison. When the Revolution finally broke, he was Nechayev to my Bakunin, my hollow-eyed and sublime disciple, berserk — but predictably, consistently berserk. A really dangerous man. I was frightened of him in absentia then; and I was frightened of him when he tore away from the good socialists of Mexico City in 1912; and I am frightened of him at my imaginary moment in the late fall of 1914, as he stares so somberly into Casasola's lens, looking, in his rusty black suit and tieless celluloid collar, like the Archbishop of Hell.

This Antonio Díaz Soto y Gama has been with the Zapatistas only since last August, when he made his way south across the Sierra de Chichinautzín into Morelos, to Zapata's temporary headquarters in the old Dominican convent of Tepoztlán. Manuel Palafox, acting as the general's chief of staff (a position to which he had named himself), appointed Antonio a private secretary to the general. Palafox had no idea of Antonio's importance, but Gildardo Magaña knew of him by reputation, treated him with due respect, and — insofar as one could do so, with someone like Antonio — befriended him.

Antonio told Gildardo how he had been trying since the outbreak of the Revolution to keep things stirred up, to prevent the political wounds from healing. He had fought against those who were satisfied simply to get rid of Porfirio Díaz, and were ready to make do with Madero. Then, Madero murdered by Huerta, Antonio had called for Huerta's overthrow, and had tried to rally the Capital's workers against the usurper. Almost single-handedly he had founded the *Casa del Obrero Mundial*, the House of the Workers of the World, hoping that an organized proletariat might join a rebellion against the state, and that eventually the workers might unite with the peasants to bring about the ultimate great people's Revolution. From his readings, from *me*, he had learned that this was inevitable, once both the workers and the campesinos were shown the logic, the truth, of our beautiful, simple design.

For a few months in 1912 and 1913, once Huerta had been run out of the Capital, Antonio's workers' movement had appeared to blossom. Unions began to form. Antonio himself opened the Escuela Racional on Calle Londres, to be modeled on the pedagogic principles of the Spanish anarchist martyr Francisco Ferrer. Here, workers were to teach workers. There would be no grades, no degrees. The lessons would be practical, the indoctrination simple and direct. Women were to be admitted, and treated as equals. There would be no talk of race or caste.

But within a few months everything Antonio had accomplished with his millenarian zeal began to come unglued. "The workers were not angry enough, Don Ricardo," he told me. "As soon as they believed they would be clothed and fed, they saw no reason to struggle, least of all for the campesinos or for the multitudes of jobless peones in the city. They only smiled and shrugged at me. They admired the way I yelled at them, and applauded, and walked by me saluting me with respect on their way home to eat, and to marvel over the new homes we were beginning to build for them. They wouldn't listen to me: they listened to those peacemakers, all our old friends gone soft with socialism, all those who were saying that the time for hatred was over." Antonio never spoke; he only orated: every impulse that came into his brain was translated immediately into a speech.

At the Aguascalientes Convention, two months before the time of my imaginary photographic session in Xochimilco, he had his first chance to orate before a large and important audience, and he'd almost pulled the whole damned Revolution down around him. I suppose you could call his speech (or performance, I should say) a success. I hope we never have another success like that.

Venustiano Carranza, having declared himself First Chief of the Revolution, had called for a Grand Convention in Aguascalientes, to which all the revolutionary chiefs should send delegations. The aim was to decide, once and for all, who was to lead us. Carranza, of course, assumed that he would be named; but just in case, he tried to pack the convention with Carrancistas, who were for the most part the same old Porfirista hacks and petty functionaries, now dressed as Liberals. (You've got to hand it to those birds for flexibility: two months before, they'd been solid with Huerta; two months before that they'd been firm Maderistas; and until the day in 1911 when Madero entered the Capital, they'd been loyal supporters of the old dictator.)

Antonio knew, for I had told him, that all these had to die. And he wanted to kill them now, in Aguascalientes. The trouble, though, was that the hacks, most of them, didn't make it to Aguascalientes. Antonio's audience turned out to be a hall full of the toughest warriors of the Revolution, soldiers from the victorious armies of Villa and Obregón. They were all armed, and by far more easily aroused than any group of bureaucrats assembled by Carranza would have been.

Both Villa and Zapata had of course been invited to the conference. But Villa chose to remain in Zacatecas with his latest bride; and Zapata stayed in Morelos, sending word to Carranza that he could come down to Zapata's camp in Yautepec if he wanted a conference. Both generals sent a delegation to Aguascalientes, however, realizing that if any sort of peace were to be reached now, it had its best chance there, with the gathered delegations. Zapata sent two of his generals, a squad of troops, and five of his advisers: Paulino Martínez, as chairman, Gildardo and Octavio Magaña, Manuel Palafox, and Antonio — who was, it turned out, tired of being pushed around and silenced by Palafox and anxious to display himself as the Danton of this Revolution.

The conference had already begun when the Zapatista delegation arrived at the old Morelos Theatre in Aguascalientes on October 26, and the audience of warriors fell silent as the little group entered, led by Paulino, all dressed in sombreros and white pajamas, all carrying their Mausers and Colt revolvers, all tiptoeing as though they were crossing a dangerous ravine, expecting an ambush. When the chairman of the conference called out a welcome to the Zapatistas, the seated members indicated their approval by cheering, pounding their rifle butts on the floor of the auditorium, and firing their pistols over their heads. Gildardo told me later that the delegation should have known, from the smell of tequila lacing the smoky air of the hall, that a certain amount of restraint was called for; but there was no way they could hold back Antonio Díaz Soto y Gama, who could hardly sit still while Paulino made his tidy little speech of thanks for the delegates' warm welcome.

As soon as Paulino had finished, Antonio leapt to the stage and ran to the special Convention flag being displayed there, next to the speaker's podium. Obregón had presented it earlier, and every delegate had signed it reverently, most with pious protestations of devotion and commitment. Antonio grabbed the flag, waved it above his head, and shook it at his audience.

"What are you doing with this filthy rag?" he hollered at his listeners. "Look at this shit-eating buzzard it's got on it!" he cried, pointing to the figure of the sacred Mexican eagle.

Gildardo said that the noise from the audience began as a low roar, or growl, rising as Antonio spoke to a great outcry of rage. Men jumped from their seats, pounding their chests with their left hands and reaching for their pistols with their right. Shots echoed through the auditorium. Splintered putti flew from the ornate ceiling. Bottles crashed against the podium. Antonio kept on, shouting that he and his comrades had come here not to write their names on some dirty, obscene flag, but to announce their honor as men, as individuals. "We are waging a great Revolution," he exhorted, "against the lies of history, a Revolution that will expose the historical lie this flag represents. What we call our independence was not independence for the Indian, but only for the Creoles, the inheritors of the Conquest, so they could continue laughing. . . ."

A hundred pistols aimed at Antonio. The roar increased. "Let go of the flag! Savage! Imbecile! Bastard! Barbarian! Renegade!" General Villareal, the presiding officer, cried out, "More respect for the flag!" Antonio stood his ground, his arms crossed, his head held back, his eyes shining, enraptured at the commotion he was causing. The Zapatista delegation, anxious for the safety of their orator, drew their pistols and stood on their chairs (all but Palafox, who had disappeared), ready to fire into the crowd of enraged conventioneers.

The crucial moment passed, as it does so often in Mexican confrontations (though it just as easily might *not* have passed, Gildardo reminded me: Antonio might have been blown full of holes, the convention stampeded, bodies strewn about like discarded banana skins, the Revolution abandoned — and the whole evening recorded as a typically Mexican political event). The boos and hisses died down, the catcalls and explosions ceased, General Villareal pounded on his bell for order, and the audience resumed their seats, ready to see the rest of the show.

Having achieved the effect he had desired, Antonio returned to his speech. The flag of the Convention, he said, was worthless because it was being used to hide the avarice and ambition of Carranza and those who supported him. (Obregón, who had already decided to side with Carranza and against Villa and Zapata, flinched a little at this.) The only honorable hope of the Convention was to accept Zapata's Plan de Ayala, and to elect a leader who would carry it out. At this the Villista delegates (who had already conferred with the Zapatistas before the Convention) applauded, and shouted their support for the Liberator Army of the South. All that remained was for the delegates to bring forward a candidate for president who was acceptable to Villa and Zapata, and the Convention would be a success. Still at the podium, Antonio smiled benignly out at the audience, looking as though he were about to make the sign of the cross over it and say softly, "'Ite, missa est.'"

Gildardo told me he had no idea whether or not Antonio knew what he was doing, whether or not his speech had been planned or extemporaneous. The latter, I think: this kind of divine madness was something we anarchists prayed for, a kind of Pentecostal fervor that promised salvation just this side of violent immolation.

It will perhaps not surprise you, Protestant gringo reader of my notebooks, to learn that in the latter days of the Revolution Antonio Díaz Soto y Gama became a mystical Catholic who tried to *pray* our enemies dead. But you might be surprised to read that today, in November of 1922, as I write these notebooks for you, the same man is a member of the Chamber of Deputies in Mexico City, and is trying day and night to have me freed from my American prison.

Casasola twists his camera on its tripod once more, this time to the right of the figures of 'Miliano and Amparo, and comes upon another small cluster of men. These are 'Miliano's generals, Indians and mestizos all, and it hurts me that I can tell you no more about them than their names, what they look like, what they have done and what they will do. This is not from simple biographical ignorance, for I have studied their lives and achievements very closely, as closely as one could study them from a prison in the United States. (Why would I not try to learn as much as I could about them? They were, after all, along with the intellectuals, the men who would allow my Revolution to succeed or fail.)

Nor have I failed to know them because of some romantic foolishness about "inscrutable Indians." I'm mostly Indian myself, remember? Maybe there simply is no essence to such men; maybe they really are no more than what is superficially measurable about them.

That's ridiculous, of course: why should Genovevo de la O, squatting in the sand fifteen feet from the camera, squinting up into the sun behind Casasola's head, lack something that, say, Gildardo Magaña possesses? Yet it is true that I can tell you only certain things about Genovevo: that he was from the mountain town of Tres Marías, north of Cuernavaca; that he had led a guerrilla band against Porfirio Díaz even before the Revolution began; that he was really a rival of 'Miliano's more than a subordinate, choosing for the moment to submit to 'Miliano's authority; that he returned to Tres Marías last year, in 1913, to find that the Federales had burned it down to punish him, and that he discovered the charred and still-smoking body of his infant daughter in the ruins.

I can also tell you that I might look into the black eyes of Genovevo de la O, and watch him smile at me, and listen to what he says (yes, he talks, almost as much as Díaz Soto y Gama), and mark his movements and his gestures, and still know nothing about the man. And I can say the same for Juan Banderas, who lies stretched like a great cat at Genovevo's side, basking in the December sun. I know that Banderas kills unpredictably and with feline pleasure; but I can't tell you what's going on in his mind, even when he's describing for me what he swears are his deepest fears and aspirations.

The same is true for Abraham Martínez, who sits close by the other two generals, straight and expressionless now in a cane chair, his rifle across his lap, his sombrero at his feet. Martínez looks at me: there is nothing behind his eyes, neither animosity nor fondness nor humor nor even boredom. I do not know whether he is relaxed or tense; I can tell you only that he is awake. That he lacks a mustache. And that his hair is cropped close, probably because he has just been released from a prison in Puebla where Carranza's soldiers were holding him.

What is most remarkable about all three generals is, in fact, that they are absolutely motionless, static: they give off nothing that might mark them as human, not at least as I understand the word. They can talk; they can move, with a swiftness that can terrify. It is not just that they are still because they are posing for Casasola. I can say of them only that they are on the "other side"; they are over there; they are wherever I am not. I shall call them the Others, they and the army of twenty thousand campesinos they lead for Emiliano Zapata. Perhaps I am afraid of them, and my fear closes them off from me.

"What's the matter, Florecito?" says a hoarse voice behind me.

I turn, surprised. I am supposed to be the only one outside Casasola's photograph. There he is, of course, Eufemio Zapata, 'Miliano's incorrigible older brother, taller than anyone here, gangly and knobby-kneed as a colt, always about to smile but seldom smiling, eyes scarcely focused, perhaps about to stumble, perhaps drunk. His saber has worked its way between his thighs. He holds himself up by leaning on his Winchester, its butt in the sand, its front sight barely reaching his belt. He is wearing the black business suit of a smaller, shorter man. His coat sleeves reach only halfway down his sunburned forearms; his waistcoat lacks most of its buttons. His trousers are stuffed into leather gaiters that he or someone has had trouble buckling. He is looking at me, but his eyes travel often to the figure of Amparo, who is about to bend toward the figure of 'Miliano, who continues to seem unaware of any of us.

"What's there to be afraid of, Florecito?" Eufemio asks, smiling almost sweetly at me. He is, I know, even more lethal than 'Miliano's other generals: it does not do to relax when he smiles, not even here in tranquil Xochimilco.

"You're at home here, man," he says. "These are all only your people, even I. You wanted a Revolution: here it is. You wanted revolutionaries: here we are. There's nothing complicated about us, not even 'Miliano and Amparo. We just want whatever you tell us to want. All we are is characters in your private opera."

Eufemio kneels, picking up a handful of black sand. "Look at this dirt," he says. "Do you see how at home it is here, in my hand?" He tosses the sand at my feet. "Look around you, cabrón."

He raises his free hand, palm up, and moves it expansively around him, from the volcanoes to the east, the dim outlines of the Capital behind us to the north, and the sierra to the west and south. A vision pops into my head of the vast jungles beyond the sierras, of the enormous sugarcane haciendas in the rolling green farmland of Morelos between us and those jungles, of the mountain ranges that rise sharply up out of the Morelian plateau, like dark rocky islands in a sea of green. Somewhere far to the south, below Morelos, is the state of Oaxaca, where I was born but of which I know almost nothing.

Eufemio shouts suddenly, making me jump. "Hey, you old cabrón, you see all this? All this is only fucking old Mexico. It's just more dirt, or, if you like, it's just the setting for your opera. What the fuck are you scared of?" He is no longer smiling.

"Are you afraid of our cruelty? We kill one another for the guerra, man, because it's there. But you don't kill us. You don't pull any fucking triggers. No, you just *order* us to be killed, for some fucking *idea!* Which of us is the crueller, tú pinche gordo?"

He stands, and I see that his right hand is in the trigger guard of his carbine. Its front sight is wavering toward me. It's another one of those Mexican moments: he may shoot; or he may not.

He does not. Now he holds the carbine as though it were a guitar, strumming its imaginary strings. He smiles seductively at me, and sings softly, as if it were a lullaby:

> *La vida no vale nada,*
> *No vale nada la vida.*

He laughs, and disappears.

The photograph curls and begins to turn from sepia to black. In a moment it dissolves and disappears, and so does Casasola, and they're all gone, 'Miliano and Amparo and the others, intellectuals and generals, and the volcanoes and jungles, and finally even Eufemio's laughter; and I am no longer even the mere spectator I was for a little while, but only a sad fat man in a gray prison suit in Leavenworth, Kansas, with tired eyes and a stiff hand from writing all day.

Notebook 4

November 5, 1922

That last little photographic jaunt took a lot out of me. I had not thought to raise so many ghosts, nor to have them affect me so strongly, after all this time. Let me assure you, whoever you are, I am not usually so easily overtaken by fantasy — unless it is ideological, that is. From day to day I live as one firmly rooted to the real world. I am a phlegmatic man who perhaps unwisely wedded himself to a frenetic destiny. I should have been a pharmacist, not a polemicist. Now, when I should be teasing a flock of grandchildren while sitting in a comfortable lawn chair on the veranda of a tiny villa, possibly overlooking the dusty city of Oaxaca, I find myself instead seated on a thin striped mattress that smells of disinfectant, toying with its embroidered label, which tells me I am liable to prosecution if I remove it.

Mr. Biddle, the warden of Leavenworth Prison, has classified me as "Highly Dangerous." (The prison gossip, usually very accurate, has also classified me as having an affair with his forty-year-old daughter, and says that this circumstance, as much as any other, is responsible for my solitary confinement. This rumor is untrue, and is liable to remain so — unless my health improves and I am allowed to resume my duties as prison librarian, a post that gave me frequent access to the poor young lady.) Perhaps I can convince you that I am at least not physically menacing if I copy out for you the description made of me in 1906 by Mr. Thomas Furlong of the Pinkerton Agency:

RICARDO FLORES MAGON
Height: five feet, eight inches
Weight: approximately 225 pounds
Color of eyes: very black
Color of hair: black and curly
Color of complexion: dark olive
Does he smoke? He is a great smoker of cigars.
Does he talk much? He is very serious, but he has the ability to speak and to express himself with elegance.
Does he speak English? Very little. (This is a lie. Even by 1906 I spoke better English by far than Mr. Thomas Furlong who, by the way, knows nothing whatever of elegance.)
Does he have much hair? Rather a lot.
How old is he? He appears to be forty-four. (In 1906 I was thirty-two.)
Is he married? No.
What other things can you tell me about Mr. Magón? That he is a very intelligent journalist, industrious, orderly, that he types very well, that he is respected by the people around him, that he has a very resolute and energetic character, and that he is fanaticized by the cause he pursues, with that brutal and dangerous fanaticism that anarchists have.

There, except for the inaccuracies, you have me. There, but for the taint of anarchism, you see one of the gentlest (and fattest) of men.

But because I am highly dangerous they have taken my cellmate, Librado Rivera, from me. I am no longer allowed to circulate, or exercise. My lawyer, Harry Weinberger, finally convinced the warden last week to grant me a physical examination, to establish that I am far too ill to be imprisoned. But the prison doctor says I am not ill, only overweight — though I now weigh only 155 pounds. I can, as I have written you, scarcely see. My chest hurts. My legs are numb. Urination is difficult and painful. And this morning my guard has come to tell me that from now on I must sleep with my head against the bars of the cell door, instead of lying along the far wall, as other prisoners do. He could give me no explanation for this new edict, but I know the reason: lying so, I can easily be reached through the bars as I sleep.

Bueno, enough of that: you are not to use these notebooks to whimper, I must remind myself. Go back to Mexico. Tell about the Revolution. Tell about the beginnings of your exile, your life as a fugitive. Show them you have something to match against the exploits of the Zapatas. Something perhaps a little subtler.

So: When my brother Jesús and I emerged from Belén Prison at the end of April 1902, we were met at the exit opposite the ciudadela by the ever-faithful Enrique, and I assumed for a moment that the three of us could now unite to form the final vanguard against Porfirio Díaz. But Jesús had lost his afición as true revolutionary, and wanted to start setting himself up around town as a good, clean liberal. "All right, hermanos," he said, "that's enough. I've gone along with it all up until now. I got you set up with *Regeneración*. I introduced you to everyone you need to know. You have the benefit of association with my respectable liberal name. I just went to jail for a year for you and your cause. Ya basta: Now keep my love, but leave me alone. I wish you well, but not too well. Voy a buscarme la vida. I'm off to find my own life."

And off Jesús went, to resume his marriage and his law practice and his connections among the politically ambitious Liberals of Mexico City, and his eternal membership in the bourgeoisie we were bound to pull down and destroy. Much later on, from his position of great influence under Madero, he worked very hard to arrange some sort of clemency for us hard-core anarchists; but we were too bad, too intransigent, for even poor Jesús to help us.

Enrique had put on a little weight while Jesús and I were away, but he was still like a puppy, bouncing around me, eager to show me the new bone he had found for us. *Regeneración* was stopped for the time being, but that was all right: I was to become the new editor of the satirical magazine *El Hijo del Ahuizote*, and Enrique was to be on its board of directors.

This did not at first seem the best way to mount an attack of words against the dictator, or to put before Mexicans the theories of Bakunin, Kropotkin, Reclus, Malato, and all the others whose works I had read in Belén. Anarchist thinkers may be deep, but they are seldom witty — to put it mildly. I did not know yet that to laugh at a thing is as good a way as any to bring it down. I knew then only that *El Hijo del Ahuizote* was mainly a magazine which published grotesque political and social cartoons, surely a trivial thing to do in so doomed a time as ours.

So when Enrique took me to the offices of the magazine, on Calle Cocheras, and introduced me to Daniel Cabrera, the old man who was its editor, I took a high tone with him. "Look here, Cabrera," I cringe to remember saying, "this can all be very easy: I do the thinking, and you do the drawing. You can draw to prescription, can't you?"

"Indeed yes, young gentleman," he answered, looking as servile as he thought I wanted him to be. "I've been wondering for fifty years of editing what to write and draw about. How fortunate we are that you've come to us at last."

Enrique, who had been learning a little tact while I was in prison learning political philosophy, coughed at this and asked me if I had heard of Posada.

"Who's he, another *artiste?*" Oh, what an awful, ignorant fool I was, then.

Enrique lifted his eyebrows at Cabrera, who kept a straight face. "That's José Guadalupe Posada, my assistant, or my master, I'll let you decide. I'm sure he'll learn a lot from you, Licenciado Flores Magón," he said.

Well, this Posada was of course none other than . . . Posada, who was to Mexico what Goya was to Spain and Daumier to France; and for most of the next year this obese Indian with a head so huge it made me shudder worked with me at ridiculing Porfirio Díaz and his friends; and it may well be that this Posada did more damage to the Porfiriato with his spidery cartoons than all my fiery editorials in *Regeneración*.

He had come to the capital fourteen years before, out of Aguascalientes by way of Guanajuato, where he'd worked in one dingy atelier after another, learning to do homely little lithographs for matchbook covers (*A Soldier's Farewell, A Mother's Prayer*), congratulatory cards, even enlistment posters — always executed in full sentimentality, without a trace of irony. My comparison of Posada with Goya and Daumier does not go beyond good intention, for he was never more than a genially bad cartoonist. But by the time he turned to political satire, he had discovered the thing that was to make him a more authentic portrayer of the Republic than all the dozens of local academics, mock-Spaniards all, who laughed at his poor technique.

Posada found that the way Mexicans most like to see

themselves depicted, satirically or not, is as a nation of wobbling bones and grinning skulls. He gave us the calavera, the death's head, the animated skeleton, and we knew when we first saw it that it was us.

Posada and I did not take to one another, at first. Posada, I am sure, thought of me as a pompous young ass, which I was; and I found him physically repugnant, which he was. His very apt nickname for himself was *la Garrapata Atracada*, the Engorged Tick. He never bathed; and, like many people with severe halitosis, got pleasure from standing as close as possible to his listeners, especially if they were as squeamish as I. (My two terms in Belén had, oddly enough, made me almost morbidly fastidious.) We were not a likely pair of collaborators.

But collaborate we did, Posada and I. Our first efforts for *El Hijo del Ahuizote* were rather bad, chiefly because of my penchant for heavy-handed symbolism. Typical was one that I had him do of Porfirio Díaz disguised as Alexander the Great, looming over a skeletal figure in a barrel, with the caption "Independent Journalism."

"Do you think it's a little obscure?" I asked Posada.

"No," he breathed in my direction. I suppose he reckoned his fetor was criticism enough.

After I learned to leave him alone, Posada abandoned such devices as captions and arch titles, and concentrated on his stark depictions of one calavera after another prancing across the face of Mexico. It was his aim to make our quotidian lives look so ridiculous that we appeared all the more fatuous when we took ourselves seriously, as statesmen or generals. So he would give us a *Calavera of Street Sweepers*, or a *Calavera of Water Bearers*, and show us scenes of perfectly banal normality in Mexico City — but the fact that all the actors in his scenes were skeletons, leering and clanking their way through their chores, swaying about in a particularly embarrassing *danse macabre*, made us all seem simultaneously clownish and menacing, true grotesques in fact.

Posada gave us death as both obscene and farcical, but never dignified; and he was never better as satirist than in a cartoon like *"Calavera Catrina,"* in which the usual grinning skeleton wears an enormous flowered hat, a feather boa, and a French evening gown, presenting herself as the perfect specter not only of Porfirian society, but also of a country governed by death. Behind her peeks the fleshless face of Coatlicue, Aztec goddess of the earth, whose nourishment consists of the hearts of sacrificial victims.

Posada, as I say, knew how to get us all in, all of corrupt present Mexico standing before our violent, death-enthralled past. My God, how we *love* death! What is one to do about a country in which the highest form of entertainment is the funeral? Perhaps one day someone will account for the lurid savagery of our Revolution by connecting it to the practices and predilections of our bloodthirsty Aztec ancestors, coupled with those of our sadistic Spanish forefathers, the conquistadores and missionaries; but for now it is enough to look at the cartoons Posada was shortly to make of Emiliano Zapata, as a skeletal charro, mustachioed and bandoliered, leading a grisly troop of phantom cavalry into battle, through forests in which from every tree hangs a comical corpse.

The real Revolution was still eight years in the future, but we all sensed that Posada knew precisely what it was to do to us. We did not of course know it yet, but Posada was the prophet of doom for our time.

It was impossible to befriend Posada, assuming one should have wanted to do so. He sidled into the offices of *El Hijo del Ahuizote* twice each week, carved out his cartoons, and then disappeared back into the narrow streets of the old city, where he was supposed to have made his lodgings in the entrance hall of some crumbling palace. In fact, though, he, his wife, and an indeterminate number of children lived in a thoroughly unromantic tenement on the old Avenida de la Paz, near the Tepito market. The building Posada lived in was no different from any slum in the area: four or five floors of hundreds of rooms, with for each building a tiny court-yard with open-air washbasins and a pile of dirt for the children to play in.

Posada even had a place of business, a dark, grimy little store with an awning over it labeled simply Taller de Gra-bado, Print Shop. He was seldom there, though, because he was never famous enough to have editors looking for him. Each day he had to seek them out, to take his lithographer's tools to them and ask to draw whatever illustrations were needed for that afternoon's newspaper. I will not bore you with how arduous this was (and anyway, who cares about lithography now that there's some Casasola lurking behind every streetlamp with his camera?); but even you children of the twentieth century must know that a lithographer had to draw on stone and then offprint the image he had made onto paper. For years Posada had to send his sons (he called them all "Perrito," "Puppy," which is the term we use for a flunky who fetches and carries) out before dawn to solicit commissions from the editors of the dailies and the maga-zines, then come running back to him so he could start cut-ting on his stones.

Eventually Posada learned to speed things up by cutting on wood, then moved on to lead or type-metal engraving, until around the turn of the century he discovered what the Englishman William Blake had discovered ninety years ear-

lier: zinc etching. I am scarcely the man to tell you exactly
what this meant technically to Posada, but professionally it
was his making. Now he could leave his shop in the morning
with a couple of his perritos in tow, each carrying a bucket
of acid and a handful of resin-coated plates. He'd turn up in
the publisher's doorway, ask what was wanted, make his
drawing on the plate, dunk it in the acid — and in a half hour
hand the print to the publisher, ready to go with the copy it
illustrated.

And what copy! The men Posada worked for knew
what the public wanted, and those of you who live long
enough to watch Posada become famous will be able to see
illustrations of his drawings of *Horrible and Iniquitous Act
Perpetrated by a Priest Against Two Unmarried Sisters*; or *The
Grand Ball of the Forty-one Masculine and Coquettish Queers on
November 20, 1901*; or (my favorite, after all these years)
After the Horrible Crime He Ate the Remains of His Son, which
looks more like an irate and hungry campesino biting into
an overstuffed enchilada than like Goya's *Saturn Devouring
His Sons*.

But when you are able to look at a book that will probably be called *The Great Etchings of José Guadalupe Posada*, you
will begin to notice among all such grand guignol ephemera,
coming along slowly at first, then increasing in frequency
and power as the Revolution approached and finally broke
over us, the real drawings, the silent ones he made in spite
of my clumsy attempts at epithets and labeling, believing as
I did then that the Revolution needed words more than it
needed pictures. They come to haunt you: the one that showed
an hacendado and his mestizo overseers, whipping to death
clumps of little Indians they had tied to trees as though they
were bunches of bananas; or a rear view of a campesino,

hands tied behind his back, being marched to his death by a mounted squadron of rurales, the men Porfirio Díaz organized and paid to do the hacendados' dirty work; or — worst of all — the neat little field before a lovely hacienda where, as the ladies of the hacienda look on, fans fluttering, mestizos urged on by an overseer swing their scythes, harvesting a most bizarre crop — the shaggy heads of fifty wide-eyed and incredulous Indians, buried to their necks in the rich black soil of Morelos.

More and more often as the war approached, Posada did drawings of Emiliano Zapata and other men who were taking up the struggle that was not so silent anymore. That was almost a decade and more after our time together on *El Hijo del Ahuizote*, of course, and in 1902 neither Posada nor I had ever heard of Zapata or Villa or that curious little Liberal (again I use the word pejoratively) from Coahuila named Francisco Madero — which is just as well, because Posada came to love Madero as much as I would hate the pious little fraud who popped up from nowhere to take the Revolution away from me in 1911 and claim it as his own. If you press on through these notebooks, you will learn that if they have a true villain it is not Manuel Palafox or even General Victoriano Huerta (whom Posada was to depict as a giant, hairy scorpion clutching the skulls and bones of his countrymen), but Francisco I. Madero, that gentle, sweet, honest, weak . . . Liberal.

But all this specific politicization of Posada came after our association on the magazine. When I knew him best (and we never so much as shared a drink together), he was only just beginning to do his calaveras, to learn how to stand them up and prance them about as though they enjoyed their Mexican lives and wanted to amuse their public, not frighten it. There might be those who will tell you that the calaveras represented for Mexicans their lack of personal security over the centuries, or their awareness of the constant proximity of death. I don't know: the only thing Posada ever said to me about his calaveras was that they were ellos que lloran al hueso, "those who weep for the bone," who celebrate death.

I *can* say that I learned as much about Mexico and its Revolution from mute, sour-breathed old Posada, printer's apron over his ticklike girth and green sunshade stretched tight around the great globe of his shaggy head, as I ever learned from all the anarchist scholars who were to take me in hand in the years to come: rigorous men and women all, but none of them Mexicans. Except one, and that was Amparo Urdiales; and what she knew, she never needed to learn from books.

But I must get on with this tale of myself: the *Pachorrudo* (the scraggly old man) of the woeful countenance, Quixote's mind in Panza's body, because I'm writing neither for art historians nor for ideologists, but for you. Who are you, by the way? Who reads the notebooks of a failed anarchist (*there's* another redundancy for you), a forgotten zealot? Are you looking for shootings and hangings, the display of viscera? They will come, any moment now. Amour? Well, I'll try; but you must remember that I am a very minor amorist from a country in which every capon crows like a rooster. Or maybe you're just the sort of person who'd thumb through this as he waited his turn in a barbershop, and who'd prefer to read instead the story in *La Patria Ilustrada* that goes with Posada's drawing of "Woman Gives Birth to Three Children and Four Animals."

Who's the sad clown in *Commedia dell'Arte?* Pierrot? Do you like him? How about ridiculous, cross-gartered Malvolio: like him? Read on, then. *But*: Remember the caution I gave you in the first of my notebooks: I am not a man to take entirely lightly. What your grandchildren are, may be because of me.

November 6, 1922

Not even *El Hijo del Ahuizote* should be taken too lightly (as I took it at first) simply because it was ostensibly nothing more than a magazine of satirical feuilletons and cartoons by people like me and Posada. Within a couple of months of taking it over, we had almost 26,000 subscribers. Most, I'm sure, wanted to laugh at the calaveras; but someone must have read what I was writing (the standard young man's inflammatory rhetoric, which I needn't rehearse for you, except to recall that I gave specific names and dates to the rotten events the Porfiriato was forcing on us more heavily than ever, instead of just repeating the chisme, the gossip, as it came down the street, which is what all the other dissident writers were doing.

Our little club of real radicals was growing quickly, too; and we made our headquarters in our offices on Calle Cocheras — a stupid place for a cell to meet, since it should have occurred to someone that *El Hijo del Ahuizote* must have been as well staked out as any trouble spot in the city. Nevertheless, we met there almost daily: Enrique and I, Librado Rivera, Santiago de la Hoz, and four or five others, most notably the Sarabia brothers, Manuel and Juan, whom I had met the year before on the occasion of my oratorical triumph in San Luis Potosí.

It amuses me now to recall that Juan Sarabia was the hottest firebrand of us all — he who was later to become as

tame a Maderista as my brother Jesús. It was Juan who
insisted that we call him Ravachol, after the French martyr
who went to the guillotine in 1892 screaming, *"Vive l'anar-
chie!"* It was Juan, too, who kept after me to write up a plan
for our Revolution, insisting that no real rebellion could hope
to attract attention to itself without a pronouncement, a
statement of purpose, a plan. When I would protest a little
at this, he would strike a Ravacholish pose and announce:
"I have never seen, nor, probably, will I ever see a revolution without the propagation of ideas as a preliminary and
the shedding of blood as the inevitable means of deciding the
outcome."

Invariably we would all applaud such rhetoric, and I did
indeed begin scribbling bits of my Plan at this time. "The
shedding of blood" meant little to me just then. Even the
kindly Kropotkin spoke of this as an unfortunate necessity
in revolution, yet I suspect that if I imagined bloodshed then,
I imagined but a few bodies stretched out before a firing
squad. I saw no fields drenched with blood, no piles of bodies tossed into shallow arroyos for burning.

But before I got too far along I made a couple of very
serious tactical mistakes.

Up in Monterrey old General Bernardo Reyes decided
he wanted to be governor. Some fool cousin of his tried to
run against him, and Bernardo called out his troops and had
them fire over a rally his rival was trying to conduct. The
rival fled, of course, and the election proceeded as smoothly
as Bernardo and his patrón, Don Porfirio Díaz, had planned
for it to. But we got wind of this whiff of democratic impulse
at *El Hijo del Ahuizote,* and wrote it up as high comedy. We
had forgotten that Bernardo was not just another general,
but was then occupying the sinecure of Secretary of War.
So we were quite surprised when agents of the Porfiriato

appeared one morning in the middle of September, shut down the magazine, and hauled us all off to the military prison at Santiago Tlatelolco, where we were charged with "Insulting the Army." My friends were let off with a warning, but the Army kept me for four months.

I had not been in prison a week before the first issue of *The Grandson of Ahuizote* appeared in the kiosks of the city. It lasted a week until it was closed down — to be reborn a week later as *The Great-Great-Grandson of Ahuizote*. This, too, disappeared as quickly as the censors could identify it. Only to reappear, more modestly this time, as *The Great-Grandson of Ahuizote*. We all thought this was very funny, and apparently so did all of Mexico City except its leaders. On January 1, 1903, they released me, with a warning I was too enthusiastic to take very seriously. On the evening of my release, we gathered in our old offices of *El Hijo*, and hung from its windows a large banner that read, THE CONSTITUTION IS DEAD.

The next morning's newspapers had a photograph of us and our banner on their front pages. We thought this was very funny, too. (I know now, of course, that this prankishness is absolutely typical of the enthusiastic early stages of serious uprisings, and that Porfirio and his henchmen were taking us just as seriously as they should have, given the trouble we were about to cause them. But oh, God, we were happy in those few short months more of relative freedom they allowed us.)

Happy, and busy. At nights I worked on my Plan, which I now knew would encompass much more than the simple replacement of Don Porfirio and restoration of the old Constitution — that it would have to call for nothing less than a new Mexico, with all its old institutions torn down and reborn as something entirely new.

What did I think my newborn Mexico would be like? I blush today to write this down, but what I envisioned then was a kind of prelapsarian Garden of Eden, an idyllic community of rich farms and healthy, happy campesinos, all guided (should they ever need guidance) by white-bearded elders, wise old men beloved by all. In short, I saw all Mexico as simply a larger version of my father's ideal pueblo. No great, sooty factories, only shops, little more than cottage industries. No huge cities, no slums. Water for irrigation. Open ranges for cattle.

Today I know that to hold such a vision is not only naive, but culpable — regressive, infantile even. Or perhaps worse even than that: if Goya was right about the sleep of reason producing monsters, then what were all my child's dreams but a kind of sleep of reason, from which monstrous forms would emerge? From my true and final cell, now, not the jaunty célula of my youth, I say: beware the idealist; beware the man with a cause.

There's a fine Spanish irony for you: ideals and causes produce revolutions, which turn into monsters. Goya knew this, all right. So had old Posada known it, but of course no one (especially me) took him very seriously.

In the mornings we put out a new magazine of dissent, *Excelsior* (which lasted three issues, more than most did). And in the afternoons my cell and I worked at reorganizing the old Confederation of Liberal Clubs of the Republic, which we saw as our best hope to launch real anarchism across the whole country.

They let us play at this until mid-April of 1903, when they came to get me, and suddenly nothing was funny anymore.

Two uniformed agents came to the door of our offices (why do they always send *two?* In both Mexico and the United

States, when the arrest was serious, they never sent three, or four: always *two*), and they headed straight for me and Enrique, ignoring the rest of our crowd. Two hours later we were back in Belén, charged with "Ridiculing Public Officials." And this time there was no fourteen-man dormitory room for us, but an airless little cell with three straw petates laid on the floor: one for me, one for Enrique, and one for a man who lay on his back with that perfect stillness only the dead enjoy.

I do not know who this man was. Neither I nor Enrique went near him. It is one thing to laugh about death in a Posada cartoon, and another thing entirely when death is lying four feet from you in a cell that never gives more than three or four hours of crepuscular light each day. Three days the body lay with us, growing, then shrinking into itself, turning each day (so far as we could tell) from gray to green to black. Then they took him away. But the stench had not completely left the cell by the end of November, when Enrique and I were released. In fact, it is with me now, if I let my memory work on those months long enough.

They let us out of the cell once, briefly, to see Juan Sarabia, who had bribed his way in with the last of the magazine's funds. For the moment his Ravachol persona was gone. He looked scared.

" 'Manos," he said, looking around him to make sure the gate through which he had entered was still open, "we're all fucked now, but especially you, Ricardo."

"Calm down, Juanico," said Enrique, "and stop looking over your shoulder at the police. They don't like to be looked at. What's wrong now that wasn't wrong before?"

Sarabia looked at the mud beneath our feet (which were bare, and the city gets cold in the November rains), took a deep breath, and told us our pals had tried to start up *The*

Father of Ahuizote, but that the Federales had come the first day, roughed them up, hammered the press into pieces, padlocked the door, and thrown them all out into the street. Then he looked at me and said, "A month ago they put out an edict against you, Ricardo. No one in the country can print anything by you, or even print your name. I think they are getting ready for you to be dead, Ricardo."

From the hindsight advantage of all these years, all these prisons, all these police, I know now that Sarabia was right, just as I know why they left that cadaver with us for three days. "Death is ugly, and lasts a long time," they were saying to me. "And this is what you will look and smell like, if we choose."

Juan Sarabia left, walking as slowly toward the exit as his sense of machismo would let him, not quite trotting but more than walking; and Enrique and I returned to our cell, to wait for whatever was going to happen to us. Or maybe only to me: they would have been capable of leaving Enrique alone in that cell for a few days with *my* cadaver, too.

Two nights later one of our jailers, suddenly full of conspiratorial bonhomie, came into our cell as we sat on our mats, silently hiding from despair by avoiding one another's eyes. He squatted beside me, offered us cigarettes, and grinned at me so broadly that I could see the whiteness of his teeth in the near darkness.

"I have come from the jefe of the prison, Señor Villavicencio. He has asked me to tell you, from his heart, Señor Flores, that he wishes you well, and that he is disposed to free you. But he wants to be sure you know this: if you write one word in Mexico again, you are a dead man. You know 'dead man'?" He nudged me in my trembling ribs, to be sure I knew this little joke was a nonjoke of the most serious kind.

I nodded. I knew. No more striking of revolutionary poses. Now it was all real: I could become like my brother Jesús, a member of the only-faintly-disloyal opposition; or I could continue as a journalist, appearing very earnest, hoping that in a few years everyone would have forgotten my disreputable past, my childish opposition to the Porfiriato, my months in jail, my brush with death. I could grow fat again, squeeze into the wicker chairs at the cafés on the Alameda, drink cognac and smoke good Cuban cigars with the other timid ones, discussing maybe the poetry of Rubén Darío.

Or I could walk away from Belén, grab myself by my balls, go up to Yankeelandia, and put out a reborn *Regeneración* that would come flying down out of exile back into Mexico, free to hit not only at Porfirio Díaz but also at everything corrupt in my country — which was to say, *every*thing, excepting only the land and the people. To be anarquista entero: the whole thing, bombs and all.

Well, I've already told you what I did. Two weeks later we were freed; and a week after that, as 1903 ended, Enrique and I and one of our gang called Santiago de la Hoz (one of the few of us who had not only zeal but a little money as well) bought train tickets to Nuevo Laredo. Our aim was to swim the Rio Bravo (which you gringos, if you *are* gringos, call the Rio Grande), and fetch up on the Texas border, in the land of hope and promise, where any man, of whatever race or creed, could express his deepest hopes and convictions without the slightest fear.

Irony must be tiring. Or maybe it's the memory of that corpse who shared our cell in Belén. Anyway, I'm exhausted. No letter to Lilly Sarnoff today, no complaint to the warden, not even a wave to Librado Rivera across the courtyard. Sometimes even heroes need to rest.

Notebook 5

Looked at from a great distance, not necessarily from Olympus, but just, let's say, from Boston or Washington, D.C., the carryings-on of the Zapatas and their friends may seem not tragic or grand but only comic, something to be managed by a Latin Mack Sennett. Do you, my good old reader, see the Revolution as slapstick comedy or (if you're slightly more cultured) as opera *bouffe?* Do you watch us as if we were figures in your newsreels?

There are the pajama-clad guerrillas on a hillside, pointing their rifles down into the barranca where the Federales are waiting in ambush. Then, bang! and the campesinos all flop over, looking like clumps of dirty white cotton as they fall, little balls of fluff against the dusty gray of mesquite and chaparral. Next, with the scissors-click motions the camera gives us, the victorious Federales pace around us, whipping their cigars up to their mouths, snatching up the rifles of the dead men, forming up into ragged ranks, and quickstepping off to the next confrontation.

Or here's the guerrilla chieftain, hands tied behind him, smiling at the firing squad drawn up only five feet before him. He shouts something (the camera can't hear), the rifles blossom smoke, and the guerrilla tumbles backward like a rag doll thrown down by a petulant child, into the grave that has been dug for him. Other prisoners shovel him under with maniacal haste, and the newsreel ends.

That's the Revolution, is it? *Silly* Mexicans, are we not?

But we Mexicans remember the harder images: the deaths that come from beatings, with ruined kidneys and crushed skulls; and those that come from shootings that are not almost funny, like tossing a big doll down: brain-shot men thrashing for hours in the arms of the women who have followed them for years, and who look as they embrace their men not into some gringo's camera but just into the dirty sand, their faces without expression. Or men with holes in their lungs vomiting blood like bulls hacked at by clumsy matadors. Or men slumped against pocked white walls, staring at the messy spot in their lap where their genitals had been.

But you probably don't want to read about that sort of thing. After all, you've latterly had your own Great War, albeit for only a few months and on someone else's continent; and you don't need some Mexican to tell you that war is hell. If you have to read about us, you'd prefer to learn how Pancho Villa, after the battle of Casas Grandes, executed sixty prisoners by lining them into files of three and firing one bullet through each file: one bullet for every three men. Very economical, and an interesting theory, but not really a success. You can line men up in neat rows three deep, but you can't make them all the same height: shoot the first man in the heart, and you get the second through the navel, and the third in his ear.

Or perhaps you'd prefer to read about how Rodolfo Fierro, the Villista general who was to die in quicksand, executed three hundred prisoners single-handed, running them like cattle through a corral, picking them off with his Colt one by one as they broke for a fence, and pausing only when his trigger finger cramped. Stick a sombrero on his head and a cigar in his teeth, and you've got the Mexican Revolution, right?

Well, that's what you'd get if General Eufemio Zapata were writing these notebooks, but he isn't. I'm the author, and what I remember, what sticks in my mind as I sit here in Leavenworth, an anarchist monk in perpetual retreat, is what I saw myself: nothing really of battle itself, but only of battle's leavings — bodies everywhere, bodies hanging from every tree, wherever we went, drying and shrinking fast in the desert heat, their heads bent onto their chests or shoulders at improbable angles, their tiny feet dangling scarcely more than three inches above the sand; bodies gathered up and set in repose against one another around the base of a tree, dozing away in their last siesta; bodies stuffed down into some village's single well; bodies anywhere at all, until you scarcely noticed them. Or horses, so overridden in combat that their saddle blankets were glued to their shredded flanks, grazing casually over the battlefields, unaware that their entrails were dangling beneath them until they tripped over them. So much for silly Mexicans and laughter at our antics. And don't nod sagely at what I write, and tell me that you knew of all this from your viewing of Goya's etchings. Unless you saw it and smelled it, you don't know.

I am so angry now that I am going to whisk the war in Morelos away from you, and turn you back to me and my adventures in your country, after I arrived on the north bank of the Rio Bravo in January 1904, ready with my compañeros to bring down the Porfiriato from some new stronghold in the United States. Be patient: my career as an expatriate journalist and erstwhile warrior is turbulent but brief, and relatively bloodless. You'll encounter a lot of beatings but few deaths, your country being so much more civilized than mine. Another sort of comedy: Flores Magón and the Keystone Kops.

When Enrique and I fled across the river with Santiago de la Hoz, we knew that he had money, but we did not know that he could not swim. Unfortunately, his money went under with him, so that my brother and I arrived in the United States as poor as all the rest of our fellow wetbacks (as you have taken to calling us) who were coming north in ever greater numbers, in search of the peace and plenty we were sure was available to all.

NO: that is still my anger speaking. Santiago was a good young man, a poet, and his death hurt me and Enrique a great deal. And only fools thought that life in the United States would be easy. There was already a large colony of Mexicans in each border town, forming a permanent under-class. Life for these expatriotas was hard, perhaps even as bad as it had been back in their pueblos. At any rate, no one was under any illusions for very long after arriving. In Mexico we had read in Yankee newspapers that "Mexicans are an integral part of Texas life"; within a week we knew just what that part was: the lowest one.

And even though the colony in Laredo welcomed the two of us (we were known everywhere by now, as symbols of protest, wrath, and hope; and those who could read delighted in showing us copies of *Regeneración* they had brought with them into exile), no one was prepared to feed or shelter us for more than a day or two. We had to find work. With luck, we did: Enrique (always the stronger) as a digger of ditches, and I as a dishwasher in a big gringo restaurant.

We lived like peones, dressed in denim work shirts and overalls we bought on credit from a compatriota who ran a cast-off dry-goods store, and tried to save our money against the time when we could resume our proper calling as revolutionaries. One of the few illusions our first weeks in America left us was our belief that here there was true freedom of the press; and we were eager to resume publication of *Regeneración*.

But without knowing it, we had made an enemy already. There was a woman in the community named Juanita Gutiérrez, a member of the Liberal party of Laredo. We thought she was our ally, and even more than that: Enrique was sure I was sleeping with her, and I was sure that he was. Perhaps the trouble was that neither of us was. In any case, this Juanita began circulating rumors that we had drowned Santiago de la Hoz for his money. When we went to her to complain about this, she denied everything — then left for Mexico City, where she repeated the same lies about us to any journalist who would listen. (Most did, of course.) I never knew whether she was a spy for the Porfiristas, or just a hysteric; but she made it necessary for us to leave Laredo within a month of our arrival there. For reasons I can't explain, revolutionaries seem to attract such women.

We moved two hundred miles north to San Antonio, found work as peones de campo on some Texan's ranch, rented a one-room adobe hut on the edge of town, worked all day and schemed half the night, waiting for luck to come to us. At the end of summer it did, in the form of the Sarabia brothers, Juan and Manuel, who had learned our whereabouts from our brother Jesús in Mexico City, and had come to join us in our struggle. Juan no longer wanted to be known as "Ravachol," and appeared to have matured considerably since his brief visit to us in Belén nine months earlier. He arrived speaking soberly of our need for "working capital" (an expression I never liked), and within days he produced two men who were eager to help us. The first of these was genuine: Camilo Arriaga, a patriot who knew how to funnel money to us from various liberal magazines back in the Capital, and who had many valuable connections in both countries. The second man was an American, an agreeable, even unctuous Texan named P. J. Birdwhistle. (Can there be such a name?) The first thing he did when Juan Sarabia brought him to our hut was to decline to sit in our one old chair. "Shit, brothers," he said to us, "if I was to sit in that ole chair it'd chew my ass to ribbons. Lookit them splinters."

Mr. Birdwhistle (I can't write that name without giggling: the guard is going to think I am abusing myself if I don't stop) was right about the chair, which we had already baptized "El Cocodrilo," the Crocodile; yet it seemed to us that he had committed a breach of etiquette which no Mexican would have made. But he offered to proofread the English editions of *Regeneración* for nothing, so we welcomed him.

With Arriaga's money we bought paper and ink and rented a press, and I set to work on composing the first issue of the magazine to come from the United States. By early November it was ready, and we printed a run of 10,000 copies. Arriaga gathered up all but a thousand of these and took them with him to the border, where he concealed them in other newspapers, copies of the Montgomery Ward catalogue, church flyers, anything that would get them past Customs and out over the country, where all the new Liberal clubs were waiting for them.

My lead essay was not bashful. In fact, one might say it was exalted. I can, in fact, remember declaring war. "Here we are," I wrote, "with the torch of the Revolution in one hand and the program of the Liberal party in the other, declaring war. The weapons of Caesar's mercenaries will not harm the citizen who heeds his responsibility. The bayonets of the rebels will answer, blow for blow . . . Mexicans: to war!"

I can to this day recall much of what I wrote next, so great was my exaltation at being able to write once again:

> Workers, listen: the infamous peace we Mexicans have suffered . . . will soon be broken. Today's calm conceals the violence of tomorrow's insurrection. Revolution is the logical consequence of the thousand crimes of despotism . . . It has to come, unfailingly, fatefully, with the punctuality of the sun banishing sorrowful night. You will see, you workers, the force of Revolution. Your hands will grasp the gun . . . The Revolution must come, irrevocably, and better still, it will triumph. By blood and fire it will come to the den where the jackals who have been devouring you for thirty-four years are holding their last feast . . . Proletarians! Keep in mind that you are the nerve of the Revolution. Go to it, not like cattle to the slaughterhouse, but as men conscious of all their rights. Go to the fight. Knock resolutely on the doors. Glory waits impatiently . . . Break your chains on the heads of your executioners.

Great stuff, no? Yes, I know how florid it sounds to you, sophisticated reader of a dead man's notebooks, snug in your rich man's club in Boston or wherever. But what if you were a Mexican campesino, hungry and exhausted from fourteen hours of working the fields or the mines of some fat hacendado or some gringo entrepreneur; and someone, a poor peón like yourself except he had been to a couple of years of school, were reading this over an illicit fire to you and your compañeros in Oaxaca, or Chiapas, or the Yucatán, or Sonora, or anywhere at all in my sad, benighted country? It would sound better to you then, no? How would you like it if you were young Emiliano Zapata in Morelos, hearing it as read to him by old Otilio Montaño, and you had just been beaten by some mestizo overseer at the Hacienda de Hospital, near Anenecuilco, for stealing some of your own family's straw to feed your horses? There was an audience for such prose, amigo mío; a large and appreciative audience.

My euphoria at being back in business again did not last long. One month after that first issue, as I was seated very tentatively on El Cocodrilo, giving a brief lecture on violent overthrow to my friends, the door burst open and in rushed a little man none of us had seen before. He leapt straight at me, and swung a knife at my shoulder. He missed, and before he could try again Enrique wrapped his strong arms around him and threw him to the floor. I grabbed the knife, and Juan Sarabia ran howling for the police.

They arrived within minutes, four of them, accompanied by none other than P. J. Birdwhistle, who was waving his ten-gallon sombrero, brandishing a revolver, and yelling, "Kill the little cocksucker!" I thought he was referring to my assailant, but he meant me, apparently; because the policemen grabbed not the intruder but me and Enrique, and hauled us down to the Courthouse, where I was released with a warning, and Enrique charged with Disturbing the Peace. It cost us thirty dollars to free him. We never saw the little man again. Nor Mr. Birdwhistle, happily. I am sure now that both were agents of the Porfiristas, sent to disrupt our efforts with *Regeneración*.

Worse things by far than this assault have happened to me, but I recall it for you now so that you may see how long Don Porfirio's arm was. The ropes that tied the Mexican government to that of the United States were very strong. For a long time gringo financiers had been passing over the border, and Díaz had been receiving them with great affection. The petroleum companies, especially Standard Oil, had been grabbing all they could for years, in open competition with Pearson of Great Britain. The richest mines were in North American hands. We still owned our railroads, but Yankees controlled and ran them. In order to maintain "la buena voluntad," Díaz had given huge stretches of our best land to American publicists. The great friends of Wall Street were certainly not about to permit a few Mexican intellectuals, weighed down by poverty, to ruin that goodwill just to give back to Mexicans what was theirs.

Nevertheless, even after this silly attack, we still believed that there was such a thing in the United States as freedom of the press — only maybe not quite so much in the border states. So we decided to move again. We packed up our equipment and caught a train to St. Louis, Missouri, in the heart of the nation. We believed that the farther from Mexico we traveled, the safer we would be. It would be months before we learned that ever since our arrival in Laredo we had been under the closest scrutiny by one Enrique Clay Creel, hacendado and governor of the state of Chihuahua — and de facto chief of Don Porfirio's international intelligence services. Señor Creel had from the first minute been monitoring not only all our movements, but all our correspondence as well. From 1904 until the fall of the Porfiriato in 1911, he read everything we wrote, and everything that was written to us. In this he had the full cooperation of the United States postal and wire services.

And he had hired as his chief operative in the United States a citizen of St. Louis, one Thomas Furlong, on leave from the Pinkertons for the sole purpose of bringing me down and silencing *Regeneración*. As you will see, this Furlong was very good at his job. He not only hounded me mercilessly; in his seven-year campaign against us he succeeded in apprehending 180 anti-Díaz Mexican expatriates. Some he took through the legal processes of extradition, but most of these he rounded up and drove across the border, where firing squads were waiting for them. I am sure Señor Creel paid him very well for all this.

Furlong's first move against us, early in 1905 as we were setting up our offices in St. Louis, on North Avenue, was to send us one of his undercover operatives, Mr. Ansel T. Samuels, who volunteered to be the advertising solicitor for the magazine. We accepted. Why we did so, I can't imagine, after our experiences with P. J. Birdwhistle. Let's just say that we were fools, or that we were busy — or let's tell the truth, which is that in St. Louis I had for the first time bigger things on my mind than overthrowing Porfirio Díaz, or bringing a just government to Mexico, or getting out a subversive newspaper. In St. Louis, I went international. I also became one of the big-time lovers, but you'll have to wait a few minutes to hear about that.

There was no barrio latino in St. Louis, but there was what seemed to me an enormous international colony. Wherever I walked I heard Italian, German, Russian, and what I soon learned to identify as Yiddish. And even if I couldn't understand most of what was being said around me in the working-class district where all these exotic languages were being spoken, I could tell a political meeting when I saw one — and they were everywhere, right out in the open, advertised in newspapers and on posters, conducted in cafés and hired halls, and in good weather even in the middle of parks. Middle European zealots of vague provenance, wearing black overcoats and fedoras or derbies, and formidable women draped in shawls, their heads covered by babushkas, gathered in steamy, low-ceilinged rooms around samovars to shout and shake their fists at one another. I could at first understand almost nothing of what they said, but their

debates were obviously polemical, to judge only from words
that bounced out at me from time to time: words like Bol-
sheviki, Narodniki, Mensheviki. And names, some of which
were of course familiar to me, like Bakunin and Kropotkin
and Grave and Reclus; and some of which were new, like
Czolgosz, Most, Berkman, and — most often, perhaps — Emma
Goldman.

They seemed very angry with one another, these foreigners. All talked at once; no one listened. In what looked to
me like fits of rage, they would stick their fists in one another's faces, spray their spittle at one another, throw their arms
around one another and burst into tears, stalk off indignantly into the night — only to return minutes later, hurling
themselves dramatically through the doorway into the wel-
coming arms of their friends, who had been sobbing discon-
solately for thirty seconds over their cups of tea. These people
had no sense of decorum, but they were indeed fascinating
to Mexican eyes.

I took to attending such meetings whenever I could get
away from *Regeneración*, first as spectator, and then — when
I learned that many of the participants could holler almost
as well in English as in their own languages — as participant.
Slightly to my surprise, I was taken seriously. They already
knew of the situation in Mexico, better in fact than did most
Mexicans; and when one day I announced my name to them,
they shouted even louder, threw their arms around me, thrust
tea, cigars, and remarkable pieces of fish covered with phlegmy
sauce at me, and called me their brother, their comrade.
Through all this I kept looking over my shoulder for the
police, but none appeared; nor did my new friends appear
to expect them. In this they were wrong.

I was so excited at being taken up by these ardent refugees that I scarcely listened when Enrique and the others

complained to me that we had spent all our savings in the move from San Antonio, and that there was no money to resume printing the magazine. I remember turning to Camilo Arriaga and saying, "Dip down into your Mexican pot and pull us up some pesos, compañero," in such a way as to suggest that mere financial matters were of little interest to me just now, so occupied was I with my important *mitteleuropaisch* political meetings.

To do them credit, no one denounced me for the pompous ass I was becoming at that time. Camilo only shrugged, disappeared — and returned, a week later, saying that he'd found a new friend for us. He described this friend as very short, about thirty, a member of the *Partido Liberal Mexicano*, and the scion of an important landowning family from the state of Coahuila. His name was Francisco I. Madero, and Camilo thought it might be easy to pry some money out of him, if we could make him feel like one of us.

"He loves *Regeneración*, Ricardo," said Camilo. "Why don't you write him and tell him you need two thousand dollars to get it going up here?"

So I sent a note to this enano, this midget, called Madero. He answered promptly, saying that he would be happy to lend us $2,000, but only if Camilo, not I, signed the note, since he was sure that I had nothing with which to guarantee a loan. He was right in this, of course; but his stipulation did nothing to endear him to me. As far as I was concerned, this Madero was just another señorito who wanted to hang around us authentic firebrands, to get an occasional vicarious whiff of danger. I would accept his $2000, but taking him seriously was out of the question.

Besides, I had more important matters to occupy me these days than catering to the sons of the rich in Mexico. I left the magazine in the hands of Enrique, the Sarabias, and two

new additions to our group, my old friends Librado Rivera
and Antonio Villarreal, and went off in search of my new
European fans. I was not the first Mexican to abandon his
compatriotas for the company of glamorous foreigners. (The
glorious emperor Moctezuma II comes to mind. So does
Porfirio Díaz.) Why on earth do we persist in doting on
things European? When has Europe meant anything but
trouble for us?

And what was so glamorous about this particular bunch
of mine? Certainly, they were far from attractive, physically
speaking: mostly, they were poorly clothed, badly shorn and
shod, with muddy complexions and bad breath. Their man-
ners were deplorable. Any kind of subtlety was alien to them.
Their voices were loud and strident. The women were em-
barrassingly forward, especially to Mexican sensibilities. I
suppose they seemed glamorous to me because I must have
seemed glamorous and exotic to them. I was their first Mexican, their first Indian. That I had, like most of them, been
imprisoned for my ideas enhanced my appeal. That I could
write, and that I ran a political magazine, made me a very
desirable acquisition. I was a delightful new toy, and potentially a very useful one.

I must have seemed comically naive to them, in spite of
all the reading I had done in Belén Prison and elsewhere.
Basically, my theories were nothing more than those of Prince
Pyotr Kropotkin, that sunniest of revolutionaries, that secular saint. From two of his books, *The Conquest of Bread* and
Mutual Aid (which I had caused to be printed in Mexico three
years earlier, and which even now young Emiliano Zapata
was having read to him in Anenecuilco by Otilio Montaño),
I had conceived a notion of anarchism almost as guileless as
my father's theories. Kropotkin believed that, contrary to
Darwin's theories of survival of the fittest, animals practice

mutual assistance. Citing Rousseau, he asked why it should be that animals could live in peace, while only civilized man tormented his fellows.

Kropotkin studied all the genera of animals, and noted the friendly relations among these, until he arrived at Man. He decided that we were capable of living, like the animals, in harmony; and that our wars were caused not by any innate aggressive impulse, but by the corrupt nature of society. From this perhaps optimistic conclusion, Kropotkin developed his moral creed of mutual toleration, cooperation, and aid, which in the Ideal State would lead to the true Brotherhood of Man.

I had been guided in my ideological life thus far by Kropotkin's theories, to the extent that I believed in the innate goodness of all Mexicans, once they should be freed from the bonds of the Porfiriato and allowed to return to the land. All systems of oppression, whether called the Roman Empire, or the Inquisition, or Czarism, or Capitalist Exploitation, or Porfirismo, were nothing more than a *danse macabre* of hatred and cruelty, the repudiation of man's true nature, a nature that in a free society would conduct itself with the same principles of mutual aid that Kropotkin had observed in the animal kingdom.

It was a lofty theory, the most elevated expression of a truly refulgent mind. I think now, as I sit on my cot, staring through the window of my cell in Leavenworth Penitentiary, that Kropotkin knew little about animals, and less about Man.

Kropotkin had trouble accounting for violence. He finally and reluctantly accepted it, because it occurred inevitably during revolutions, which were unavoidable stages in human progress. In this he resembled his much more sanguinary predecessor, Mikhail Bakunin, who had written that bloody revolutions are often necessary, thanks to human stupidity; but that they are always evil, a monstrous evil and a great disaster, an affront not only to Man but also the idea of Purity, and to the perfection of the purpose in whose name they take place. But Kropotkin could never bring himself to believe in the necessity of evil. Revolution, he thought, alternated, in the great scheme of things, with evolution — was, in fact, little more than accelerated evolution. Both belonged to the unity of nature, and were therefore good.

With Bakunin, Kropotkin believed too that revolutions were not made by individuals or by secret societies, but came automatically: the power of things, the current of events and facts, produced them. They were long preparing in the depths of the obscure consciousness of the masses — and then they broke out suddenly, often on apparently slight occasion. Revolution was natural, spontaneous, mystical in its origins, and unstoppable once begun. All the revolutionary leader had to do (all *I*, Ricardo Flores Magón, had to do!) was to tell the people, clearly and simply, that they had only to rise up and destroy the social system that was oppressing them, and they would do so, joyously and with impeccable violence should it be necessary. They had only to know that their moment in history had arrived, and their good impulses would do the rest.

Bakunin believed that when the Revolution came to Europe, it would explode in one of the more economically backward countries — Italy, Spain, or Russia — where the workers, though untrained, unorganized, and illiterate, with no understanding of their own wants, would be ready to rise because they had nothing to lose. (And how much readier to rise would be the Mexican peasants, I thought; how much less than their European counterparts did they have to lose.) To impel the masses to action, Bakunin (and Kropotkin after him) called for "propaganda of the deed": not only by the word, but also "by dagger, gun, and dynamite." Thus began the terrible anarchist practice of relentless, remorseless terrorism in the service of the New Millennium.

As leaders of his Revolution, Kropotkin called for "men of courage willing not only to speak but to act, pure characters who prefer prison, exile, and death to a life that contradicts their principles, bold natures who know that in order to win one must dare." Was I not such a man? I was; and I had proven so, first by prison and then by exile. And I proposed to be daring. I needed only to be told how to go about doing so.

In early spring of 1905 my refugee friends introduced me to a newly arrived Spaniard named Florencio Bazora, perhaps hoping that this articulate, flamboyant Andalusian would take me under his wing and sharpen my understanding of what we anarchists were really up to. Bazora had been alcalde of Cazalla de la Sierra, a town in the hills northeast of Sevilla. The Guardia Civil had run him off, in the big *Mano Negra* scare of the nineties, and he had surfaced again in Barcelona, where he became a disciple of Francisco Ferrer, the soon-to-be-martyred founder of the Escuela Moderna (the Mexico City branch of which had as one of its young maestras a Tehuana woman named Amparo Urdiales). Bazora was just what I needed: he spoke Spanish, he knew his theory, and he was never pesado, boring, heavy — as, I must admit, many of my Russian and German friends were.

Bazora and I would stroll through the balmy April nights of St. Louis, I in my shabby black suit and floppy fedora, and he in his Spanish intellectual's costume of beret and shabby tweeds. He would put his hand on my shoulder, and laugh, and say, "'Look here, Ricardo: do you know what anarchism *really* is?'"

I would of course say that I had no idea.

He would point to the nearest wall and say, "In Cazalla, if I painted on such a wall a notice that said, DO NOT PISS ON THIS WALL, do you know what would happen?"

I would of course say no.

"By nightfall, every man in the village would have pissed on that wall. *That's* anarchism. And if I went to the cliff at the edge of the village, and stuck a sign in the dirt that said, DO NOT THROW GARBAGE HERE, by morning every woman in Cazalla would have tossed her garbage there. *That's* anarchism."

I thought perhaps that this was not anarchism, but infantilism; but I said nothing.

Then Bazora would laugh, pound me on the back, and lead me to a café where we could talk more seriously. I enjoyed these springtime frolics with Bazora: not many of my new friends cared much for humor, and none of them spoke otherwise than chastely. Bazora could profane and blaspheme almost as well as a Mexican, and I was grateful to him for this.

"Look, Ricardo," he said to me one evening, as we walked arm in arm down a crowded sidewalk, drawing glances from annoyed Missourians, "you have to think of all this anarchist shit as a sort of mad spectrum. At one end is the solitary rebel, the single anarch, opposing all, denying all, rejecting confederates — and getting nowhere. He's an imbecile, but we think of him as the holy fool of anarchism. He's the one who delights in the *acte gratuit*, the bomb tossed at anyone. He's an interesting, repellent phenomenon. Nothing more. He's what the public thinks of when you say the word *anarchist*."

I replied that such a man, though glamorous, was no true

anarchist, because he had only the desire to destroy, whereas the real anarchist always had a view of a desirable future society, and sought ways of bringing it about.

"All right," Bazora said. "But what do you do about someone like this man Czolgosz, who pulls out a pistol and shoots the gringo president McKinley?" This had happened in 1901, at the Pan-American Exposition in Buffalo, New York, and was an event to which we in Mexico had paid little attention, political assassination being a fairly common occurrence to us. We had not known that Leon Czolgosz, when arrested after the shooting, revealed himself to be a poor halfwit — but a halfwit with a motivation, a goal, in his statement to the press and the police: "I killed President McKinley because I done my duty . . . because he was an enemy of the good working people. I heard that woman Emma Goldman say in a speech that all rulers should be exterminated. . . . That set me to thinking so that my head nearly split with pain. . . . I am an anarchist. I don't believe in marriage. I believe in free love." Few of us had noticed even the headlines after the assassination: CONFESSES TO HAVING BEEN INCITED BY EMMA GOLDMAN. WOMAN ANARCHIST WANTED.

"The man's a fucking idiot, right?" said Bazora. I nodded. "But he had a view of a future society, right? And he sought ways of bringing it about, right?" Again, I nodded. "Then Señor Czolgosz becomes an authentic anarchist in your book, right?" I nodded — then shook my head. Bazora laughed.

"And what about the effect on the United States of Czolgosz's *attentat?*" he asked. ("Attentat" was what we anarchists called our violent acts.) "Here was the whole fucking country on edge after the Haymarket Riot in 1886, when eight of our people tossed a bomb into a crowd of police.

And then this silly shit Czolgosz comes along and blows a hole in the president, and what happens?"

I gave Bazora my earnestly ignorant look.

"Que eres otro idiota, tú culo sucio," he said. "The trouble with you Mexicans is that you don't think you need to know anything in order to be an intellectual. No wonder we Spaniards abandoned you."

Bazora's notions about Mexican history were not the same as mine, clearly; but he was not a man who liked being corrected, so I kept silent.

"I'll tell you what happened after the assassination, Magoncito, and you're going to wish someone had told you this before you came to this shitty country. What happened was that the new president, this Roosevelt, got up in front of his Congress and said that anarchism was a crime against the whole human race, and all mankind should band against the anarchist."

"Isn't it good for us that Roosevelt said that, though?" I asked. "Isn't the government *supposed* to be against us?"

"In theory, of course," said Bazora. "But look at the trouble Czolgosz has allowed the President to make for us. He's got the Congress to pass laws making all our speeches and writings be considered seditious. We are no longer to be allowed at large. If we're found out, we're to be deported. If we try to come here, we're to be kept out. They've got an Immigration Act now that says all this. We're not just dissidents now, Ricardo. Now we're fucking criminals, and they can throw our asses out whenever they want. And you can believe that's what they want for you. You're a gone greaser, Ricardo. Any day, and they're coming for you. How do you feel about all your theory now, mariposa mia?"

I told Bazora that what I felt right then was just a little trapped. We had to get out of Mexico, Enrique and I and

the others. Where should we have gone? South, to Guate-
mala, that madman's land? Over to Cuba, that American
colony? No, we had to be right where we were; and even if
we were criminals here, we were in less danger now than we
had been in Mexico. Bazora laughed again at this.

"All right, my Mexican stud bull," he said. "Let's get
back to our anarchist spectrum for a moment. Ignore the
single madman. Let us say that saner anarchists recognize
the need for a contract of some sort, after the manner of that
fat frog, Proudhon. Let's call them the mutualists. They want
individual freedom just as much as the bomb thrower does;
but they know they can attain that freedom only if they band
together to build a new society."

"What happens to the old one?" I asked.

"Forget that, idiot. Pay attention. Next come the collec-
tivists, like Bakunin, who want to insert their anarchist attitudes into a society of growing industry, where voluntary
organizations would pursue the individual good of each
worker. Stop yawning, stupid Mexican. What's next, tú puta
madre?"

I said I had no idea. I was thinking that I liked theory
all right, but perhaps a little less than I had thought.

"Coño, it's your man Kropotkin, with his anarchist communism. He wants to take wages out of the hands of the
workers, and distribute them on the basis of need. Everybody happy to work hard, everybody happy to share. Do
you believe that, mocoso, you mucus-head?"

I shrugged, hoping to convey some doubt, but no cynicism.

"Shit. Then do you believe in the next lot, the anarcho-
syndicalists, who think that a system of trade unions is the
best means of distributing wages fairly? I'll *tell* you what you
believe: you don't believe in any of that, because it's all a lot

of shit. Don't listen to what those goddamn Russians down the street in their piss-smelling tea gardens are yelling at you. I'll fucking *tell* you what you fucking believe in, you Indian pig." (You must understand that Bazora was smiling amiably at me as he said these things. He was talking to me as an equal. I cannot imagine how he spoke to those he considered his inferiors.) I smiled inquiringly at him.

"You'd probably go for Tolstoy's flabby ideas, wouldn't you? You're probably a pacifist, aren't you?" Bazora knew better than this: I had shown him my eloquent calls-to-arms in *Regeneración*. "You probably want to found some goddam liberation community, don't you?" he continued. "Some happy farm, full of smiling peasants, right?"

I nodded, sure that Bazora would leap at me for nodding.

He did. "Stupid *fuck!*" he shouted. "Who protects the happy farmers from all the predators who want what they have? How far will your little band of campesinos get with their nonresistance? Do you know why Tolstoy believes such shit? Because he's a fucking *Aristocrat*, that's why! One of the great hacendados of all time. Are you going to trust *him?*"

I shook my head. Bazora was not such a relief from my middle-European friends, after all. I wondered why they had sent me to him for instruction.

"All right, compañero," Bazora sighed. "There is no dogma that will suit anarchism. By definition, no theory fits our philosophy. If one did, then there wouldn't be anarchism. All anarchism is, all it *can* be, is a state of mind. It is the voice of the peasant, or the worker, who says to his chief, not 'What do you want me to do?' but 'What would you want me to do if you thought you could make me do it?' What makes a real anarchist is not some stupid fucking theory, but constant *anger*, and the refusal to accept any direction except

that which suits him. The inclination to say *Fuck you* to anyone at all. You give me a society of men like that, and *there's*
your Revolution. Is that too simple for your theoretical Mexican mind?"

I said nothing, but reflected that most of the conquistadores had come from Andalucía, a region of tough men who
would say Fuck you to anyone at all — who had, in fact, said
it to a whole continent, and got away with it. I had to smile
a little at an image that flickered across my mind: of Bazora,
seated opposite me, wearing not a Basque boina on his head,
but a peaked and plumed steel helmet; and around his shoulders not a worn tweed jacket, but a suit of rusty armor. He
looked just right, so.

"That's right, laugh, you silly fart," he said, rising. "Time
for tea with the Lithuanians. The lesson's over."

The lesson wasn't really over, though, because Bazora's
harangue stayed in my mind permanently. I began to think
now that men like Kropotkin were too gentle, too naive, too
humane, to understand just how total, how furious, the authentic Revolution would have to be when we finally brought
it about.

November 10, 1922

Perhaps I shall have the opportunity, in the little time I have
left to me, to tell you more of my ideological indoctrination.
But right now I must introduce you to Emma Goldman, queen
of the anarchists, my own Lithuanian Jew, but far from mine
alone, and mine for a very, very short time.

Emma had come to the United States from Vilna by way

of St. Petersburg in 1885, aged sixteen. She worked as a seamstress in Rochester, New York, until 1889, and married and divorced there. She moved to New York City, and took up with a Russian Jewish community on Suffolk Street. There she was befriended by a tall, handsome man named Alexander Berkman, who had come over from Vilna the year before. They became lovers, co-agitators in the nascent Labor Movement, and leaders of the Jewish organization called Pioneers of Liberty. One day in 1890, "Sasha" Berkman took Emma to hear a speech given by the famous Johann Most, editor of the anarchist weekly, *Freiheit*.

Young Emma was captivated by Most. He was 44, with sympathetic blue eyes that (as she later told me) "radiated hatred and love." The rest of him was impressive, too: his spine was permanently twisted, so that he had to walk with a gliding, crablike gait; and the lower part of his face was contorted to the left by a permanently dislocated jaw. Emma found him irresistible, especially when she read his editorials in *Freiheit*. They were, she said, "like lava shooting forth flames of ridicule, scorn, and defiance, and breathing hatred." Most worked part-time for an explosives factory in Jersey City, which gave him the expertise he needed to publish a manual on the manufacture of bombs; and when he expounded in his newspaper on the uses of dynamite and nitroglycerin, Emma was his.

This did not please Sasha Berkman, who sought to regain Emma's favor by a particularly audacious *attentat*. In 1892 the news broke of the shooting of striking workers at the Carnegie Steel Mills in Homestead, Pennsylvania, near Pittsburgh. Andrew Carnegie's second-in-command, Henry Clay Frick, had ordered in a private army of Pinkertons to break the strike. Berkman saw Frick as a symbol of capitalist oppression, and resolved to commit a pure act of

"Propaganda by the Deed" on him. He bought a pistol and
a knife, took a bus to Frick's mansion on Fifth Avenue, and
burst into Frick's office there. He fired two rounds into the
surprised capitalist, then stabbed him. Frick, aggrieved but
not dead, called for help; and Berkman went off to a fifteen-
year term in the Western Penitentiary of Pennsylvania.

Berkman's inept *attentat* had one effect that must have
seemed salutary to him, however. Johann Most, contemp-
tuous of Berkman's clumsiness, denounced him in a public
speech. Emma Goldman, enraged at this, grabbed up a buggy
whip, leapt out of the crowd onto the podium where Most
was hiding his twisted face in his hands, and lashed him
severely. Emma went to jail briefly for assault and battery,
and the affair was over. She and Berkman corresponded often
during his incarceration; and, when he was freed in early
1906, they became partners, if not lovers, once again. With
money she had earned helping to manage Pavel Orlenoff's
theater troupe, Emma founded her anarchist journal, *Mother
Earth*, in March 1906; and Sasha was her editor.

I never met either Most or Berkman, but I did indeed
get to know Emma, through the good offices of Florencio
Bazora. He took me one night to another of those steamy
cafés that reeked of boiled cabbage and cheap tobacco, and
steered me through all the smoke and impassioned speeches
to a table where sat a gigantic, red-faced Irishman, and one
of the homeliest women I had ever seen. This was of course
Emma Goldman, anarchist heroine, militant journalist, lady
libertine, and advocate of free love. The Irishman, Ed Brady,
was too drunk to notice our arrival; but Emma stood up,
smoothed her starched white blouse over her ample bosom,
squinted at me through her pince-nez, and stuck out her hand.

"You the Mexican boy?" she asked, running her little
black eyes over me casually, as a vaquero might appraise the

becerro he is about to rope and brand. Emma was thirty-five, only four years older than I; but she made me feel like a clumsy adolescent — which, in a way, is just what I was. I was as close to being a virgin as it was possible for a grown Mexican to be. I knew almost nothing of the big world; Bazora had shown me what a naïf I was, politically speaking. And I had a vocabulary in Spanish and English that might do for the pages of *Regeneración*, but was of no use at all to me as I stood cowering under the gaze of this formidable woman. I nodded, running my fingers over my fly buttons and staring at that bosom. I was the Mexican Boy, all right.

Emma sat back down, crossed her short, sturdy legs, hitched her black skirt up so that I could get a glimpse of her plump ankles, and pointed to the chair on her left. Brady, on her right, had put his head on the table. Bazora gave me one of his patented sly-devil Andalusian leers and moved away, leaving me to Emma's feral attentions.

As I say, she was no beauty. Her dun-colored hair was pulled back in a bun, making her broad face seem all the broader. Her wide nose appeared to have been broken, and her tobacco-stained teeth were chipped: mementos of some brawl with cossacks? She looked, all in all, like a pugilistic schoolteacher. But she gave off a powerful scent of musk, a smell of recent sex, or sex foretold, a wild and salty Baltic breath that reached me through all the clouds of smoke that filled the room.

"You got a little Mexican girl somewhere, Peedro?" she asked, leaning forward to put a granitic hand on my knee.

"No," I lied. (As I have been lying to you a little, my poor old reader. I have said nothing to you of my young friend, María Talavera, who had come to San Antonio from Mexico City in hopes of joining the Struggle, and who had become my companion almost overnight, so simple and honest was she, so easily seduced. I had left her in Texas, where she was waiting for me now, believing absolutely in the easy promises I had made to her, ready to be loyal to me for the rest of my life. I have not mentioned her to you, reader, because I am ashamed to bring so decent a girl — for that is all she was — into so scabrous a tale as this one. And besides, she is still waiting for me, even now, in Los Angeles, hoping each day that Librado Rivera will be able to smuggle a note from me out of Leavenworth. May we not speak of her, please?)

"What are you, then, some kind of *fehgeleh?*" Emma asked. "You don't like the girls?" She squeezed my knee. I winced.

"Oh, yes, señorita," I said. "It is only that I have never met a woman until you who — "

"Knock it off, Peedro," she said. "Don't give me that pretty-boy crapola. You come with me now, and little Emma will teach you a few things you don't know." She stood again, pulling me up with her, that fearsome grip now around my arm. She marched me across the street and up a narrow flight of stairs into a tiny one-room apartment. I remember a table with a washbowl and pitcher on it, an overstuffed chair covered in a waxy cloth of a noxious green, and a bed that was littered with magazines and newspapers, in German, Yiddish, and English. These she swept to the floor with one wave of her left hand, without letting go of my arm with her right.

Then she released me and turned away, reaching behind her back to pull her blouse over her head. "Don't look," she said. "You don't look when ladies take off their clothes." Then, a very quick second later: "Now look, Peedro."

I turned and looked. Oh, God, this was all too much for me. This was not seduction as it was practiced in Mexico (or so I believed). Emma, tough, hard, homely Emma, stood there

in nothing but her thick black knee-length stockings and her
run-down, heeled-over black boots. She raised her gristly
arms, backed her broad behind against the edge of the sagging bed, took a deep breath, gave me a grin that plunged
me into despair, and fell backwards, throwing her feet into
the air. Then she gazed at me coyly around her pale thigh,
and said, "Come and get it, Mexican."

Well, I went and got it. And that's all you're going to
read about *that*, my gringo friend. As a man, my lips are
sealed.

Emma's weren't, though. She laughed during the act, but
not as loud as she laughed afterward, as she dressed; or as
she laughed later, back in the café, as she told all her friends
about her new Latin lover, her "speedy little lover-boy," as
she called me the rest of the evening. (Later on, it was short-
ened to "Speedy," but everyone knew what was implied by
this.)

There was no malice in her mockery, though — or, if there
was, it was directed not at me personally, but at me as a
man. Once she had got what was for her the silly necessary
business of sex out of the way, Emma was as good a friend
to me as I had in St. Louis. Somewhere in the rough school
of her upbringing she must have come to believe that you
bought your equality with men by taking them to bed; after
which you became, if not a man, at least worthy of being
taken seriously by men. Once I realized (or chose to realize)
that Emma's predatory voluptuousness was only assumed, I
was no longer so afraid of her. And she could talk to me
without all the mannerisms of slangy salaciousness, of what
really concerned us both far more than sex: the Revolution.
(I know I wrote in my first notebook that I was a sensualist;
but the truth is that I am a sensualist of ideas, not of the
flesh. Even Amparo, whom I continue to desire to distrac-

tion, is for me primarily a symbol of *The Desirable Woman,* rather than the object of my sexual urges. At least, this is what I have made myself believe, sitting here in my cell.)

We had many discussions, Emma and I, in the late spring of 1905, about what was to be done about Mexico. I discovered that she was an even more ardent and naive Kropotkinite than I. Like him, she thought that modern technology, and not a pure rejection of the capitalistic world, would be the basis for a communism of abundance. I could never make her realize that there was no such thing as modern technology in Mexico, and that there was no way the Revolution in Mexico could make any use of the capitalistic world — not so long as Mexico was controlled by Yankee plutocrats and a very few rich Mexicans. She insisted on believing there must be a volatile industrial class in the country, and that it could be galvanized into action by the revolt of the peasantry. Once this had been accomplished, she insisted, the urban and rural underclass could assume control of the capitalist machinery and operate it for the good of the masses.

It was useless to argue with her: she did not know our Indians; she did not know our Porfirio Díaz. She did not know what centuries of Spanish oppression had done to our people; she did not know how deeply into the country were rooted the fingers of the gringo capitalists. I learned from Emma, but her fond intractability made me see how great the gulf was between European theorists of anarchism and the reality of Mexico. Our problems were uniquely our own: we revoltosos would have to construct our own ideology, one purely Mexican. I had no idea what this should be. And to this day I do not know — except that our Revolution, as horrible as it was when it finally arrived, was not awful enough to succeed.

I began to spend more time with my own people, who

had been waiting patiently for me to conclude my flirtation
with those sophisticated refugees. I went back to the Chan-
ning Street offices of *Regeneración*, and embraced Enrique and
Antonio Villarreal and the Sarabias and little Librado and
the others, and told them that the time had come for us to
march.

They had anticipated me: two weeks before my reunion
with them, they had held a meeting and begun the Partido
Liberal Mexicano. I had been elected president, Juan Sarabia was vice president, Villarreal was secretary, and Enrique
was treasurer. Librado and the others were vocales, "talk-
ers": committee members who were expected to contribute
to all discussions, but were expected also to defer to the of-
ficeholders. If only from my new authority as a European-
ized sophisticate, they did defer to me. I was the jefe, there's
no doubt about that.

The first thing they wanted from me was a Plan, something which would establish formally just who we were and
what we stood for. We would publish it in *Regeneración* and
send it south, so our countrymen would know we meant
business, and were not just a shabby bunch of dissidents.
Well, I wrote it, telling myself that it was possible, could
succeed, and pushing my doubts to the back of my mind. I
did not let myself see how it might do for somewhere else,
but not for Mexico.

The Plan is famous today, and everyone accepts it as the
model for the Mexican Constitution of 1917 (though fewer
recognize it as the model too for Emiliano Zapata's Plan de
Ayala of 1911). I don't need to go into all its fifty-two pro-
visions for you. Let me simplify.

What our Plan called for, first, was no reelection of the
president. (Díaz had himself proclaimed this, and agreed that
the president could serve no more than one four-year term;

but he had amended the old Constitution so that *he* could be reelected, for as many six-year terms as he chose.) Next, no more obligatory military service. Then, the closing of all religious schools. Education must become wholly secular: no more repressive indoctrination by the Church. Children were to attend state public schools until fourteen, and not be allowed to work until that time. Absolute freedom of the press. A minimum daily wage of five pesos. An eight-hour workday. The debts of campesinos to their bosses forgiven. No more tiendas de rayas, company stores. Protection of Indians. (Under Díaz the Mayas, Yaquis, and Tarahumaras, among others, had been goaded into rebellion, ruthlessly beaten, and sold into slavery — all so that their lands could be confiscated and presented to important hacendados and gringo opportunists.)

And, most important of all for the rebirth of Mexico, land reform. The vast tracts of land taken from the campesinos must be taken back, reparceled, and returned to their original owners. You will begin to appreciate the magnitude of this task if I tell you that the Terrazas and Creel families now owned 14,000,000 acres of Chihuahua; Vice President Ramón Corral controlled most of Sonora; and the Escandón family, soon to be the enemies of Emiliano Zapata, regarded all but a fraction of Morelos as theirs. Among foreigners, for instance, William Randolph Hearst's Babícora Estate covered more than a million acres; the W. C. Greene holdings in Sonora amounted to more than 600,000 acres; and the Colorado River Land Company owned more than 700,000 acres in Baja California. All this land had been stolen, and must be returned before anything else was done, once the Revolution was accomplished and the Porfiriato destroyed.

Do not underestimate the importance of this Plan. Incorporated into *Regeneración*, it went out quickly into all of

Mexico. Everyone who could read, read it. For those who could not read, there were itinerant lectores — lawyers, schoolteachers, journalists, printers, all of those que tienen ideas — who fanned out all over the country, ready to read the Plan to los de abajo, the underdogs, the illiterate campesinos and the poor of the cities. They took great risks, these men: the government hated them, as did the hacendados and the Church. More than a few disappeared, plucked from the campfires or alleyways where they were reading, gone forever into Belén or San Juan de Ulúa, or simply stood up against any wall by rurales or Federales, reviled, and shot.

In the United States, as well, our Plan became known. The circulation of *Regeneración* reached toward 25,000, and we began receiving congratulatory mail from the International Workers of the World (your "Wobblies") and the Western Federation of Miners, and from individuals from Los Angeles to New York. Emma Goldman wrote on our behalf to her friends Samuel Gompers and Mary Harris, an influential old woman who called herself "Mother Jones" and who took up leftist causes all over America. A newspaperman named John Kenneth Turner was so moved by what I had written about the Indians that he traveled clandestinely throughout Mexico and on his return to the United States wrote a splendid series of muckraking articles. Now I was truly the Voice of the Revolution, a man to be reckoned with, a man to be taken seriously.

Unfortunately, Turner's articles caught the attention of William Randolph Hearst and Harrison Gray Otis, who published denunciations of Turner — and of me — in their newspapers; and who then wired Don Porfirio that I must be silenced.

I had written an article earlier in the year denouncing

the activities of the political chief of Pochutla, Oaxaca. Two weeks after we published the Plan, this man, Manuel Esperón de la Flor, appeared in St. Louis to demand that the American authorities institute proceedings against *Regeneración* for defamation of character. The police came immediately, arrested me, Enrique, and Juan Sarabia, and destroyed our presses.

In the ensuing hearing, just as we seemed about to win for lack of evidence, the wife of de la Flor appeared in court, dressed in full mourning, to claim that we had defamed her as well. She was a good-looking woman of about forty-five, and cried beautifully, and we were sunk. Bail was set at the ridiculous sum of $10,000: Don Porfirio and his stooge, Enrique Clay Creel, wanted us put away for a long time. But, to everyone's amazement, all our new socialist friends came to our rescue, and the money appeared — plus $4,000 extra, to help pay for our lawyer. My friend Emma was, of course, behind all this largess.

I repaid her kindness by jumping bail and fleeing St. Louis. The loss of the $10,000 must have been a cruel jolt to those who had come to our rescue, and I felt very guilty about it; but the moment we were set free, Thomas Furlong and his Pinkertons resumed their campaign of harassment, and it was obvious to us that if we wanted *Regeneración* to continue, we would have to draw Furlong away from St. Louis, and lure him as far afield as we could. My generous friends could not afford to lose the bail money; but I could not afford to lose the magazine, and I knew that its survival meant more to the Revolution than their money or my conscience. So Enrique, Juan Sarabia, and I took the $4,000 that was to have gone to our lawyer and bought train tickets to Toronto, Ontario. We left Librado and Antonio Villarreal in charge of the mag-

azine, and told them we would be back as soon as we had
thrown the Pinkertons off our trail.

Why did we go to Canada? As I recall, that country
seemed to us so distant that we could not imagine Don Porfirio's tentacles reaching us there. And I'd grown very suspicious of the Land of the Free and the Home of the Brave,
by now. When Furlong persuaded the Postal Service to deny
our privileges of using fourth-class mail, we lost hope that
we could be treated fairly in the United States. Canada was
not only distant: it was vast as well, and we hoped that we
could lose our pursuers among the ice floes and glaciers we
fancied would be awaiting us in the far north. We were wrong
on all counts, of course. There was no ice, no snow; and the
Pinkertons found us immediately. When we tried to find jobs
in Montreal, they persuaded our bosses to fire us. They ran-
sacked every hotel room we slept in. They convinced the
local police that we were dangerous, and ought to be deported to Mexico, where we were wanted for murder. We
tried to elude them by moving to Quebec, but they made
things tough for us there, too. The $4,000 went rapidly. By
May of 1906 it was almost gone, and we had to think of
finding another hideout.

Our minds were made up for us by several occurrences
along the Mexican-American border. The appearance of the
Plan had provoked strikes all over Mexico, but it was one at
the mines of the Consolidated Copper Company at Cananea,
in Sonora, that showed us it was time to launch the rebellion.

There were more than 5,000 Mexicans at Colonel W. C.
Greene's mines at Cananea, and on the first of June they
struck for a five-peso hourly wage and an eight-hour day (as
I had told them in the Plan was their right). Greene ignored

their requests and, when 2,000 of the strikers marched on the mine's lumberyard, he ordered his security police to open fire.

A riot broke out and the strikers fled, setting fire to Cananea's buildings as they ran for the mountains. The well-connected Greene called for a troop of rurales to help him restore order; and, when these were not enough, asked the territorial governor of Arizona to send his Rangers across the border and down to the mines. The governor refused to send official troops, but he did nothing to discourage a band of rowdy adventurers who were waiting at the border near Bisbee, spoiling for the chance to ride down into Mexico and shoot up a pack of Reds. Together with the rurales, they put down the revolt. Colonel Greene declared martial law.

Twenty-three men had been killed in the strike, and twenty-two wounded, most of them Mexicans. The governor of Sonora, always eager to give Greene whatever he wanted, shipped fifty of the strike leaders off to the dungeons of San Juan de Ulúa in Veracruz.

A kind of peace was restored at Cananea; but the strike had an inflammatory effect on the rest of Mexico. Other strikes erupted in the textile mills of Puebla, Tlaxcala, the Federal District, and Veracruz. Owners of mines everywhere shut down, fearing a repetition of what had happened at Cananea; and more than 25,000 men were put out of work by July.

At least a thousand of these found their way to the border, where they hoped to join the fight I had been proclaiming for so long in *Regeneración*. Suddenly I had an army. It was bedraggled and untrained, but I did not mind. I believed that all I needed now were a few rifles and a little ammunition, along with a lot of audacity and shrewdness. The time for the Revolution had come.

Enrique, Juan Sarabia, and I headed south from Canada, picked up our colleagues in St. Louis along the way (including the highly suspect Ansel Samuels, who was probably getting word daily to Thomas Furlong about our movements), and by August 1 were in El Paso, ready to mount an attack on the city of Juárez. To the Liberal clubs in Mexico we sent a message: "We rebel against the dictatorship of Porfirio Díaz on September 2." Furlong and Creel of course intercepted the message, and warned garrisons all along the border. But we did not know this, and probably would not have cared had we known, so full of martial zeal were we.

The Liberal club of miners in Douglas, Arizona, planned to seize the custom house across the border in Agua Prieta. But one of the miners was in the pay of the governor of Sonora, and exposed them before they could move into Mexico. We still refused to see how thoroughly we had been infiltrated, and went right on with our plans. In El Paso we used the house of a friend, Modesto Díaz, as our command post. Friends in Mexico City smuggled arms to us, which we hid just across the border. My strategy called for a hundred of our volunteers to cross the border under cover of darkness, recover the arms, overcome the garrison in Juárez, free the jail's prisoners, and set up the first anarchist stronghold in the city.

But the Mexican consul in Juárez, one Francisco Mallen, learned of our plans and alerted the police of El Paso, who watched us closely. All unaware, we waited for the moment to strike. We had to delay the invasion until September 26 because of a shortage of arms and ammunition (we could not fight until we had our weapons; and our weapons — such as they were — were in Mexico, and we would have to fight to reach them: a logistical and tactical problem that I could not get my intellectual's mind around). But on that date thirty of my rebels crossed into Mexico, briefly occupied the town of Jiménez — and then were forced to retreat across the border, where they were arrested by the El Paso police.

We waited another three weeks, hoping to acquire more arms. By then most of my small army had melted away, as armies do when you cannot arm them, or pay them, or feed them; and when, on October 19, we marched on Juárez, we were a company of exactly five men: Enrique, Juan Sarabia, and I, and two Mexican army spies. We were halted and arrested, of course. Enrique and Juan went to jail (as did Antonio Villarreal and Librado Rivera, seized in the El Paso office where we had been hoping to reestablish our magazine). But I, lucky Ricardo Flores Magón, escaped.

I scuttled back across the Rio Bravo and trotted off, hiding behind bushes and sand dunes, until I fetched up at our headquarters east of El Paso, where our host, Modesto Díaz, was expecting our return. We hid out together there for a night, then sneaked into the city and jumped aboard a freight train headed for the West Coast. Or, rather, Modesto jumped. I was too fat and nearsighted to make it aboard on my own, and Modesto had to reach down and drag me into a cattle car, behind first.

So that is your hero's first combat, gringo voyeur. Not quite up to the standards of the Zapata boys, is it? But I have just written for you how the Revolution *really* began, and you will have to make the most of it. I was off for Los Angeles, with a bounty of $25,000 on my head, placed there by Don Porfirio Díaz himself. I had friends in California who would shelter me until our forces could regroup. I had a name, a reputation, now: I was much more than a simple dissident journalist. I was far from defeated. It was just going to be a little more complicated than I had imagined.

Notebook 6

═══════════════════════════

November 12, 1922

Because of my occasional despondency, or because of my suspicion that my jailers mean to kill me, you might by now think that I have abandoned hope. But this you must not believe. Weinberger the lawyer sends me encouraging notes almost daily, telling me of the growing furor in Mexico over my ridiculous incarceration. President Álvaro Obregón, backed by his Chamber of Deputies and his Parliament (prodded constantly by the virtuous, mad Díaz Soto y Gama), continues to send wires and emissaries to Washington, urging that Librado Rivera and I be freed and allowed to return home. The state legislatures of Yucatán and Coahuila, several workers' syndicates, the Mexican Federation of Labor, the Young Communist League, and the *Partido Comunista Mexicano* are all pressuring Obregón, and taking out notices in the press describing our mistreatment in Yankeelandia. Enrique, operating from Los Angeles, has encouraged a general strike and a boycott of all American goods. The people have not, after all, been allowed to forget me.

Even the intellectuals call for my release, and speak of me as an important *precursor* of the Revolution — which is absurd, because I am precursor to *nothing*: I *am* the Revolution. (It is true that I had *my* precursors, forgotten pedants who vaguely anticipated what was to happen in Mexico; but it is not my intention now to write about these ancient shadows to you.) I began the Revolution, and led it — until, too weak and confused for itself and its time, it fell away and became a dwindling plaything for a new generation of intellectuals.

Any day now, therefore, one might expect that my cell door will swing open, Warden Biddle will apologize in the name of President Harding, and I (and Librado, of course) will be escorted in full dignity back to my people (our people, of course), who know at least that Ricardo Flores Magón has given all his years and all his health to them, and who now wish to reward him, not with money (it is two years since I spurned Obregón's offer of a pension) but with recognition, with at least a modest place in their pantheon of heroes, along with Villa and Emiliano Zapata and the rest. (Librado, too, must have his reward: little burrheaded Librado, as loyal to his cause as a dog to its master.)

Possibly, of course, there are still men in Mexico, those we call la gente extranjera de categoría, foreigners who count, who remain stronger even than Obregón and his old gang. I mean all the big gringo capitalists with names like Hearst and Buckley, men who still own half our land and all our resources. These men are surely writing to Harding too, to say that I must *not* be freed, lest I reinfect Mexico with the disease of anarchism, and demand that they give back the mines and oil wells Porfirio Díaz tossed away to them so long ago, so he could pay for yet more additions to his palaces, more frenchifications of the capital, more jewels for his adolescent bride. Not only not be freed, moreover, but eradicated once and for all. It pleases me that I have not, even in Leavenworth, lost my ability to frighten such powerful men.

Lest my uncharacteristic lack of humility today upset you,

I shall abandon for the moment my little *apologia pro vita mea*, and turn your attention back once more to those other, more obvious heroes, the Zapata boys of Morelos, of the village of Anenecuilco, population 371, "indígenas" (as Amparo told me we should now call the Indians) and mestizos — to see how they became what they were to become.

If I were as florid in my rhetoric as my critics say, I could write for you (as some Mexican historian is bound to write) that "the history of the Revolution begins like a wound in Anenecuilco." Such a statement, though gorgeous, is of course not strictly true; because, as we all know, what happened in the South was only a small part of the Revolution, often peripheral rather than integral, more of an abrasion than a mortal wound (and not the first part, either: the Revolution began much earlier, with Ricardo Flores Magón in Belén Prison). But history and I love paradoxes, so I shall say also, less gorgeously but more accurately, that Anenecuilco was the heart of the Revolution, the sole and final bastion (saving myself) of its integrity, the scene of its saddest failure.

I shall take you there, as I went there myself after we all left Xochimilco at the end of 1914, that crucial time to which I keep returning in these notebooks.

Pancho Villa had taken his armies north, to do battle with the divisions there that claimed loyalty to Venustiano Carranza, who had assumed power after Huerta fled and was now calling himself "The First Chief of the Constitutionalist Army." Carranza himself had gone into hiding down in Veracruz, waiting for his one competent general, young Álvaro Obregón, to fight his way up from Veracruz through Jalapa and Perote along the route taken four hundred years earlier by Hernán Cortés, past Puebla and back into the Capital.

Emiliano Zapata had promised Villa that he would attack Obregón, stop his advance at Puebla, and push him back into the Gulf of Mexico. But this he never did, for two reasons: first, Obregón would have been too strong for him, whatever sort of campaign Zapata had mounted. He had a real army, booted and trained and well-officered; and he had equipped this army splendidly from the mountains of weapons and ammunition left in Veracruz by the American marines, who had just ceased their infuriating occupation of that city.

And, second: Zapata's Liberator Army of the South wanted just then not to fight, but to go home to Morelos to see to their crops. Emiliano sent Eufemio and three battalions down to Puebla to await Obregón's advance; and the Zapatistas milled around for a couple of weeks, looking over their shoulders at the two volcanoes and the rain clouds that were gathering over them, and thinking longingly of the fields of corn that lay just beyond those volcanoes, needing their care. So they just drifted off, singly or in small groups from one village or another, taking their rifles and their women with them, and assuring their generals that they would return to the fight whenever they were needed — after the harvest, of course.

There was nothing much Emiliano could do, then, but set up a thin perimeter of defense in the hills south of Xochimilco; send occasional forays into the Capital to keep it subdued against the time when his ostensible ally, Villa, should care to reoccupy it; remove his headquarters farther south, disband his remaining troops, and enjoy the peace.

Thus it was that I descended into Morelos, that intricate little garden, that oasis of semitropical greenery that had seemed so paradisal to Aztec royalty and then to Cortés, and then to the missionaries who moved swiftly onto the best land they could wheedle away from the Spanish viceroys, and finally to the ten or twelve big hacendados who divided the state into enormous sugar plantations, which they ruled like feudal barons — until Emiliano Zapata came to take the land away from them and return it to the indígenas who had lived there even before the time of the Aztecs.

We were not retreating from the Capital, the Zapatistas and I: call it rather a reabsorption. The army was simply melting back into the land, soldiers and soldaderas and guachas — the tough, barefoot women who did the cooking and carrying for the army, trotting along all day in the warm winter sun, coated with dust thrown back over them by our horses, laughing and scrabbling as they ran.

With Zapata and his estado mayor, his general staff, rode — just a little apart — his scruffy brain trust, his squad of advisers and ideologues: the sturdy and earnest Magaña brothers; the furtive and oily Manuel Palafox, riding as close as he dared to the chief, who nodded benignly at him from time to time; poor doomed Otilio Montaño, soon to die a traitor; gaunt, pale Díaz Soto y Gama, appearing as always just this side of exalted hysteria, scarcely aware that a horse was beneath him, waving his arms to emphasize whatever crescendos of rhetoric he was delivering to whatever invisible audience; demure and discreet Serafín Robles, 'Miliano's private secretary, known to us all as Robledo, who had been with the chief almost from the beginning, giving to him in the most inconspicuous ways all his loyalty; and I, Flores Magón of the tight, dirty black suit, the missing buttons, the torn sleeve, the aching thighs, and the blistered behind, fat but willing, scheming as always for the good of the ideal state (which at that time for me meant only the conversion of Emiliano Zapata to something like anarchism).

And one other, just now. Sometimes behind me, sometimes out on either flank of our little band of intellectuals and rogues, sometimes terrifyingly right beside me, rode Amparo Urdiales. When she was near, I could turn my head toward her and see that she, like Díaz Soto y Gama, was carrying on her own interior conversations. Every minute or so she would smile and nod, or shake her head in fond disapproval (causing that marvelously long, straight hair to flow back and forth over her shoulders in such a way that I had to gasp), or almost silently sing a few words of what I was to learn was likely to be either a lullaby or a poem by some old Aztec priest or other — or a bawdy and murderous marching song, full of chingar and cabrón and coño and culo and mierda. Occasionally she would come out of her reverie and her huge, dark hawk's eyes would focus on me, and we would speak.

"How goes it, caballero? Is your horse hurting you more than you're hurting him? Have you fallen into the rhythm yet?"

Now, in the first days of our acquaintance (oh, God, how I wish I had another word to use here, like "love" or "affair": am I going to have to settle for something as tepid — and as inaccurate — as "friendship"?), I scarcely noticed what she said, so hypnotized was I by the movement of her lips, by the tiny lines on either side of her mouth when she smiled gently at me with only a hint of mockery, by the way she sat her saddle so effortlessly, by her unconscious ability to seem at the same time both subtly aloof and mischievous. I could only bob along mindlessly across the hills and arroyos of northern Morelos, stupid and desperate with desire for her, cruelly aware how foolish I must look to her, surrounded as we were by real horsemen, real warriors. (Yes, reader, I know how soppy and infantile I sound to you now. I know I present myself like a character in some young girl's sentimental novela. I wish I could say that I was able to draw myself up in my saddle and exclaim something mature and witty and ironic to Amparo, something worthy of my years of struggle and authority.

"Oh, how my ass aches," I'd say instead at such moments. "I'm hungry," I'd say out loud, and she would laugh and pull away to ride apart again; and what I'd *really* said, in my own private speech to her, was "I am dying for love of you," or "You are my heart's desire," or "Oh my God, I love you! *HELP!*" Amparo knew I was crying out these things to her, of course, just as she knew with great precision how she looked, how she moved, what her voice sounded like, what effect she was having on me. That she was artful made me desire her even more.

And I might as well admit now, in the privacy of these notebooks (which not even I, with my nearly blind eyes, can clearly read in the faint light that comes through the window of my cell in Leavenworth), that beneath this chaste, impassioned speech to Amparo was another, far less chaste and just as true.

"I'm going to throw you off your horse," this deeper voice would holler at her. "I'm going to hurl you down onto the sand and rub my nose in your hair and bite those lips and squeeze those breasts and whip that skirt up over your belly and grab those strong thighs and pull them apart and I'm going to leap inside you, Amparo, and I'm going to EAT YOU UP!" I am sure Amparo heard this speech, too, and liked it, and laughed at it. Don Juan Carnivorio.

Eufemio, lolling along in a stupor beside his brother and the other generals, jerking his body erect from time to time just as he was about to fall out of his saddle, snoring and belching and groaning on the road to Anenecuilco, would have heard me, too. Once only, as we were approaching the village of Tepoztlán, he pulled himself together enough to call over to me.

"Forget it, Florecito," he said. "How many men do you think that one can handle?" He nodded in the direction of Amparo, who had moved her horse closer to Emiliano. "Get in line, Florecito, and wait your turn. Another little year and I'll be gone, and a little after that so will 'Miliano. Then maybe you can have her for a moment. Keep your cock in your hand till then, or find a guacha to do for you — or maybe a nun in Tepoztlán. You know what they say about nuns: Cara cubierta, culo abierto." ("Face covered, twat open," Yankee reader.) General laughter passed among the Zapata vanguard (including Amparo and Emiliano, who both turned to look back at me, smiling their usual gentle, mocking smiles). I met it with my characteristic attempt to appear both dignified and self-deprecatory.

There is a kind of shrug that we Mexicans make, and a sort of rueful smirk, that come in handy at such times; and I was getting a lot of practice at this sort of thing. It was a new and necessary rhetoric for me, who had spent my life in words only. A tricky rhetoric, too: earlier I had tried to raise my arms with the palms of my hands held up in surrender, but I forgot that doing this would cause me to let go of the reins. I had to be saved from falling off my horse by Gildardo Magaña, who grabbed me by the collar as I was sliding from my saddle.

Anyway, there weren't any nuns in Tepoztlán when we got there. I doubt whether there were ten nuns left in Morelos by this time: like the priests, they had mostly gone to earth by then, or immured themselves in the basements of their convents, against the time when Jesus should declare the Revolution (and the Constitution, for that matter) null and void, so they could come out and resume their pillaging of the poor.

All right, all right, mea maxima culpa, I'm sorry for that last business. I admit that the clergy of Morelos was more enlightened than most. It was a priest who helped Emiliano and Otilio Montaño translate the ancient Nahuatl parchments containing all the deeds and rights of Anenecuilco; and several priests and deacons rode with the Zapatistas, as bloodthirsty as anyone else.

I was to learn something historians of the Revolution would surely decide to forget: that in the South the Revolution was regarded as a crusade, a sacred war. The land was holy, and the Virgin of Guadalupe, just as surely as the old Tlahuican and Aztec gods, presided over the land. Here we sewed her medallions on our sombreros; and we galloped into battle behind her blue and white banner, shriven and blessed as all get-out.

I never mentioned this curious anachronism to Emiliano. Nor do I know whether he supported this notion of a peasant holy war, or only ignored it. Certainly I never saw any signs of faith in him (except on the night his brother died), or in any of his generals. In fact, among us only Díaz Soto y Gama was pious; and *he* would flop to his knees at the slightest provocation, and cross himself and pound on his chest until the air was clouded with his dust.

We set up our camp in the old Dominican monastery of Tepoztlán. Emiliano (and, I supposed, Amparo) took a large corner room, one with a huge black crucifix on an interior wall, and with scars from Zapata's own artillery on the outside walls, large holes covered over now by sheets of canvas. The rest of us, officers and staff, ranged ourselves along the corridors in the tiny, windowless cells so many generations of monks had inhabited until the Revolution drove them away. Eufemio had disappeared, as was often his practice when Emiliano was exercising his prior right to Amparo. (At least, this is the way I thought then that the three arranged things, with Amparo going to whichever brother the two had decided on. It did not occur to me until much later that Amparo had any say in this pairing — that in fact she might be the one who decided which of them she would stay with, or even whether she would stay with either.)

Zapata's troops spread out through Tepoztlán, relaxed and laughing now that they were out of the Capital and back in their patria chica, their little homeland of Morelos. Their camp fires sprang up throughout the town, then out into the dark green vega that lay to the south, and even partway up into the sheer cliffs that sheltered Tepoztlán from the north.

This was a sacred place to them, more sacred even than if it had been blessed by the Virgin of Guadalupe; for this was the birthplace of their great man-god Quetzalcóatl, the ancient Feathered Serpent revered by every Indian nation in Mexico. The conquistadores and missionaries had tried either to stamp out veneration of Quetzalcóatl or, failing that, to identify him with Jesus Christ; but the Feathered Serpent was still up there in the sierra over Tepoztlán, looking down on his Zapatistas with benign ferocity and causing them all (yes, even me a little) to walk quietly that first night, and look up often into the blackness that hid the cliffs from us.

For the first time in years, the Revolution seemed far from me just then, as I stood in the entrance to the convent looking out into the darkness, counting the camp fires, listening to the soft, heartbreaking songs sung by various little clusters of troops as they watched their women cooking their meals. I would hear a few chords from a guitar far to my left; then hear an answering refrain from another, far to my right.

Slowly, almost imperceptibly at first, I began to feel the tension of years slipping from me, all the strident and thwarted time of jails and escapes and humiliations, the wild hopes and their inevitable frustration. I thought then that this was the first moment of real peace that I had known since childhood.

I know now that what I felt was not peace but the calmness that often accompanies despair. I sat on the steps of the convent, and put my head in my hands. My eyeglasses fell from my face to the granite stone beneath my feet, and cracked yet again.

I did not hear her come up behind me, but at some point in my grieving — for that is what it was — I knew that Amparo was sitting silently beside me.

She said nothing until an owl hooted from the direction of the cliffs. Then she murmured, close by my ear, "Cuando el tecolote llora, el indio muere." When the night owl cries, the Indian dies.

"Have you heard that saying, Ricardito?"

"No."

"It's a common dicho, hijo mío. Every child down here knows it."

I took my head from my hands, and gave Amparo my forlorn look, one I'd had modest success with in the past, among Yankee camp followers of anarchism.

"Is that your forlorn look, pobrecito?" Amparo asked, her expression one of fond solicitude. This was not quite fair: I *was* forlorn, truly so. It was simply that I wished to convey my mood to her as accurately as possible. I nodded, forlornly.

"Then let me play to it, Florecito," she said, smiling her fond, compassionate smile at me. (And where had she got this particular diminutive for me? So far, only Eufemio had called me that. Had the two of them spoken together of me, perhaps disparagingly?)

"Do you like poetry?" she asked. I shook my head. What did I know of poetry? Where in my turbulent career would I have found time to read poems?

"I've been too busy with politics for poetry, Amparo," I said, shifting a little into my beleaguered statesman voice.

"Como no, Florecito. Let me tell you then of another politician, earlier than you but of no less importance. Do you know of Nezahualcoyótl, king of Texcoco?"

I shook my head again, though in fact I did recall hearing the man's name in my Mexico City school days; and I knew that he ruled the tiny kingdom of Texcoco around the time of that clumsy fop, Moctezuma II, and that he had become something of a vassal to Moctezuma before Cortés came to make Moctezuma *his* vassal. I told Amparo this much.

She laughed. "Those are not the important things about Nezahualcoyótl, Florecito. You should know that he was two vital things besides a king: he was a magician, and he was a poet."

I registered great surprise: it seemed appropriate.

"I thought of him when we heard the owl just now," Amparo said. "He could turn himself into an owl, or a quetzal, or a zopilote, and fly over all his kingdom, day or night, to watch over it. But that he was a poet is for me the best thing. He wrote beautifully, but very sadly, about how swiftly our lives fly by, but how marvelous life is while we have it — and how the little bit of beauty we have is worth all the pain, which after all doesn't last long, either. Shall I say one poem of his for you, Florecito?"

I nodded again: why not?

"I translated it from Nahuatl. The title is for you. It's called 'Una Muerte Florida.' "

A florid death. Mexicans love to pun, horribly sometimes. I gave her just a bit of my martyr's smile. And Amparo said Nezahualcoyótl's poem for me, as I now write it for you:

> I, Nezahualcoyótl, ask this:
> By any chance is it true that one
> Lives rooted in the earth?
> Not always in the earth:
> Here for only just a while;
> Though it be made of jade, it breaks;
> Though it be made of gold, it breaks;
> Though it be made of quetzal plumage,
> It shreds apart.
> Here for only just a while.

Even if I listened only to the sound of her voice, and not to Nezahualcoyótl's meaning, the poem took me far away from my own temporary despondency, and even distanced me momentarily from my longing for Amparo. I rested my head in my hands and resumed staring out into the velvet night, where the camp fires still burned and the voices of the resting army murmured all around me. Even when Amparo's hand touched my shoulder, and her hair brushed for a second against my cheek, and I heard the faint scraping of her sandals on the stone steps as she moved away from me, I was dropping into a mood that was deeper by far than melancholy. I recognize it now, as I say: it was despair — what the pious among you would call the "sin against the Holy Spirit."

This was a condition I had almost always managed to

avoid before, even in Belén, even when my magazines were burned and my presses destroyed, even when I was being hounded from one American city to another, even when my friends and allies deserted me and joined the enemy. I had always been able to keep my *cause* before my eyes, even as my cynicism grew; and this cause became as sacred to me as any Indian's belief in either the Virgin or Quetzalcóatl. Anarchism had kept me from despair, time and again. The worse things got for me, the more I could say to myself that the final cataclysm was upon us, and the Millennium at hand: the State was about to be blown away, and a splendid new dispensation would blossom. Man would know his first freedom since the Fall.

Through all the years I had held fast to this belief, even as my eyes and ears brought me sure evidence that we were not advancing toward the New Millennium, but retreating from it. Nevertheless, my innocence had held out against my experience until that night. Even in the messy time of the past December in Xochimilco and the Capital, I could almost convince myself that there was still hope; that I could sneak my own brand of Anarchism, under the guise of Agrarian Reform, into the camp of the Zapatistas, and cause it to flourish there.

The path to the new Civilization would lie through the same Indian primitivism I remembered my father shouting at me and my brothers when we were boys in Teotitlán, past the sophistications of Kropotkin and Bakunin, and on to my own nascent theories of sacred rage. Guided by my wise and gentle counsel, Emiliano Zapata would become Mexico's secular messiah, and lead his Indians and mestizos out of slavery into a land of happy people, just and kind and bold and free. (Isn't that lovely, gringo reader? Even as I write this, listening for the guard who brings my supper, I shiver a little with excitement.)

But then, as I sat in the doorway of the convent in Tepoztlán, with only a small, jagged sierra between me and the revolutionary chaos to the north, I came to know it was all impossible. For the first time in my adult life, I was out of all the strident racket that I had gloried in — that I had, in part, caused. Here, looking out at peaceful, lazy men bedding down around their fires with their smiling, dusty women, as I listened to Amparo recite her dead king's words, I knew that the gulf between this world and the one I belonged to was impassable. I could not bring these people to the Millennium. I was part of what was keeping them from it. I saw myself suddenly not as the liberator of the Indians, but as their contaminator. I was no better than Cortés, who had professed to bring with him salvation, but brought instead pestilence and death.

In the days and weeks that followed, the more my new friends accepted me, and showed me their lands and told me their stories, the more in fact the Morelian peacefulness descended on me, the more aware I became of my radical fraudulence. "Don't trust me," I wanted to cry out to them. "I'm only using you!" But of course I said nothing.

I wandered slowly back to my monk's cell. The thick stone walls of the monastery silenced the voices and guitars of the army camped around me. What did I have to do with these people, these Tlahuicans and Aztecs? Amparo had told me that, before the hacendados took their lands and enslaved them, these gentle Indians (I'm sorry, I can't call them indígenas: that's another of those artificial words that liberals like to poke in our faces) had walked about in their fields with bunches of roses clasped in their hands. "And have you noticed their hands?" Amparo had asked. "Like their feet, so small and delicate?"

How could I understand that these delicate carriers of bouquets could suddenly turn vengeful and lethal, so unpredictably cruel that they might appall even other Mexicans? And, accepting that — for the carefree cruelty of the Zapatistas was well established — how could I suppose that such a volatile, tricky people might ever be mine to convert? I was up against one of anarchism's fundamental paradoxes: to succeed, the Revolution needed men and women who were at the same time innocent of ideological taint and yet eager for ideological illumination. We had to have an army of enlightened, violent innocents. Supine on my pallet, the moldy walls of my cell close around me, I nodded off, anguished by this absurdity.

The agony of despair lessened daily, as we rode south. The air, hot by day and cool by night; the scent of thyme, straw, sweat, and leather; the long, somnolent hours; the steady plodding of the horses' hooves — all had a powerful curative effect on me, so that my mood went from despair to despondency to something very like complacency in a matter of days. Was this shallow of me, reader? Is it that I am capable of strong emotions, but not for very long? Am I too curious about what is coming next to brood for more than a few hours over even the sorriest tragedy? Is any man different from me, in this respect? I may even be guilty of being, *au fond*, a man of rather sunny temperament. So might Eufemio have been, for all I know. Between all the killings and rapings, he might have been bathing in a veritable sea of tranquillity.

I followed my new friends down through Morelos, growing a little accustomed to my horse, losing the odd kilo of fat from my waist, cleaning myself up gradually whenever we stopped at a stream, even abandoning my ruined black suit (my close companion of many years) for a campesino's white jumper and baggy trousers.

A smiling Robledo, Zapata's majordomo, brought me these last, as we camped one evening just north of Yautepec. "Put these on, Don Ricardo," he burbled, "and you're one of us."

I did. I peeled off the black suit, my shirt and socks, and — at Robledo's insistence — my knee-length woolen drawers; scrubbed myself off with handfuls of the sandy soil on which I was standing; and put on my new peasant's clothes, which were still wrinkled from having been carried in someone's saddlebag.

Robledo crowed with delight as I tied the strings of my calzones around my ankles. He was always a merry little man, temperamentally the very opposite of the sour Manuel Palafox, whom Robledo resembled closely. And who would try to betray Robledo, just as he was to betray Otilio Montaño. "Now you're a true campesino, Don Ricardo," he said. "Now you're truly our compañero."

Whatever Robledo thought I was, I looked now like a fat bourgeois in white cotton pajamas. Even after Robledo found me a straw sombrero and a pair of huaraches, I looked like a plump, middle-aged gentleman ready for bed but caught out-of-doors by mistake. But it was too late to go back. Within the hour, someone had buried my old black costume, for reasons of hygiene, I'm sure. A pity, in a way: that suit had been part of my signature, just as much as the spectacles that made my eyes look buglike, or the shock of thick, wiry hair that grew anyhow across my broad skull.

The dwindling army moved slowly south throughout that first week in January, past Yautepec to the city of Cuautla, and then from Cuautla farther south a few kilometers until we came to the village of Anenecuilco, where it all had started. There could not have been more than fifty of us left that January of 1915 — staff officers, the zany brain trust, minor functionaries — when we finally pulled up in Emiliano's birthplace, ten days after leaving Xochimilco.

That Emiliano should have moved so slowly (this was really only a day's jaunt for a man who could, if pressed, ride all across Morelos in a day and a night) was not, as I first thought, out of consideration for those of us who were not horsemen, but rather because this was something of a procession: wherever we went, especially in small cities like Yautepec and Cuautla, the populace turned out to cheer, kiss, and touch their warrior chieftain. And it seemed to me, impatient as I was, smarting from my saddle and embarrassed by my ludicrous peasant's getup (to say nothing of my lingering attack of despair) that the chieftain knew everyone in the throngs that pressed around us whenever we paused along the route. He'd kiss babies, nod deferentially to elders, cause his horse to rear at young women as he appraised them with his connoisseur's eye — do all the things an accomplished politico knows how to do. There was little I could teach him in this regard, certainly.

That there were so few of us was fortunate, because there was not enough room in Anenecuilco for even our small band. Five kilometers south of Cuautla the village appeared, hardly more than a cluster of small houses strewn about, with perhaps three dusty little streets — alleyways, really — running between them from the main road up to the barren hills that lay just to the east.

Do not expect much when I write "houses," reader: you would probably call them sheds, and wonder how humans could live in them. Most were built in jacal style, from stalks of tall cane, roofed with thatch. The cane was bound together so loosely that birds could fly through the walls without hindrance. A few dwellings, like that of the Zapatas, were the homes of Anenecuilco's families of substance. These were tiled, made from the caliche mixture of adobe and lime which reflected the sun. They had one or two earth-floored rooms.

Every house, however poor, had its small yard and garden, and some could take shade from the eucalyptus and poplar trees that grew at random throughout the village. Here and there I could see a fruit tree or a corn patch. As I stood at the entrance to the largest alleyway, pounding the dust from myself with my new sombrero, and exchanging baleful glances with my horse (who was either a mare or a gelding; how should I know of such things?), I caught the strong scent of eucalyptus leaves, cooking, and urine. In the midday quiet, the only sounds were the inconsequential barking of invisible and anonymous dogs and the constant slap-slapping as women in their open doorways shaped moist corn paste into thin tortilla cakes. Here, in his own village, the chieftain's return was a pleasant but not remarkable event.

Our small band scattered almost immediately. I saw Emiliano standing in front of his family's home, his face as always darkly shaded by his enormous sombrero. He lounged against a tree, with his caballero's posture of casual alertness, as he appeared to examine me and my new outfit. After a long moment he nodded gravely to me, drew himself up, and stepped into his house.

It is only now, from a distance of seven years, that I can read Emiliano's signal to me. I believe that he was saying, "Look here, Ricardo: this is my place. This is where my war is: not Mexico, not even Morelos. Anenecuilco."

Eufemio had once again disappeared. So had Amparo. I marched up the street looking for them, but was stopped by

Otilio Montaño, the old schoolteacher from Ayala. He smiled, put his arm through mine, and nudged me gently.

"Leave them all alone for a while, Don Ricardo," he said, giving my arm a little squeeze. " 'Miliano must visit his wife, and the other two have business of their own." This was the first I had heard of Josefa Espejo, the childhood sweetheart Emiliano had married in 1911, full of his first victories.

"Very well, Otilio. When do we eat, then?"

Otilio laughed. "Do as I do, hombre. Let your belly growl away a little of your fat, first. They'll feed us before we starve."

I grunted. I have always been a man for whom hunger was not so much a hardship as an affront.

"Let me distract you, Don Ricardo," Otilio said. "Let me show you our river, so you can begin to understand us." He led me toward the road we'd ridden down that morning. After a minute he stopped me and said, "There it is, the Anenecuilco." He indicated a narrow stream, not much more than a trickle of muddy water, that ran in the ditch between us and the road. I shrugged. Give me the food first, and then you can give me the moral, as someone had said, or would say.

"Anenecuilco is a Nahuatl word that means 'The River That Twists Like a Snake,' Don Ricardo. That is what it does. Look how it slides away, how you don't even notice it until you're about to step in it. If we followed it, you'd see how it twists along through dry beds of stone and sand, and how it wells out for no reason into tiny ponds, and how sometimes it narrows into nothing and dives into the earth. It's a complex little river, no?"

I shrugged, waiting for the substance of the metaphor that was obviously on its way.

"What does the river *mean*, Otilio?" I asked in my naive voice, the one that is ready to slip into awe when the meaning is explained. (You see the pattern, now, gringo? It's only my body that's the buffoon; my mind is always scheming, deriding, supersubtle. I am anarchism's Iago. Was Emiliano Zapata my Othello? And Amparo?)

Otilio smiled, squinted, clasped his hands behind his ample hips, and leaned toward me, the very picture of the wily old schoolmaster about to make his telling point to a roomful of slow but earnest students. "Why, it's obvious, Don Ricardo," he said. "The people of Anenecuilco are like their river, just so."

My eyes widened as far as I was able. "How so, Otilio?"

"Oh, clearly, Don Ricardo, because they are quiet, persistent, able to hide or disappear, sometimes generously swelling out into ample groups (the ponds, you see, Don Ricardo?), sometimes (as you'd see if we were to walk farther south, where the river widens) rushing along so fiercely that they carry all before them."

I was speechless, of course. Otilio grinned, happy at having laid this elegant trope at the feet of his not-too-bright pupil.

In the week that followed I was to have many conversations with Otilio, who was a walking chronicle, and I believe an accurate one, of everything that had ever occurred in Anenecuilco, from before the Aztecs to the present. You will surely forgive me if I pass it all on to you in truncated form.

Otilio told me, as we walked along the river, or through the hills behind the village, or up the road toward Ayala, of all the centuries the people of Anenecuilco had struggled to keep their town and lands from the greedy hands of Aztec nobles, conquistadores, priests, and Creole landlords; how relentlessly those landlords had stolen their terrain to grow their sugar on, breaking the old laws and inventing new ones, so that by the end of the last century the Anenecuilcans had been left nothing but their flimsy huts and a few fields of rocky sand, with no way to survive except by becoming bonded servants, medieros, of the hacendados — who treated them not as free men, nor even as fellow humans, but as mindless slaves, la gente de la casa, those who belonged to the estate.

Otilio told me how the villagers had always regarded the Zapata men as leaders — had asked them to act as intermediaries with the hacendados; or to take their pleas for help to Mexico City, to be heard by whatever bored functionary they could get to listen to them; or, finally, to lead them in armed revolt against the hacendados once it became clear that not even the great Don Porfirio Díaz would come to their rescue.

He told me of Gabriel Zapata and his wife Cleofas Salazar, who had ten children, the fourth of whom was Eufemio, and the ninth Emiliano, who was born in the late summer of 1879, with the faint outline of a hand marking his tiny chest: the insignia of a leader. He told me how this infant Emiliano had one day come upon his father weeping helplessly behind his rough stable, and asked, "Father, why do you cry?"

"Because they take our land from us."

"Who?"

"The landlords."

"Then why don't we fight them?"

"Because they are powerful."

"Well, when I'm big I'm going to make them give the land back."

Yes, reader, I know this little anecdote sounds as though it were the invention of some secular hagiographer, and perhaps it is; but this is what Otilio told me, and he swore to its veracity. And it is what the people of Aneneculico believed. A lot of heroes have to coalesce in order to produce one Emiliano Zapata: Robin Hood and Roland, Quetzalcóatl and Moses; and we must not be too critical of the process.

The parents of this Wise Child died when he was sixteen, and he and Eufemio were left the task of raising their eight brothers and sisters. Eufemio soon departed for Veracruz, where he worked at no one knows what, while Emiliano stayed in Anenecuilco, working the family's small farm and using his savings to buy a string of ten mules. As arriero, muleteer, he carried corn from the farms to the mills, and lime and bricks to the nearby hacienda of Chinameca. And he prospered: by 1910 he was worth more than 3,000 pesos — not rich, but richer by far than, say, the Flores Magón brothers, two of whom were by then fleeing from the police of two countries.

Some of his money he saved; some of it — a lot of it — he spent on becoming Anenecuilco's idea of a charro among charros, a proper macho with enormous mustachios (to distinguish himself from toreros and friars, he said) and glittering horseman's outfit. He was the delight of fiestas and charreadas, rounding up horses, riding bulls into the ground, staging cockfights, performing feats of marksmanship — and impregnating, or so it seemed, half the young women of Morelos. (Otilio admitted that this last claim was a trifle exaggerated. What he did verify was that in 1908 Emiliano had kidnapped a woman of Cuautla, Inés Alfaro, with whom he set up house and sired a son, Nicolás, and two daughters. The father of Inés, Remigio Alfaro, denounced Emiliano to the authorities, who had him drafted into the Seventh Battalion of the Army, where he served five months before being released, probably grateful at having his conjugal life disrupted.)

By this time, Otilio said, Emiliano's political activities had already begun. He had joined the Cuautla chapter of the Club Liberal Democrático de Morelos; he had come under the instruction of none other than Otilio Montaño of Ayala, who schooled him in the doctrines of Prince Pyotr Kropotkin (from a textbook printed six years earlier in Mexico City by yours truly), and read to him my editorials in *Regeneración*; and he had been elected president of the Comité de Defensa of Anenecuilco. The village elders, sensing that real trouble was coming, and knowing that they were too old to lead others in combat, had naturally chosen Emiliano as their young jefe for the bloodshed to come.

In January 1910, Emiliano was plucked off the streets of Anenecuilco and jailed for three days, on a charge of "loitering in a state of drunkenness." All this meant, Otilio explained, was that the army had decided to take him back. Once again, though, Emiliano did not stay long in the ranks. He was spotted at his barracks in Cuernavaca by Don Ignacio de la Torre y Mier, hacendado and son-in-law of Porfirio Díaz. This Don Nachito knew Emiliano's reputation as a horseman, and had him released from active duty with the understanding that Emiliano would become his chief groomsman in the Capital. Emiliano lasted four months at this post, then quit because, he said, "I couldn't stand it that this rich man's horses lived better in their stalls than my own people in Anenecuilco."

Once again in his village, Emiliano studied (with the help of Otilio and a friendly priest who knew Nahuatl) the fueros, the old parchments that contained the land rights of his people. He memorized them, so that one man from Anenecuilco should forever know what was theirs since before Cortés. He gathered the able-bodied men of the village around him, and trained them to be a cavalry troop of guerrilleros. He armed them with a few rifles, machetes, knives, scythes, anything at all they could use against the hacendados and their goons when the time for battle came.

It came quickly. The word was out that Francisco Madero had begun his rebellion in the north, and that his Plan de San Luis Potosí called for total agrarian reform, in which the land the hacendados had stolen from the campesinos would be given back to them immediately. In Morelos, supporters of Madero gathered around Pablo Torres Burgos and none other than Otilio Montaño in Cuautla; and in Tlaquiltenango, with old Gabriel Tepepa, a veteran of the war against the French. In neighboring Guerrero, the cacique Ambrosio Figueroa assembled his men and awaited a signal from Madero. In Anenecuilco, Emiliano Zapata, now joined by his brother Eufemio, commenced tearing down the fences the hacendados had put up around the town's land.

The first fighting of the Revolution was hardly impressive. On November 16, 1910, Maderista troops in nearby Puebla were defeated by Federales, who then moved southwest into Morelos, in search of the newly constituted bands of guerrillas. To everyone's surprise, Emiliano cautioned the rebel leaders against hurling themselves into combat straightaway. At a meeting in Jojutla he took the floor, and began explaining to his fellow jefes what course the Revolution ought to take; and, said Otilio, he sounded precisely as though he had got his theories from a communist manual of guerrilla warfare.

First, Emiliano said, the rebels had to organize themselves into cells. This should be done secretly, with care given both to political and military preparations. Once this organization was accomplished, then the second phase could grow out of the first: armed rebellion by guerrilla forces, in which the populace would rise up and, led by the members of the original cells, fight a series of small battles, always attacking the enemy on his flanks or from his rear, avoiding open confrontation with the main body of the army. Only then, after the guerrilla troops had disciplined themselves sufficiently and grown in numbers and matériel, should they aspire to full warfare against the enemy, acting as a regular army.

Success, Emiliano said, depended on completion of each stage before the next was attempted. The rebels should fight no pitched battles until they had become a cohesive force, able to meet regular troops in open combat. And the organization and leadership of the Revolution had to be sufficiently strong and flexible for a reverse to be absorbed: they had to be able to shift back from the second to the first stage if necessary. They should also know, Emiliano told them, that the moment of greatest danger for their Revolution would be the point of transition from the first to the second stage — the emergence into the open.

If all this sounds pretty complex for a semiliterate campesino, a man who had spent his young life farming, driving mules, raising hell at fiestas, and getting children on the community at large, then so be it. But Otilio was there, and this is what he heard. Where did Emiliano get it? Not from Kropotkin, whose interests lay more in agriculture and economics than in warfare; nor from anything I had written in *Regeneración*, certainly: I had mostly preached about the need for bringing down Porfirio Díaz. I can only conclude that Emiliano was a natural: he made it up.

You will perhaps not be surprised to learn that his fellow chiefs paid no attention to him at all. Off they galloped in all directions, full of piss and vinegar (as my cowboy friends say), with hardly a score of rifles and pistols among them, riding into the face of the Federal Army as it advanced over Morelos, screaming *"Mueran los gachupines"* as they attacked, and steadily losing one town after another and scattering into the brush after every encounter. Within two months, old Gabriel Tepepa had been gunned down — not by Federales, but by the Figueroa brothers from Guerrero, who hoped to take over the whole Revolution in the South. And Pablo Torres Burgos, nominally Emiliano's chief, was shot to death as he slept at his siesta in Villa de Ayala, victim of patrolling Federales. The Revolution in the South was about to blow itself away in reckless enthusiasm.

It was saved from this fate by Emiliano Zapata and his lieutenants, who lay back and organized, trained, and gathered ammunition. Other erstwhile chiefs rose and fell; Zapata waited. By April 1911, he commanded fifteen hundred men, well trained in the principles of guerrilla warfare. To indicate that he was ready to fight, he issued no proclamations, but — true to his dramatic self — made two gestures.

In late April, as the rebels were about to abandon Jojutla to the Federales, Emiliano had just ridden to his position at the head of his troops when a shot rang out. This was nothing unusual: his men were accustomed to firing their weapons at any time, out of enthusiasm, or annoyance, or hunger — you name it. But Emiliano took off his sombrero and showed his men the hole that had just appeared in it. Someone looked up, and saw the tiny figure of a man climbing about on the roof of the building of the jefatura política, far above their heads. Emiliano shouted, "No one move!" and, in the silence that followed, rode his great black stallion up the steps of the building, carbine in his hand, through the entryway, into the lobby, and then slowly up the steps inside the building. Some minutes later the onlookers heard a single shot. Then Emiliano appeared again, cigar in mouth, slowly riding his horse back down the steps, out the entryway, and into the street.

Otilio almost wept as he told me this tale. "They would have died for him then, Don Ricardo. Qué arte, no?"

The second gesture was a most fateful one. Several weeks after his feat in Jojutla, Emiliano received a dare from the hated Spanish administrator of the hacienda at Chinameca (whose lime and bricks the young muleteer Zapata had carried only a few years earlier): "If you're so valiant and such a big man, then I have enough bullets and carbines to give you what you deserve."

Though an attack on Chinameca had no place in Emiliano's plans, there was no question about his attacking the hacienda: to do so at once was a point of honor. The result, according to Otilio, was a frightening slaughter. The Zapatistas roared through the brick buildings, firing and hacking at anything that moved. They shot every man and woman, then beheaded them, then hurled their bodies into the river that ran outside the hacienda.

By these two gestures, Emiliano Zapata showed his friends and his enemies that he was a man of style, and a killer. He hoped that his allies would pay attention to his theories, and fight the sort of guerrilla war he had in mind; but this other, this posing and killing, was just as important.

And there was one other thing, Otilio insisted to me. This was the extraordinary cariño, affection, that Emiliano inspired in almost everyone who followed him. He seldom raised his voice; he never bossed anyone. He never needed to.

"Some of his generals were animals," said Otilio. "They wanted blood more than they wanted land or liberty. Let me tell you of one time, early on in the campaign, as we were beginning our first siege of Cuernavaca."

We were returning from one of our long walks, from Ayala back to Anenecuilco. Otilio drew in his big stomach, and looked briefly at the first houses of the little town ahead of us.

"The artillery of the Federales had been tearing us up, as we approached the first big barranca of the city. I was just behind Emiliano. Together we noticed that a bunch of our forward troops, maybe fifty of them, had stopped advancing about a hundred meters ahead of us, and had clumped together, as if to look at something. We spurred our horses and rode up to investigate. The noise of the cannons staring down at us from the ramparts of the city was fearful.

"Emiliano rode among the men, parting them from whatever they were clustering around, oblivious to the battle. There, crouched at the center of the huddle, was one of Emiliano's generals, on his knees, sawing with his saber at the neck of a fallen officer of the Federales. As we watched, this general pulled the officer's head from its body, held it up before him by one of its ears, laughed that loon's laugh we know so well down here, and gave the severed head a lusty kiss on both its cheeks. The men around him commenced laughing too, until Emiliano spoke out, not loudly but very clearly, 'Stop. This is a shame. Stop.'

"The crouching general stopped," Otilio said, "and, still holding the head by its ear, looked up at Emiliano. At first he only stared. Then he drew back his arm, as though he might toss the head up to Emiliano. Then he laughed his loon's laugh, dropped the head into the sand, and struggled to his feet. Someone handed him his saber, and led him to his horse. He mounted, grinned happily at Emiliano, and resumed leading his men against the ramparts of the city. Emiliano led me back to the hillock we'd been directing the battle from, and never mentioned what had happened to me or, I think, to anyone else."

"Who was it?" I asked. "Genovevo de la O? Juan Banderas?"

"No, hombre," Otilio said quietly. "It was closer to home than that." He glanced quickly over at the tiny main street of Anenecuilco, then looked back at the green canefields that lay beside the highway we'd been walking down.

I turned toward the village and saw Eufemio Zapata, General Eufemio Zapata, sauntering toward us, his long arm around the waist of Amparo Urdiales, who walked with her lovely head on his shoulder. Eufemio waved at us amiably. So did Amparo. Then he performed a quick little paso doble step, one of his trademark gestures, and Amparo followed him, her skirts and petticoats swirling about her long, long legs. The two turned off the cobblestone street into the garden of the home of the Zapatas, and their happy laughter hung in the air after they had disappeared.

Notebook 7

Let me tell you something about la guerra, Florecito,"
said Eufemio Zapata to me one evening in the early spring
of 1915, as we warmed our hands over a low brazier in the
center of our one-room adobe hut in Tlaltizapán, where
General Emiliano Zapata had established his winter headquarters.

Eufemio of course knew nothing of war in its grand or
strategic sense. What he meant was the little war, the guerrilla, about which he was as expert as his baby brother. I
was happy to listen. So far as I was concerned, Eufemio was
probably a madman, and certainly a drunkard, and a prophet
of dismaying accuracy; but he saw practical things, things
right around us, with a painful sharpness; and I knew that
when he bothered to speak to me more or less calmly and
rationally, with a minimum of insult, he could tell me things
I wouldn't hear from anyone else — even Amparo, of whom
I saw little these days, so busy was she setting up her "escuelas racionales" throughout the pueblos of Morelos. She
was convinced that if she could teach the campesinos how to
read and write, they would be ready to assume their proper
roles in history.

The winter had been for us one of those anomalous times

of relative peace that occur in the midst of even the most barbarous of wars. Morelos was just then a small oasis of calm, while all around us swirled the awfulness of the Revolution. Up in the north Pancho Villa was being pursued, and regularly defeated, by the divisions of Álvaro Obregón, still allied firmly to the cause of Venustiano Carranza, the new High Chief of Everything. This Carranza had set up court in Veracruz, waiting for Obregón and others to clear up the mess in the rest of Mexico before he assumed control of the Capital — which was no place to be in the winter and spring of 1915.

A few detachments of Zapatistas has remained in the Federal District, raiding here and there and even entering the city whenever Obregón was away on his northern forays. One of these marauding bands blew up the water-pumping station at Xochimilco, which caused great hardship in the Capital. Its inhabitants could have water for only one hour each evening. There was no water to work the sewers or flush the filth from the streets. People fainted from the stench.

I know that General Obregón is a hero in Mexico today; and from my position in Leavenworth he looks in many ways like the sanest and most benign of us all (except Emiliano — except Emiliano); but the citizens of Mexico City did not care much for him in 1915. Nor he for them. Perhaps he was motivated by the rural man's instinctive hatred of city folk. Or maybe he was angry because of the way they cheered the Villistas and Zapatistas during their occupation the preceding fall. Whatever the causes of his animus, he surely did decide to punish them. Not only did he not repair the water pump, he set in motion a deliberate program of humiliation as well.

Money all but disappeared, or was worthless when one

tried to use it. The few newspapers that remained open were allowed only to chronicle Obregón's victories, or to publish editorials on such trenchant topics as why cats could see in the dark, and whether fat men were really happy. They could on no account say anything about soaring food prices, hunger, or disease. Regular supplies of food to the city dwindled, then stopped. People trapped rats for supper. Shopkeepers shot hungry women who begged for food. Rampaging crowds trampled children underfoot. The Panteón Dolores conducted a daily cremation for the corpses of those who had died from hunger or disease. Every block in the city knew typhus and smallpox.

The Capital's foreign colony formed a relief committee to bring in food from the provinces. Obregón refused to provide trains to haul the food they bought. It rotted at railheads no more than twenty miles outside the city, its existence unknown to the citizens.

The people appealed to Carranza, who was biding his comfortable time in Veracruz, sitting on mountains of tropical fruit and fresh harvests of corn. They begged him to rein in his surrogate in the Capital, Obregón. He ignored the appeals, and exported all the Gulf Coast's food products to pay for arms for Obregón's troops. Foreign agencies sent food shipments to Veracruz, intending them for the starving capitalinos. Carranza confiscated it all, and sold it back to the shippers.

He closed the government offices and schools in the Capital, and ordered all their furnishings sent to him in Veracruz. With Obregón in the North, he sent General Pablo González to enforce his decrees. González, unable to win in the field, was eager to display his ferocity among civilians. He made all the merchants open their safes at gunpoint and give him what little remained of their money. He decreed that anyone suspected of hoarding money should spend his days sweeping offal from the streets. He ordered the clergy to contribute 500,000 pesos for "relief of the poor." When the money could not be found, he jailed 168 priests. He stripped the hospitals of all their bedding and supplies, which he sent north to Obregón.

This was the reward the people of Mexico City received for supporting the Revolution and for helping Villa and Zapata (and Obregón) overthrow the vicious Huerta. Wintering in Morelos, we heard of these things, but they seemed far away from us at the time, so snug were we in Tlaltizapán, a thousand meters up in the foothills of the rugged sierra that runs down through the center of the state. On good days we could sit in front of our huts and, warmed by the winter sun, look northeast across the plains below us toward the distant white specks that were Cuautla and Anenecuilco; or southwest toward the shimmering blue shadow of Lake Tequesquitengo, just beyond the towns of Jojutla and Zacatepec. (An entire village lay just below the surface of this newly formed lake, flooded into oblivion by some hacendado's desire to have a lake *just there*.) Thirty kilometers to the north, hidden in its own sierra, lay Yautepec. And twenty kilometers farther along, out of sight and usually out of mind, was the capital of the state, Cuernavaca, which the forces of Emiliano Zapata had already taken once in this war, and would take again before the collapse of everything.

To one such as myself, whose life had been one long noise, these days were halcyon, almost preternaturally silent. I would sit for what seemed hours, listening to the wind sigh through the tall eucalyptus trees above my head, watching the duels of hawks and jackdaws far above me in the wintry blue sky. Great white clouds, blown by winds from the Pacific, moved slowly from sierra to sierra along the horizon,

trailing enormous blue-gray shadows across the plains beneath them. I would drowse or lie, listening to the rumbling
of my stomach, dimly aware that I could eat when I chose,
as much as I chose. From time to time I would hear the
vague, soft voices of the few soldiers who remained with us;
or the clink of crockery, or a lazy horse's whickering. I missed
Amparo, but in an unhurried, nonspecific way. There would
be time, I told myself with some mild surprise: for the first
time in my life there might be time. (I knew better if I thought
about it, of course; but sometimes I chose not to think about
it.)

Perhaps, instead of lying so lazily in Tlaltizapán, I should
have been in Cuernavaca, where there was indeed activity of
the sort I knew well. Leaving Mexico City six months after
us, González Garza's tatterdemalion Convention, which had
tried to govern the country ever since the Aguascalientes
meeting the preceding autumn, had established itself there.
It met daily in the old Toluca Theatre, and tried to behave
as though it represented all Mexico; but — except for a few
lingering Villistas, who must have preferred the mild Morelian winter to the harsher climate of Sonora and Chihuahua,
where they should have been fighting at the side of their
commander — the Convention really existed at the pleasure
of the Zapatistas, who lounged about in the theater as though
they, not I, were at rest in Tlaltizapán.

Wrapped in their bright serapes, they dozed as that
arachnid little invert, Manuel Palafox, pushed one measure
after another of his own invention through the Convention,
claiming that he was acting on the express orders of his ab-
sent chieftain. He called for intricate and suspicious methods
of land and monetary reform, all of which would require his
authority and participation; when all Emiliano had said to
him was, "Go to Cuernavaca. Tell them to give the land to

the people. Now. If any hacendado refuses to cooperate, take his entire hacienda from him. As for money: deal only in the silver we have mined in Guerrero. Pay no attention to the scrip they will try to use." Emiliano saw things simply (or so it seemed to me, for a long time), while the devious mind of Palafox required schemes so complex that only he could trace his way through them.

Palafox worked for the most part behind the scenes, ignoring the delegates of the Convention. But his colleague, my good man Antonio Díaz Soto y Gama, not only led the Zapatista delegation, but insisted on addressing the Convention daily. When anyone tried to debate the advantages of a parliamentary system of government for Mexico, or to discuss the fact that Obregón's army was only a day's march away, or to ask what might be done about the starving people of the Capital, Díaz Soto y Gama would take the floor and deliver long and learned harangues on Robespierre, Marat, Danton, Mirabeau, Kropotkin, Marx, and Bakunin. Or on the etymology of the word *boycott*. Or on the chastity of Mexican womanhood. (How this must have pleased the women who were perched on the laps of not a few delegates.) At one point some of the Villista delegates called for a sanity test for Díaz Soto y Gama, but they did not succeed in this. He simply threw back his shoulders, fixed his eyes on his luckless audience, and orated longer and louder.

When González Garza, that poor young man, realized that his Convention carried no authority at all throughout the rest of the country, he sought at least to govern Morelos. But Emiliano Zapata denied him even this. Morelos was too important to be managed by anyone but himself.

Villa appealed to Emiliano for help against Obregón after the Carrancistas beat him at Celaya in April. Zapata refused, claiming he could not mount an attack against Obregón's rear guard because Villa had sent him no artillery as he had promised to do. This was true enough, but the fact was that for Emiliano the war had ended — or had ended in Morelos, which for him came to the same thing. González Garza, from the stage of the theater in Cuernavaca, begged him to marshal his troops and retake the beleaguered capital. Emiliano refused, saying that he had more important business in Morelos. What was he up to, these days?

Chiefly, he was being precisely the kind of leader Morelos needed just now. I know, my logical gringo reader, that an anarchist ideologue has no business even toying with the notion that any people, anywhere, need a leader, ever. But here is what Emiliano did, during these months' hiatus from battle: he gave all his time and energy to the pueblos of Morelos. He would ride through the state each day, accompanied by a small squadron of his ingenieros, young, university-trained scientists who had come to him from the Capital, eager to help in the agrarian reforms Emiliano wanted to establish. He would stop in each pueblo he came to, set up camp, and conduct interviews with the campesinos of that village.

He would make sure that authority had been returned to the elders. He himself made no decisions, but deferred to those elders. He refused to allow his generals, wherever they were dispersed after the last campaign, to have any say in governing the campesinos.

His engineers surveyed the boundaries of each village, and portioned out land according to the old methods and records. Fields that had lain cracked and dry for years were irrigated and planted. Advised by Amparo, he established a workers' school in each pueblo, to be attended by any man or woman who desired to come. He refused to constitute a police force for Morelos, as Palafox had advised him to do: the villagers, he said, would police themselves.

When a pueblo seemed able to take care of itself in the old ways, he would climb into his saddle and move on to the next, always patient, always quiet, always deferential to the elders. Morelos, exploited by Díaz and then torn apart by Huerta, began to bloom.

In April Emiliano was back in Tlaltizapán for a meeting with Judge Duval West, who was down on a fact-finding mission for President Woodrow Wilson. Wilson was trying to figure out which revolutionary leader to support. Villa, originally the favorite, was now not only a loser but a bandit as well, in American eyes. Carranza was a possibility, but Wilson found him pompous and deceitful. Judge West was to see if Emiliano was the paragon of democratic mildness his supporters claimed — or whether he was in truth the Attila of the South, as the propertied classes (and the newspapers they supported) insisted he was.

Emiliano arrived late the evening before the meeting, tired from his ceaseless riding across the state. He nodded to me and the other members of his troupe who had gathered around him, threw an arm around Eufemio's scrawny shoulders, and drew him into the hut that was kept vacant for the Chief. The two stayed in the hut all night, talking, and now and then laughing. Eufemio appeared once in the doorway to call for tequila. Shortly after sunrise the next morning Emiliano emerged from the hut, dressed in all his charro finery, to meet this Judge West, a gaunt old man got up for the occasion in cowboy clothes. I suppose he was roughing it in Mexico.

I introduced the two. Emiliano shook the judge's hand, then steered him back into his hut. A minute later Eufemio popped out, clutching his sombrero in one hand and his boots in the other, and looking very surly. An hour later Judge West came out, and walked over toward me. Emiliano stayed inside.

The judge shook his bald old head. "What are you doing here, anyway, Mister Magón?" he asked me.

"Flores Magón, at your service, Excelencia." I had known a lot of American judges by now, from the other side of the desk, as it were; and I was not much awed by this one. "I am here to advise General Zapata in matters political, if it pleases him to have me do so," I said.

"Well, you've got your work cut out for you, son," the judge said. "Your boy don't know a damn thing."

I gave him my humble but earnest, inquiring look. "It is true," I said cautiously, "that the general's political philosophy is simple to the extreme."

"You might say that, son. Or you might say that your general is simpleminded. He seems to think the property of the rich should be taken and given to the poor."

I admitted to a certain naïveté on the general's part.

"Look, son," the judge said, squinting back at the hut where Emiliano still remained. "Your boy is worse than naive: you ought to keep him indoors, where he can't do any harm. Look: pure hell's busting loose all over Mexico, and General Zapata sits here in this little state of his, pretending he's in Paradise. I've heard people everywhere, even up in the North, talking about him like he was the Messiah. He's the Savior, they say; he's the Father. He's not just a man anymore, they say: he's a symbol. What do you make of that?"

I replied that there were also lots of people in Mexico who thought of the general as a Fiend Incarnate, whose chief gifts to Mexico had been bloodshed, rapine, and loot.

"Sure thing, son, and they're probably right enough. You don't produce any saints down in this goddamn country, so far as I can see. But look here: he goes around telling these peasants of his that they don't need a government or a standing army or a police force. He tells 'em to carry their rifles into the fields with them, and to use 'em if they have to."

I had no complaint with any of this, and said as much to the judge.

"Just what the hell kind of political adviser are you, son?" he asked. "The men in white are going to come for you, too, one of these days. Do you know what I think?"

What he thought was pretty obvious, but I shook my head. We are always polite to gringos in my country.

"I think your boy is some kind of damn fool, to tell the truth. I told him I thought all he had in mind was the earth and the air of this Morelos of his. I told him he needed to go back to Mexico City and stand up for the rights of his goddamn peasants, if he loves them so much, instead of mooning around down here in the woods. And you know what he said? 'I cannot live in the city. My home remains among my people. I have led this Revolution to give the soil and the free air back to my people. Here in Morelos, this has been achieved. Let the rest of Mexico secure its freedom and happiness in the same way.' Now what the hell am I going to tell President Wilson about a man who says things like that?"

The judge spat in the sand at his feet, and grinned a little. "Come to think of it," he said, "my man Woodrow might like all that foolishness just fine. So I ain't going to tell him. We got enough trouble in Europe right now without taking on the job of being wet nurses to a bunch of happy loonies down here. Anyway, son, your general can't last much longer: they won't let him."

The judge slapped his Stetson down on his sunburned pate, shook hands, and turned to go. He stopped, and poked me in the chest with his bony finger. "What kind of political person are you, anyway? You one of those Bolshies I heard Zapata had around him?"

I nodded.

"That figures," he said. He waved, and walked away.

I did in fact wonder at that time what my anarchist friends in St. Louis would have made of Emiliano. There was plenty of room in the Anarchist Pantheon (should such a monstrosity ever exist) for Fools of God like Emiliano — which I suppose is how Judge West saw him. We had room for Innocents, and we knew they must be slaughtered: the New Millennium had need of such sacrificial victims. But even then I sensed that Emiliano was no fool, of whatever stripe. I think now that he knew exactly what he was up to, the whole time — and that's very frightening. Because that means he was probably ready to make me — or any of us — a sacrificial victim, too.

November 16, 1922

It was after Judge West went home to make his report, and Emiliano returned to his mission to the villages, that Eufemio sat me down to explain war to me. He was sober — as sober as he got, anyway — and he was serious. I was not sure why he should have chosen me as his audience that evening. Perhaps his prescience told him I'd one day be the Chronicler of the Revolution, and he wanted to make sure I got it straight. Or perhaps he chose me as his confidant because he sensed that I not only understood, but shared, some of his darker impulses. So I sat cross-legged (not an easy position for me) across from him, with the fire between us, waited for the guacha who cooked for him to pour us out a mug of coffee and then leave, and gave him my open and attentive face.

"The thing about war, Florecito," he began, "is that when you get into it, you learn you've got three enemies instead of one. There are the people you're fighting, your own people, and yourself. You've only got one ally: el terreno, the land. Everything else is shit, a distraction, something to be ignored.

"Look at us. First we had Díaz to fight, or at least to resist. Then Huerta. Then Robles. And now, coming up this summer, that idiot González. These are the people we fight: fools, assholes, drunkards, and more fools. They're nothing to beat. They can kill a few of our men but they hurt us only when they tear up our ally, the terrain.

"Then you've got our 'official' people, the ones who think of themselves as our allies, our leaders, even — the politicos, the would-be governors, the hangers-on, like Palafox and that crazy Soto y Gama of yours. These people don't count. They bother you, you kill them."

This was where *I* belonged in Eufemio's categories, clearly. I must have looked concerned, because he laughed. "Don't worry, Florecito," he said. "No one's going to kill you. No one in Mexico, anyway." Like all those who knew him, I hated it when he said these prophetic things. Even when he said them to placate, or to allay fears, they had the opposite effect. But he only laughed again, and continued.

"Also among our own people, Florecito, I count the other guerrillero chieftains — Tepepa, the Figueroas, Banderas, de la O — all those, even Villa. Some you get to join you, some you forget about, some you kill. Fuck them, too, even the brave ones. Do anything you want with them, but don't ever trust them. Not even if they're your brothers."

"Does Emiliano trust you?" I asked (not the least dangerous question I had ever asked, you will agree).

"Sure," Eufemio said. "He can trust me to be his Chief of Staff, or he can trust me to be what I've hired out to be, or he can trust me to betray him when the right time for that comes along. Any questions about that?"

I had lots of questions about that, but more prudence than curiosity just now. I sat still.

"The real people, the only real people," he continued, "are the campesinos. You don't fuck with them. They're really part of the terreno. They know the same things you know: that the only things that really count are the pueblo, the weather, the crops, the animals, the soil, the water. If you show them you know this, they'll fight for you, hide you when you run, die without complaint for you when you tell them to. If they're for you, you win. If they're against you, you lose. Only if they turn on you, or forget you, do they become your real enemies. This is not such a hard lesson, is it, Florecito?"

"Not as you state it, 'Femio," I said. "But what if your first enemies, those who fight you and ravage your land, are much stronger than you, with more troops and matériel?"

Eufemio lay back on his straw petate and stared up at the sagging laths that supported the dirt and clay ceiling of our hut, smiling faintly at the ease of the lesson he was giving me. His carbine, its maple stock bleached almost white from all the rubbings of ash and sand that had been given it, lay at his side, never fully out of his grasp.

"That's no problem, hombre," he said. "You just don't fight them the way they want you to fight. The more they come at you with all their goddamn battalions and divisions and cannons and trucks and trains, the easier they are to beat. I'll tell you how to do that, but let me say something first about that third enemy, the one that is yourself. I won't speak of 'Miliano just yet; take me, instead."

Here Eufemio sat up, glanced quickly over at the dark corner, far from the firelight, where he stored his bottles, then swung his gaze across me. His eyes, black in this light, obscured a little by the lank hair that fell over his brow, were bright and flickering. He almost never looked at anything, I thought, for more than an instant.

"What am I?" he asked, resting the carbine now across his thighs. "Nothing. When our parents died, I ran off to Veracruz with my ten-peso inheritance, leaving 'Miliano, who was only sixteen, to raise our sisters and take care of our land. I lay about on the Gulf, drinking and fucking and doing a little dirty business here and there; and then the Revolution began, and 'Miliano called for me, and I came. He made me his Chief of Staff and so I am *General* Eufemio Zapata. I am as you see me: a drunk and a clown and a killer. A piece of shit."

And a fornicator too, I thought, and with the woman I love, too, I thought — but did not say. But Eufemio had stopped speaking, to see what effect this admission would have on me. I dismissed it: if Eufemio wanted for once to be taken seriously, I would do so. I knew, and he knew that I knew, that he was all the things he said he was; but a great deal more, besides. I said, "All right, let's suppose that is what you are. Is that what makes you one of the enemy? I don't think so."

He grinned, more at himself than me, I thought. "All right, Señor Anarquista Intelectual: you're right. What makes any of us a possible enemy is not so much bad character or bad judgment, or lack of experience, or even cowardice. We're all stupid cowards (except maybe one of us) if you look at us right. What makes us our own enemies is loss of illusion. We lose that, we start to see clearly, we see the whole thing's a lot of shit, we get tired, and we throw the whole thing away. The one who wins is the one who keeps his illusions longest."

"Do you retain your illusions, 'Femio?" And where were mine these days? I wondered. After that evening below the cliffs in Tepoztlán, did I still believe there was anything I could do for these people? If not, why was I here?

"I never had any illusions," answered Eufemio. "Look, estúpido: this ridiculous man you see is the man I choose to be. Or the man I *have* to be. We have room for only one true hero down here: little 'Miliano. But 'Miliano needs me so he can be a hero; he needs for me to be his fool and villain. The worse I look, the better he looks. In life, you can't have a 'Miliano unless you have an Eufemio, too, just a little behind and to the side of you."

Eufemio looked almost startled as he said this, as though such an idea had never before occurred to him. It seemed interesting to me not intrinsically, but because it was Eufemio Zapata who was stating it.

" 'Miliano doesn't know this," he continued. "He loves me: I'm his big brother, after all. He wanted to make me Governor of Morelos. When he announced this, I got drunk and disappeared for a week. He wants me to help him in meetings: I disrupt them. He wants me to be brave in battle. I am, but in such a way as to disturb him. You want to know how? I am *too* brave, coño: I risk everything. I behave like a brute. I would behave like a coward but that would shame him, not me. I may disgrace myself, but I must not shame him. That would ruin the game."

This admission hurt me more than I can say. I had left most of my own illusions behind me a few months before, when I decided to return to Mexico and seek out the Zapatas. But I had retained one real hope, retained it even after my heart told me that night in Tepoztlán to let it go: that Emiliano Zapata and his followers in the South represented something real, something possible, something palpable to which I could fasten the fragile remnants of my idealism. And already I was beginning to realize that what I might be offering Emiliano was in truth a kind of betrayal. But here was this savage Eufemio, this grinning animal, telling me that he knew just as much about disillusionment as I did; that the face he showed the world was a mask, grotesque enough, but carefully contrived for all that — but that, in spite of all his faults, he was loyal to his brother. There was a bond between these two that came from a kind of love I knew nothing about.

I watched him closely. He was looking directly at me as he made this speech, gauging its effect. I returned his gaze. Still looking at me, he lowered his face, then dropped his eyes and stared into the fire for a moment — and then lifted his face and smirked at me, like a little boy caught doing something naughty but lovable.

"Do you believe any of this shit I'm saying, Florecito?" he asked. "Don't you know how drunks talk? Don't you see I'm playing with you, puffing myself up, trying to make you feel sorry for me?"

I saw his hand move toward the trigger guard of his carbine. It occurred to me that he was drunker than he seemed, and that he might be ready to spring at me.

Well, I'm not quite a coward, either, as I've often reminded you. I looked as stern as I could under the circumstances. "What about Amparo?" I asked. "What does *she* believe about you? What does your brother think about you and Amparo?" I waited for his attack, which I thought was sure to come.

But Eufemio surprised me. He slumped forward at my words, dropping his head onto his chest, letting his arms fall slackly across his folded legs. I thought of one of Posada's skeletal marionettes, with the strings to their limbs gone slack. He sat like this for a long minute, while I held my breath.

Then he raised his head (his death's head, I thought), and looked at me again. His eyes looked sunken, tired beyond simple fatigue. It was a remarkable transformation. "We don't talk of Amparo now, compadre," he said. "We don't ever talk of her, you understand me? You shut up about her now, Flores Magón."

We sat silently, eyeing each other for a length of time I can't determine. Then Eufemio pulled himself together once again, laughed, shouted "Carajo!" and tossed another glance at the corner where his bottles lay. He took a deep breath and smiled at me in a way that was intended to be reassuring.

"But I was going to tell you about war, wasn't I, Florecito? That's a much simpler, safer subject, no?"

"Oh yes, 'Femio," I breathed. "Let's go back to the war."

"Well, hombre," he said, "it's been great, a huge fiesta!" Eufemio was quite recovered now (his old self, I'm tempted to write, as though I had any idea what his old self was). He sat erect, with his head tilted so far back that he seemed to be looking down at me. He gestured expansively with one hand; with the other he held the carbine lightly, upright at his side.

"Ah, you should have been there in the early days, Florecito, in the first months when it was all so simple. We hardly needed to think then, coño. Get a few hundred men together, blow up a train, burn out a couple of haciendas. Hit the garrison at Ayala, grab some new rifles, have a fiesta. Then saddle up, get some more of the boys, take Jonacatepec and Yautepec, run down to Azúcar de Matamoros, wire that pendejo Madero in the North that it's safe for him to head south any time he thinks he can get it up. Come up against Cuautla, the Federales fight like hell. We keep coming at them for three days until we lose a thousand men but they're wiped out. We burn the palace and the big hotel — ay, María, what great days!"

There was a certain discrepancy, I reflected, between this boisterous Eufemio, giving me his thug's version of what happened in the spring of 1911, and the Eufemio of a few minutes earlier. I knew better than to ask myself which was the *real* Eufemio: both were real — or both masks — and both, I knew, were dangerous. I smiled with him, now; but I watched that carbine.

"It sounds like fun for you, 'Femio," I said. "What about all the cruelty, the killing of civilians, the innocent deaths — all the things that gave you people such a terrible reputation?"

"Oh, horseshit, tú pinche gordo," he answered. "In my estimation, there wasn't *enough* cruelty. And I'm not the only one who felt that way. I remember one night after Cuautla when my fellow general Abraham Martínez got up, drunk, and said to 'Miliano in front of us all: 'Jefe, I want to toast your health and that you should live forever, but when are you going to get this fucking idea out of your head that you can fulfill your mission just by killing a few Spaniards and hacendados? Get rid of those cowards who are always preaching that we shouldn't rob, or kill, or rape a few women now and then. How else are we going to get our revenge for what we suffered under Díaz?' Martínez was right, Florecito, and everyone knew it but 'Miliano."

So much for winning the support of the campesinos, the ones you don't fuck with, I thought but did not say. "But then you moved on Cuernavaca, am I correct?" I asked, to get him back on his breakneck narrative.

"Correct," said Eufemio, beaming. "We had a race to see who got there first, us or the Figueroas's man, Manuel Asúnsolo, who was swinging up from Guerrero. We went in together, both armies, a great triumph — by 'Miliano's goody-goody standards, anyway. I have to say my brother knows how to put on a show. He had both columns, Asúnsolo's and ours, march in from the north, down out of the sierra. We generals were in front, done up like los Plateados on white horses. The troops that came behind us looked like the most ferocious desperadoes ever to sack a city, half-naked, with rifles and machetes and pikes slung all over them and their miserable nags.

"The people of the city were scared pissless of us at first, because of this bad reputation you speak of. But 'Miliano threw open the prison doors, ordered the bars closed, said he'd shoot anyone who misbehaved. Before you knew it, the streets were full of pretty Indian girls running after us with arms full of bright red flowers, which they stuck in our belts and sombreros. When they saw we weren't going to massacre them, they couldn't love us enough. Sometimes you have to hand it to 'Miliano. If we'd done it my way, instead of his, we'd have had an entirely different sort of ceremony, I can tell you."

Eufemio expected me to shudder. So I did, though I've never been much impressed by the posturings of bullies. If that is what he was.

"Yes, shudder, pobrecito," Eufemio said. "But consider, who was right? We had the wonderful mala fama of Attila and his Huns, tearing down out of the mountains to plunder, rape, kill, and all that. People trembled and ran, or gave us what we wanted, or begged to join us. We *owned* Morelos just then — and we could have kept it. But my sweet brother, so busy being the dashing caballero, insisted on behaving like some sugary acolyte.

"So what happened? Once they saw he wasn't going to eat them alive, all the hacendados and politicians and ass-kissers came out of hiding and got together and cooked up all the lies about what beasts we were (and *should* have been, if I'd had my way!), and ran up to the Capital with their stories. And everybody of course believed them, and we were fucked. We'd be a lot better off today if we'd taken all the fat bastards to the edge of the barranca and pushed them over. *That* would have shown those Maderista gordiflones in the Capital that they should take us seriously."

I was a little perplexed. "So when Madero reached Mexico City, they told him bad things about the Zapatistas, which they wouldn't have if you'd actually *done* bad things?"

"Exactly my point," said Eufemio, nodding reasonably. "Madero had his big entry one Sunday in June. We were there the next day, all dressed up and sober, to meet him, to pay him honor like everyone else. We still expected great things of him then, you know: he was the one who got the Revolution going, after all."

No, he wasn't, I thought. *I* got it going, and Madero took it away from me. And sent me to prison for my troubles, as well. Had his gringo friends in Los Angeles arrest me when I refused to acknowledge him as the leader of the Revolution.

"And when we got to his daddy's house in Berlin Street,"

Eufemio continued, "where he was staying to show how modest he was, what a disappointment for us! The man was *nothing*, Florecito, *nothing*. A poor shriveled chivo, a little billygoat, with squinty eyes and a scraggly beard to hide his baby's chin, and no taller than that slimy fart Palafox, who's probably listening outside our door right now. *This* was our deliverer? Hombre, I had to shrink down behind 'Miliano so they wouldn't see me laughing. And he was so sweet, and so sincere! What a *good* little man! What a total, sad, little prick, Florecito."

"I know what happened at that famous meeting, 'Femio," I said. "How all the frock-coated politicians were crowding around Madero, trying to tell him what to think; and how Emiliano said to Madero that he had come to hold him to his promises to give the land back to the pueblos; and how Madero said yes, of course, but we have to do these things carefully, and — "

" — And how 'Miliano picked up his carbine and walked up to Madero and pointed at the gold watch chain he wore across his scrawny chest and said, 'Look, Señor Madero, suppose I point my rifle at you and take this watch and keep it; and later we meet again, and we're both armed: would you have a right to demand that I give it back?' And Madero nodded, white-faced and scared shitless, and said, 'Of course, General Zapata, and I would expect interest'; and 'Miliano said, 'Well, that's exactly what happened to us in Morelos, where a few hacendados have taken the campesinos' land by force.' "

"And Emiliano told Madero to give the land back."

"And 'Miliano said, *with great dignity*, 'My soldiers — the armed campesinos and all the people in the villages — insist that I tell you, with all respect, that they want the return of their lands to be started immediately.' You must know that my brother behaved with great correctness at this moment, Florecito. This was a famous event, and I don't want 'Miliano sounding like some kind of stupid Indian, here."

Stupid Indian. Well, Eufemio was full of surprises. But I assured him that, as putative recorder of all this business, I would get it down accurately. I nudged him on a bit: "But then you went home and nothing happened . . ."

"Let me tell it, coño," Eufemio said. "We went back to Cuernavaca, and 'Miliano invited Madero to visit us there, thinking that if he saw for himself how things were, he'd listen to us and not to all those pachorrudos in the Capital. And we put on a real show for them there, you'd better believe. 'Miliano let me handle things, so I did it right. We had a big feast in the Borda Gardens, right between the two pools, with fountains springing up all around us, and lots of pajaritos with big tits to serve us, and three mariachi bands, and plenty of pulque and aguardiente. Madero turned out to be a vegetarian and a teetotaler, but I thought *fuck him*, let's have a good time anyway, and we did. Then I took him to a reviewing stand I'd had built just behind the cathedral, and we had a grand parade and review for 'Mexico's Deliverer.'

"The boys couldn't march for shit, of course, but they looked great as they stepped on past, all those sombrerudos in their white calzones with socks of purple, yellow, or green pulled up over their trouser legs, and every kind of weapon — and our one little cannon trailing after them. And since there weren't very many of them, I had them march around the cathedral and past the reviewing stand three times, until Madero must have thought there were ten thousand of us." Eufemio stopped suddenly and glared at me. I was wondering what Madero must have thought of those three little cannons.

"Are you laughing at all this, you fat maricón? You looking down at all the simple peasants, having their tacky parade to impress the big dignatarios? Don't laugh too hard, asshole: if you'd seen the pride and loyalty on their simple peasant faces, how grand they felt at being part of General Emiliano Zapata's army, you wouldn't feel so much like laughing. You finished laughing, now?" He continued to glare.

I wasn't laughing.

"All right, then. It was a triumph, anyway. The only person missing was 'Miliano. When he saw that all the pachorrudos had arrived with Madero on the train that morning, he went into one of his silences and crept off somewhere. He never showed up all day, not even to say good-bye to Madero. I think it was all too much of a show for my brother. He likes to look good, but only on his own terms, you know?"

I thought Emiliano had realized that it was useless to try to get through to Madero, that the little man's sweet nature made him unable to get past all his advisers; and that Emiliano had gone off in something like despair. But this was Eufemio's story, for the moment, so I said only, to prod him again, "And so you went home, and nothing happened."

"All right, we did go home, and 'Miliano had promised Madero we would disarm and discharge the army, and sit back and wait for all the land reforms we'd been promised. So we lined up the boys, and started paying them off, and collecting their weapons. And 'Miliano started thinking the war was over, and he could retire. This made him think of marriage, and that made him think of Josefa Espejo. With her, and his farm, and a string of mules, he figured he would have all he'd ever wanted. I think you fancy scholars don't understand how simply my brother sees life. You think that because he's a great man, he must have great ideas, great ambitions, no?

"Anyway, Josefa was a plump little muchacha, from up the road at Villa de Ayala. Her family had some money, so it was a big wedding, with a beef barbecue in her garden, and great clay jars filled with beans and chili, all covered over with huge banana leaves. Lots of the boys were still around, maybe not too eager to get back to their own farms; and there was some fancy shooting and lariat work. 'Miliano rode in a couple of races, and a few of us got drunk (myself included, would you believe it?); and there were showers of rice powder and blossoms, all very pretty. 'Miliano seemed not at all the conquering general, just a young farmer maybe on his way to being prosperous. It was a good wedding, Florecito, but I never believed in any of it, and I was right."

"Why? Because they wouldn't leave you alone?" I asked. Everyone knew by now the broad patterns of history made by the Revolution in Morelos: how time and again Emiliano Zapata would rise up in rebellion against whoever governed the country, win, then retire — only to be forced to rebel again, win, retire — and so on, right up to the spring of 1915, as I sat with Eufemio in our camp in Tlaltizapán. I already knew much of what Emiliano's brother could tell me; what I wanted to learn from his narrative was how I could fit myself into all this; whether there were some way the patterns could be altered to let me — us — survive. Us, and our poor necessary illusions. So I prodded Eufemio again.

"No, coño, they wouldn't leave us alone. On the very day of the wedding — the second one, the one with the priest, in August — a messenger came to tell 'Miliano that there was fighting over in Puebla City, between some of our boys and a regiment of Federales, who were now supposed to be loyal to Madero. 'Miliano sent word to all the Zapatistas to stop disarming, to form up and get ready to ride out again. No need to think about land reform for a while: first we had to do some more fighting.

"It was all confused, of course — what wasn't, in this fucking war? 'Miliano thought Madero was in trouble, and gathered up eleven hundred men to ride over to Jojutla, where he heard the little man was holed up. But the little man was in Mexico City, sitting there with his thumb up his ass, while his number one general, that old drunken Huerta, the famous Indian killer from the North, was preparing to move down into Morelos to wipe us out.

"Madero was helpless against this Huerta, this bullet-headed, half-blind old villain, who'd wiped out most of the indios in Guerrero and the Yucatán for Porfirio Díaz. Huerta pushed him around, lied to him, and convinced him that 'Miliano, who was the only honest ally Madero ever had, was really his enemy, until Madero finally begged him to lead a campaign against us. By late August he'd moved into Morelos, then across the valley and into the sierra until he had us surrounded at Cuautla — where Madero was paying a friendly visit to 'Miliano, who thought maybe there was still hope for this dwarf señorito.

"I rode out onto a hill west of the city, near the Casasano hacienda, and looked over at the road that ran down the ridge between the Yautepec and Cuautla valleys. It was the middle of the rainy season, and clouds were lying down among the brown hills. And here along the road came a whole regiment of Federales in their white uniforms, sweating and grunting in all the wetness, with the white clay of the roads sticking to their boots and to all the fancy equipment they carried with them: repeating rifles, Mausers, .44-caliber Winchesters, machine guns on wooden carts — even a few 75-millimeter cannons. Their officers were cocky as hell, prancing ahead of the column on their horses, laughing at the good time they were going to have with us.

"This sight made me so mad that I raced back to town, yelling that we should hang Madero right away as a traitor. But 'Miliano bundled him onto a train for the Capital, the poor baby, and we made ready to meet Huerta's Federales.

"Huerta was sure he had us. But when he pushed into the city that afternoon, we were gone. We just rode out the south end of town, kept to the hills along the Río Cuautla, and headed south, past Anenecuilco, and down to Tenextepango by midnight. The Federales almost caught up with us before dawn, but 'Miliano and I and a few others ran across the canefields and into the ditches along the road. We followed them until we met an arriero with a few mules which he was happy to lend us. We rode across the border into Puebla, and climbed high into the sierra there. We made camp in a pine forest far from anything, and stayed there for a month, while our guerrilleros regrouped back in Morelos."

"Is this my lesson about war, 'Femio?" I asked. "Run and hide. Regroup. Fight a little. Run and hide some more. Is that it?"

Eufemio was growing tired of my interruptions. But it was hard going, trying to keep his enthusiasm reined in, and his mind on where I wanted him to go. I wanted a set of principles; he wanted to tell adventure stories.

"Sit still, Gordito," he said. "I'll tell you what you want to know. All right, here: for the rest of the fall we let Huerta chase us. He'd come after us with his regiments of cavalry and infantry, and we'd lead him into the hills, and disappear. Then we'd split our boys up into two bunches, and send them around to Huerta's flanks, and hit him there — and then run off, letting him see our asses as we slipped into the hills and arroyos ahead of him. We never fought on his terms, only on ours; and we never held still, not even for a night, until we'd drawn him down into Puebla or Guerrero, farther and farther away from Cuernavaca and the Capital. We cut his telegraph lines. We blew up his supply trains. Huerta thought we were running from him, but we were really leading him around by the nose, wearing him down, killing a few of his men each day, stealing his horses and weapons. It was not only a great way to fight, Florecito; it was the *only* way.

"Look: we knew the terrain. Huerta didn't. The people were on our side. The more he burned their farms and trampled their fields, raped their women, and deported their young men to work as slaves on the henequen plantations of the Yucatán, the more they hated him and loved us. This was the way to fight a war, Florecito: it worked, and it was fun."

Eufemio had touched on a line I wanted to pursue with him, though I knew he would not like where it led. I decided to try him, anyway. He was leaning back on his elbows, now, as relaxed as he was likely to become. So I said, "This is the way it went for months, 'Femio, I know; until Madero was inaugurated and Huerta had to go back to the Capital to commence plotting against him. And this is the way it went again, in 1912, when *President* Madero sent Juvencio Robles down after you, to finish what Huerta had left unfinished. Robles was as bad as Huerta, maybe even worse, with all the hangings and shootings of Zapatista sympathizers (wasn't it Robles who said, 'I'm going to hang them from the trees like earrings'?), and the burning of crops, the razing of villages. But you kept to your guerrilla, and never won and never lost; and Emiliano issued the famous Plan de Ayala — "

"*Fuck* the Plan de Ayala!" shouted Eufemio, sitting up and glaring at me. This outburst startled me, not only because of its suddenness. I had assumed that he would be proud of his brother's document, which Emiliano and Otilio Montaño had written (using as their model my own Plan for the Partido Liberal Mexicano, the one I had written in Los Angeles in 1911) to make their goals plain to the people: not the ideologues, or the politicians, or the journalists, but the *people*. It spoke with quiet eloquence of the land, wood, and water which had been usurped through tyranny and venality. I remember one statement, especially: "The great majority of Mexicans own nothing more than the land they stand upon . . . unable to engage in industry or agriculture because lands, woods, and water are monopolized by a few. Therefore such properties shall be expropriated . . . in order that the villages and citizens of Mexico may obtain ejidos, colonies, town sites, and tillable lands. . . . The properties of those who oppose this plan shall be seized." As with everything Emiliano put his hand to, the plan was simple, unswerving, unambiguous. The pachorrudos and editorialists in Mexico City sneered at it as the work of a hayseed bandido, but when I read a copy of it in 1912, in McNeil Prison, I recognized not only its source in my own earlier Plan, but also the great effect it would have on the people for whom it had been intended.

I could not account for Eufemio's violent outburst, so I waited for his anger to subside once again — which it did quickly, as almost always — then asked him for an explanation. "What was wrong with this, 'Femio? Look, Emiliano did what he said he'd do: when his men captured a hacienda, he turned it over to them and to the campesinos who'd been working there. No legal schemes, no long delays: everything simple and direct. All his followers had to do was work the land, always with their rifles nearby; and come away to fight when Emiliano asked them to. What's in the Plan that goes against that?"

"Don't you hear it, Florecito?" Eufemio answered. "It's *Mexico* the Plan is talking about; no longer just Morelos, no longer just Anenecuilco. You people couldn't leave 'Miliano alone down here. It wasn't enough for him to clean up this state: suddenly he had to clean up the rest of *Mexico,* too — the whole fucking country, deserts and jungles and cities. *Mexico!* Chingado y maldito! *Mexico!* La patria de los hijos de la Gran Chingada!" Mexico, fucked and cursed; Mexico, homeland of the sons of the Big Whore.

I waited a minute for the tirade to subside, then said, "Why should you stay only in Morelos? I ask you to observe how things happened. In Morelos, Huerta came and tried to destroy you, and failed — and almost destroyed Morelos in the process. The people loved you for ridding them of Huerta. Then as soon as he was gone and you began to relax, here came Robles to take his turn in the state, and thousands of campesinos died, from murder or starvation. The towns and fields were burned, barren. Then you ran Robles out, and the people who were left loved you even more."

"That's all true," said Eufemio, beginning to settle back again. "But why does it mean 'Miliano had to protect the whole fucking country? Why couldn't he leave that to Villa and Orozco and all those other huevones in the North?"

"Because in a war, to free a country you can't just free one state and think you've done enough, 'Femio. Think, 'Femio. Think what this war has been for you. Think of how it's been a great cat-and-mouse game. You run and slap, run and slap. You get to ride, shoot, blow up trains — "

"Ahhh, yes," Eufemio said, stretching and unfolding himself, "blowing up trains." He moved stiffly over to the darkened corner, bent down, and came up with an almost-full bottle of tequila. He threw his head back, took a long pull at the bottle, gasped, and tossed the bottle across the brazier toward me. Then he returned to his place and squatted down, wiping his mustache and smiling contentedly.

"Blowing up trains. Shall I tell you something of real joy, Florecito?"

"By all means," I sighed, moving the now almost-empty bottle into the shadows behind my back.

"I said I'd tell you something about war. Well, here it is: forget all that shit about the guerrilla and cat-and-mouse and which-ones-are-the-enemy. If you can, imagine that you are one of us, and you know the Federales are going to run a train from the Capital across the sierra down to Cuernavaca. There is something on that train you want, or that 'Miliano says you must have — guns, machinery, I don't give a shit. And maybe there are a couple of cars full of Federales on it, too. You know the train will have to slow as it goes through all the bends above Tres Marías, and there'll be a lot of big rocks there the engineers can't see around. You know there's a little wooden bridge four spans long across a draw just after a big bend in the line. You know the train will come through that draw. So you stage a madrugada, a dawn attack.

"The night before, you and a couple of your handier boys climb out onto the bridge and tie eight sticks of dynamite to the supports at the far end. You bore a blasting cap into one of the sticks, clamp a fuse into it, then run the fuse back around the rocks to a little spot you've picked, a nice hideaway maybe fifty yards above the track. You and the boys feed and tether the horses, fry a few tamales, pass a bottle around, wrap yourselves into your serapes, and go to sleep looking up at the stars. It's a sharp, clear night, and they're all over the sky, with the moon so bright you can count the cacti on the hills across the draw.

"Then you wake up just before dawn, stretch, scratch, saddle up, and watch the little train as it heads toward you, rattling along around the bends. The sky is bright blue already, and you're a little hungry, pleasantly so. You have a slug of aguardiente, pa' matar el gusanillo, to kill the little worm. Maybe there's a soft breeze. Maybe the day's already hot. You can see some Federales on top of the cars, sitting behind a pile of sandbags with their machine guns, just in case we're waiting to bushwhack them.

"You know what it's like, Florecito? It's like when you're with a new woman, and you know you're going to have her, and she knows it too, and you both can hardly wait, and everything you see and hear and smell and touch is sharper than you've ever known it to be; so that every time her dress rustles it almost hurts you, the sound is so sharp, and — you know what I mean, Florecito?"

I knew. Or knew I would know, if given the chance.

"Right. Anyway, you have to be careful when you light the fuse. How long will the spark take to reach the dynamite? If it gets there too soon, the explosion will be under the locomotive, which will take most of the force, maybe not even stopping the train unless the bridge blows, too. If it gets there too late, you blow up a couple of cars, maybe, but the rest of the train keeps going. So you light the fuse just before the locomotive goes onto the central span, and the blast catches the coal car, and *Bam*! You've got it all!

"Maybe the whole bridge collapses, and the train falls into the draw. You all whoop like mad, fire off a lot of rounds, and gallop down to the wreck to see what prizes you've won.

It's great, Florecito, just great. You shoot the ones who are still alive, you take what you want and load up the mules, and off you go. Anda, que relajo!"

"And that's war," I said.

"Yes, that's war, tú puta madre. In fact, that's the very best part of war. Is there something wrong with what I tell you?" Again the black eyes fixed on me, and the carbine swung up toward my chest.

My response to Eufemio's reminiscence was all wrong, of course — from his point of view, anyway. It is never good to interrupt a man in the midst of his rapture, unless you are going to applaud it. But I could not let him off with so small, so juvenile a perception as this. It has often been my flaw to try to deal rationally with irrational men.

"With all respect, 'Femio," I said, trying one more time to placate him, "there is a part of it all that is not so good."

"Ah, you mean only dying," Eufemio began, wrestling with his anger.

"No, I wasn't thinking so simply as that," I said. "I was thinking of the people who are trying to keep alive in this playground on which you conduct your games of war. First there is a bad situation from which you must save them — exploitation, tyrants, greedy landlords, all that. You save them, and they're grateful. And then you save them again, and they're still grateful. Every time you do it, they love you more; but after a while there aren't so many of them, and there're not so many fields left for them to till. Until finally, though they still love you, they're as weary of you — and as scared of you — as they are of their oppressors. They just wish you'd all go away and leave them alone with their misery. Do you remember what happened only last year, after Robles's invasion but before Huerta murdered Madero?"

"With Felipe Angeles, you mean?" Eufemio asked. He

was still a little sullen, probably wanting to have stayed with his train wreck a little longer.

I nodded. Madero, in perhaps the only intelligent move the poor dupe was ever to make, appointed the dapper, correct Angeles (who was later to join Villa's army as his chief artillery officer, and still later to be executed by the Carrancistas) as Robles' replacement. He was to govern Morelos, and try to dampen the revolutionary spirit there, so Madero could concentrate on pacifying the rest of Mexico for a while.

Angeles was a great surprise, a professional officer who behaved with discretion, decency, and high intelligence. He saw that, if he were to behave as brutally as his predecessors in Morelos, his subjects would hate him; and, tired as they were, continue to cleave to Emiliano. So he did the one thing that could defeat Emiliano: by treating the campesinos with kindness, and by giving them what they wanted and in fact must have to survive, he rendered the Zapatistas irrelevant. They had no one to fight, hence no reason to continue existing as rebels. When Emiliano tried yet again to raise the people against the oppressors, they did not respond: they were no longer oppressed (or were not oppressed *at that moment*, which comes to the same thing).

Angeles sent them food and seed, replenished their herds, set his soldiers to helping them rebuild their villages — in short, made them content, or nearly so. And here in their midst stood their hero, Emiliano Zapata, at the head of eight thousand experienced troops, with no one to fight and no campesinos to cry for his help. (Why will tyrants never learn how simple it is to thwart rebellion? All they had to do was *leave the people alone* for a bit, and they'd be home free. . . . But they wouldn't be tyrants, then, would they?)

Needing to fight, Emiliano besieged Cuernavaca again, and took it, when Angeles withdrew to protect the city from further destruction. Emiliano then led his men down into Guerrero, taking Iguala and Chilpancingo. He was well-nigh invincible. His generals (all except Eufemio) urged him to move on Mexico City, where Huerta, having assumed the presidency after assassinating Madero, was behaving with characteristic bestiality. Emiliano contemplated such a campaign, but was reluctant to do so until Villa, Obregón, and Carranza had reduced Huerta's northern armies. (Put another way, Emiliano knew that a campaign against the Capital would require him to cease being the leader of a guerrilla band and become the general of an army, capable of large-scale, sustained activity; and this he did not want to do. He was not a soldier, and he knew it.)

Eufemio would not speak of Felipe Angeles, or of Huerta's usurpation, I knew; or of all that had happened between that summer of 1914 and this evening in the spring of 1915. Because everything that happened — the victories of Villa and Obregón in the North; the retreat of Huerta into the Capital, his flight to Veracruz and into exile; the grab for power by Carranza; the attempt by the rebel generals to forestall Carranza at the conference in Aguascalientes; and the grand meeting of Pancho Villa and Emiliano in Xochimilco — all this was beyond Eufemio. He saw more than all the rest of us, and what he saw was so terrible and so inevitable that he had to shut off his mind. His intuition told him so much that he could not bear to think about what it told him.

I looked at the tall young calavera slumped across the brazier from me, stupefied now with tequila. The dying flames caused his eyes to glitter as if they were opaque, unseeing, without depth. Pobrecito, I wanted to say to him, you're dead where you sit, and you know it. Your only life has been in Morelos, your only vitality that given you by your brother and his battles. And in your prescience you know this. You know that in the great sweep of history, you didn't mean very much — a little noise, a few gestures, a few deaths. Poor Calavera Zapatista, with your big, black sombrero on your grinning death's head, with your drooping mustache, your tight black jacket and caballero's trousers, your half-buckled gaiters and crumpled boots — and that goddamn carbine. The Revolution can't use you much longer. After the first violence, we need men who *think*.

You were wrong, 'Femio. You're not a mask, not for Emiliano, anyway. What you are is his shadow, his ghost: no substance to you at all, for all the racket you make. Is that why Amparo, the incomparable Amparo, lets you into her secret places? Because she likes to play with ghosts?

You were right, 'Femio. You wouldn't last much longer. Were you watching your death as you sat staring into the flames?

Notebook 8

November 18, 1922

As I warned you long ago, I am not to be measured quickly: more than a self-deprecating buffoon, less than a titan. I know that I am not a prepossessing figure as I sit here, hunched over these pages trying to make out from the light of the single bulb in the ceiling what I am writing for you. (And believe me, this is hard: I have to hold my left hand straight along the right edge of each page so that I will know when my pen has come to the end of a line, and it is time to return to the left-hand margin and begin a new line. For one who has, since his days with Posada, prided himself on his calligraphy, this is depressing.)

As what you would call a terminal diabetic, I am no sight to inspire confidence or optimism. But at the moment I am less concerned with my physical appearance (for, after all, who but my guard sees me here in my solitary confinement?), or the sorry state of my heart, liver, and kidneys, than I am with the self I project to you. I am a trifle embarrassed, for instance, by this pedestrian style in which I must write, lacking as I do enough time to perform with my accustomed flair. That I can still do better, let me illustrate very briefly by copying into this notebook a few lines which I penned earlier today to Ellen White (or Lilly Sarnoff, to give her real name), in answer to her request for particulars about my childhood in Oaxaca:

> The child of tropical mountains, my first impressions of life were measured by the grandeur and majesty of my surroundings, and no prince ever rocked in his cradle in the midst of such splendor as I, under the gold and purple rays of my native sun. Simply put, I breathed in beauty with my first breath. I believe that these first impressions determined my future, because for as long as I can remember, nature has been for me an inexhaustible fountain from which my soul has tried to satiate its formidable thirst for beauty.

Grand stuff, no? (Especially since, as I wrote you earlier, I recall almost nothing of my early days in Oaxaca. A real author can write well about anything — or nothing.) I know, poor gringo, how you would prefer to read such as that to the rough, vulgar prose I am hurling at you; but I have no time to write elegantly — and besides, how could I hope to transmit to you some sense of the crude but vital speech of Eufemio Zapata or Emma Goldman, if I were to surround their words with such eloquent passages as I have written to Miss Sarnoff (or Miss White)?

Because of my ability to compose words in what I hope you will allow me to call my *bel canto* manner, my admirers have assumed that my culture was broad, extending to all the arts. Little Librado Rivera, who is my fondest disciple (and my fellow jailbird), said of me once to an interviewer — a court reporter, actually — that I "adored the beautiful music of Caruso and the musical compositions of that most tragic of men: Beethoven"; and that I "recited from memory the most beautiful poems of Rubén Darío, Shakespeare, Carpio, Manuel Acuña, and Díaz Mirón." Well. Bless Librado, but he exaggerates. The truth is that I have heard about as little music, and read about as little poetry, as it is possible for an educated man to get away with in our time. I would doubtless have admired Caruso if I had ever heard him. Beethoven for me is a few snatches of a sonata played on a piano in a Mexico City bordello at the turn of the century. And of the poets, well, I've heard of Darío and I've read some Shakespeare; the others are only names. I'm sure I would have enjoyed them.

The fact is that I have not had the time — or, usually, the freedom — for culture. In my St. Louis days, I was often struck by my Jewish friends' veneration of the arts. How, I wondered, did Emma Goldman and her fellow radicals ever find time to read a book or listen to music? It seemed to me that for them even simple conversation was manic, a matter of sustained interruption. When did they ever cease their agitated monologues long enough to read a book or listen to a piece of music? So far as I could tell, they didn't even listen to one another. Culture, I suspect, is for those who have not yet begun their Revolution; or for those who have already seen theirs fail.

Enough about culture: I'll leave that for my letters to ladies from Boston and New York. The real substance of my life has been running, hiding, and going to jail, with brief spurts of frenetic and bombastic (I know it) writing in between. My detractors say that I have insisted on such a career, either out of some perverse desire to inflict suffering on myself, or because I knew I was incapable of serious, solid activity and constructed my life so as always to be compelled to dart about on the surface of things, like some clumsy black beetle skittering about on the lip of a neglected jug. Judge for yourself, now, old gringo who's become my closest companion, almost my confiteor: what else could I have done?

———

We rode the rails west, Modesto Díaz and I, in October of 1906, until we reached the city of Los Angeles. There we found our way into Old Sonora Town, as the barrio latino was called, and were taken in by our contact there, one Rómulo Carmona. There was nothing to do just then but hide. We had left Enrique behind in Montreal, working as a bricklayer. Librado was still in St. Louis, trying to keep *Regeneración* going. Juan Sarabia had been arrested in Ciudad Juárez and sent to the prison of San Juan de Ulúa in Veracruz, to serve a five-year sentence. Antonio Villarreal was on his way to us, via Santa Fe and Denver. I could not even walk the streets of the barrio: Porfirio Díaz had put a bounty of $20,000 on my head, and caused 150,000 "Wanted" posters to be pasted up all over Mexico and the southwestern United States. There I was, for all the world to admire: in full face and profile, wire-rimmed spectacles perched atop my woolly head, tight wing collar and loose cravat, black jacket, and a face with the perplexed expression of a stunned ox. With mustache. A face to terrify the multitudes.

Two days after our arrival, Carmona came to my room to tell me that three men were standing on the sidewalk across the street outside, watching our house with that air of conspicuous unconcern that undercover agents the world over like to affect. I fled through the back door, and hid at another friendly house in the next block.

A month later I learned that this house, too, was being watched. There was no back door. My host, a deadpan indio from Tamaulipas, told me to shave my mustache, then brought to my room a flowered blouse, shawl, thick cotton skirt, two petticoats, and a calico poke bonnet to hide my face. I dressed in all this, rolled my trouser legs over my calves, took up a canvas shopping bag, and stepped out the front door. Do not laugh too long at this display: consider that, though it would have been bad to be caught by Díaz's agents, it would have been infinitely worse to be caught while feeling great shame. What sport my enemies would have had! What cartoons in the Mexico City newspapers! You Anglos think we Mexicans value manly courage above all virtues; but I tell you that, with us, dignity comes first. Dress a man as a woman, and you rob him of both dignity and courage.

I went undetected, and boarded a train for San Francisco, thinking that this city to the north, still emerging from its great earthquake and fire, might be so disordered as to make a natural hideout. But I felt eyes on my back there (perhaps I was right, perhaps not: fugitives acquire vivid imaginations), and left after a week for Sacramento.

I took a room there, and waited for something to happen. The life of a fugitive is supposed to be romantic, I know; but it isn't. I could not go out to look for work. I could not go near any of the principal streets of the city, but had to slip along alleyways. Lacking money, I could go to no restaurants. Until Carmona sent me a package of bread and baloney from Los Angeles, I had nothing to eat. Like fugitives everywhere, I had to become my own prisoner: to hide all day in my room, go out only at night, and even then have to watch my every step — to look in every corner and on all sides, before making any movement. We call it walking a salto de mata: jumping from one bush to the next.

After months of this purgatorial life I returned from an evening of prowling to find Antonio Villarreal crouching in the doorway to my room. He had arrived in Los Angeles the week before, and Carmona had sent him to fetch me. We hitchhiked the next day to Los Angeles, and were overjoyed to discover that Enrique, too, had made it across the country to join us.

A week later Librado struggled in, exhausted: Thomas Furlong's men had destroyed our press in St. Louis and caused Librado to be arrested for a murder he was supposed to have committed in Hermosillo, a place he had never been. He was to have been deported, but a judge in Missouri threw his case out of court; and Librado leapt on a freight train heading west with a load of lime aboard. He was almost asphyxiated before he could jump from the train in Colorado; and he walked, choking and weeping, most of the rest of the way to join us in California.

I gave them all a day to rest, then found us a run-down house on East Pico Street to rent for thirty dollars a month. We needed to find work, to earn enough money to get *Regeneración* started up again. "This is our best chance," I told the comrades. "We're in a new world out here, in a great new city, with friends all around us, if we keep our eyes open. These are our people, here. From here we can reach in to Mexico with our words, and from here our troops can strike at the dictator when the time for the uprising comes." My capacity for optimism in the face of massive negative evidence has never ceased to amaze me. Brave words, though, right?

Foolishly naive words, of course. On August 23, as Librado, Villarreal, and I were seated at our kitchen table, the front door burst open and six men dressed as laborers poured into the house. Two were Mexicans; and another pair we knew only too well: Thomas Furlong himself, and Ansell Samuels, our faithless co-worker from St. Louis. Two others stood back and watched the assault. These last were reporters, brought along by Furlong to record — and embellish — the event. As I recall, this is what they wrote in the *Los Angeles Herald* the following day:

> Repeatedly thrown to the floor, Ricardo Flores Magón managed to get to his feet, at times with two police on top of him, and throw them off. Tied up, he broke his manacles as if they were made of string, and kept on fighting. Huge, in splendid physical condition, he struggled like a demon, and held off the police for more than an hour. Finally he was knocked down by a powerful blow to the jaw, and before he could get up, was tied with thick rope and subdued.

Antonio Villarreal, too, was a brute, wrote these romancers. He was said to have destroyed the furniture in three rooms (we had no furniture other than that kitchen table and two chairs) before being trussed up. Even poor Librado was called "little but powerful, agile as an athlete," and supposedly fought ferociously until Furlong got a grip on this throat and bore him down.

In all their account of these heroics, the reporters nowhere mentioned that our assailants had no arrest warrants, and that in fact there were no charges against us.

This was, of course, a kidnapping; and Librado shouted as much to the crowd of onlookers who had gathered outside the house during the fracas, as we were being piled into a couple of waiting cars. If he had not cried out, I am sure we would have been driven across the border and turned over to Porfirio Díaz's men, and murdered. As it was, we were taken to El Condado, the Los Angeles County Jail, and held there incommunicado while Furlong and the police added up charges to bring against us. Eventually, they decided on five: resisting arrest, homicide and theft, criminal defamation, assassination of someone called "Juan Pérez" in Mexico, and conspiring to violate the neutrality laws.

Rómulo Carmona turned up at the jail two days later with a tall, blond gringo he introduced as Job Harriman, "the famous socialist lawyer and great friend of the Mexican oppressed." For once we were lucky: Harriman was just what Carmona claimed, in spite of his very suspect surname, which in California ranked in infamy only slightly below Hearst and Otis. Harriman was a true socialist and a fervent, shrewd attorney; and he was to stick by us for years, until his political ambitions took him away from the tribal warfare in the barrios.

The charges against us were ridiculous, of course, even the last. But Harriman cautioned us against optimism: "You're what they're afraid of in this country, compadres; you're the Red Menace. Don't look for too much justice from these courts, because a scared public doesn't want justice."

Harriman was right. At the pre-trial hearing, Harriman faced Thomas Furlong, a burly, white-haired man who looked (said Harriman) like everybody's favorite uncle, and quickly brought out the absurdity of the charges — all of which were dropped, except for the last. But Harriman soon established just who had been guilty of violating the neutrality laws:

Harriman: What is your occupation?
Furlong: I am president and director of the Furlong Secret
           Service Company of St. Louis, Missouri.
Harriman: Did you detain these men?
Furlong: Yes.
Harriman: Did you arrest them without a judicial order?
Furlong: Yes, sir.
Harriman: You entered their house and searched it without a
           judicial order?

Furlong: Yes.
Harriman: You attacked them in their house and took them
             away?
Furlong: No, sir, they surrendered . . .
Harriman: Who paid you to do this work?
Furlong: The Mexican government.

That should have done it; we should have been freed, and Furlong rebuked — or even arrested himself. But Harriman was right. The last charge was allowed to stand, and we were held without bail, while evidence against us was gathered for the trial.

I wrote you three notebooks ago that I did not wish to tell you more about María Talavera, my Mexican mistress, than was absolutely necessary. Today I will amend that evasive description to say that she was not only *not* a little campesina, blindly following wherever I might lead, grateful for whatever crumb of affection I might feed her; but that her name was really María Talavera de Brousse; that she was slightly older and considerably taller than I; that she was a woman of great intelligence and spirit, just as willing to fight and be jailed as any of us; and that she played a crucial role in the events that were to follow this arrest. I will tell you why I am so equivocal about this woman: because I abandoned her, emotionally speaking, for Amparo Urdiales, and I am ashamed of myself.

I have said that I would not lie to you in these notebooks. But now you know that I may do so, not out of modesty or vanity, or political expediency, but out of shame. María was a good woman, and she loved me, and I was too busy being the Anarchist Conscience of the People to respond to her as I should have done. (When I told Amparo of María, she said, "Oh, Florecito, you men carry such a heavy baggage of guilt with you. This María probably loved you for what you represented, not for what you fondly think of as your true self. If you hadn't been such a symbolic figure, she might not have loved you at all. It's as easy for a woman to fall in love with a cause, or a symbol, as with a man." Was this why she loved Emiliano Zapata? I asked. As usual, Amparo only laughed.)

I bring up María Talavera's name only because I must tell you that, in the long months I lay in jail awaiting trial, she was my only reliable conduit to the Revolution. Once a week she would visit me at El Condado, and we would sit facing one another on a pair of long benches, separated by a low screen of wire mesh. Once a week she would drop her purse, opened, at her feet. I would bend down to pick it up for her, slipping a note into it as I did so — and word would go out to the Liberal forces along the border and to our members throughout Mexico, to prepare for what I now thought of as the Revolution of 1908.

Word to be ready went out to all forty-six Liberal clubs. The emotions of workers everywhere in Mexico had been aroused since the Río Blanco revolt in January 1907, when 800 textile workers were massacred by a company of Federales. Now, acting on my instructions passed on to them by María, bands of Liberals attacked towns and garrisons at Viescas, in Coahuila; Matamoros, in Tamaulipas; Palomas and Janos, in Chihuahua; and Mexicali, in Baja California. In July, the Yaqui Indians of Sonora rose up, attacking the mining operations that threatened their tribal land. The whole North was seething, ready to boil.

I know, I know: these were not much more than a series of minor skirmishes, with no solid results. No towns were taken, no territory held. But by the summer of 1908, all Mexico was watching us, waiting for the crucial moment to announce itself. We sent our messengers across the country, from Veracruz to Tlaxcala and Oaxaca.

There was only one obstacle, finally, in our way. And that was Francisco I. Madero, the spiritualist pollo of Coahuila, who had plans of his own for Mexico. One of our people had gone to the Madero ranch in 1907, knowing of Madero's quondam support for *Regeneración*, and intending to solicit money for arms. No, said Madero; he didn't want to do anything that would encourage the spilling of Mexican blood. He preferred that social change should come about gradually, through the education of the masses. Besides (and these were his very words to the emissary), "Díaz was not a tyrant. A bit rigid, but not a tyrant." He certainly wished us well, however, and hoped we would think of him as a friend, and assured us that we would be in his prayers. What is one to say about such a man?

In all charity, I must admit that Madero's heart was in the right place. He was not a bad man, only the prisoner of his class. Never having been face-to-face with *real* bad men intending him harm, and unable to conceive of a world without mercy and forgiveness, he had no notion of evil. He probably thought well of his fellow man until the very moment when Huerta's bullet entered his brain.

In somewhat less charity, I can say also that Madero's benign obtuseness hurt us badly from the start. While I was running and hiding across the United States, he was making discreet little forays from his family's hacienda, seeking support for his No-Reelection Party. (Díaz had promised not to reelect himself in 1910, and Madero hoped to hold him to that promise.) Men who might have joined us — good men, enlightened men — joined him instead. Madero looked safe, credible. His ideas were moderate, homegrown. Maderismo

represented the appeal of Reason; safe, middle-class, predictable Reason.

Whereas *I*, on the other hand: I was mad Flores Magón,
voice of the irrational desheredados of Mexico, the disinher-
ited ones, the poor and oppressed, who just might, if aroused
sufficiently, pull the whole edifice down: not just Díaz, but
the courts and the army and the haciendas and the industries, as well. My ideas were foreign, and violent. I was dangerous, and Madero was safe. He offered Mexico that
beguiling absurdity, a pleasant revolution; whereas I offered
them The Revolution.

From my jail cell in Los Angeles, I derided and belittled
Madero and his modest campaign; but I should have known
that he was what I called him earlier in these notebooks: the
real villain of the whole drama, all the more so because it
was impossible to hate him. Look at the way Emiliano Zapata trusted and believed him, long after he should have
known Madero would betray him. Maybe Eufemio was right:
maybe they should have strung Madero up when they had
him in their hands at Cuautla, rather than helping him flee
back to the Capital.

With no help from Madero and his well-meaning supporters, and with its leader jailed, my Revolution of 1908
sputtered out within a month of its commencement. The agents
of the Porfiriato moved along the border, arresting our people and confiscating their weapons. Enrique, who had taken
part in the raid on Palomas and then escaped to El Paso,
made his way back to Los Angeles to tell me of our failure.
There was nothing for me to do now but prepare for the
trial, which was finally about to begin — almost two years
after our arrest.

At the last moment the Attorney General arranged to have

the trial moved to Arizona, which was, he claimed, "the scene of our crime." Arizona was a territory, not yet a state; and this made it easier to buy and sell judges than in California. And in Arizona he reckoned we'd be out of sight of all the progressive organizations that were springing up out of the labor movement all over the United States, and that were especially flourishing in California. So off we all went by police van to Tombstone, for the predictable farce.

Farce it was, though not for us. Ansell Samuels was the chief witness for the prosecution, and he produced whole bundles of "evidence" that he'd collected against us: letters we had written and received in St. Louis, Canada, and El Paso; copies of *Regeneración* containing what he called "inflammatory clarion calls to violence"; an affidavit from that accursed woman in Oaxaca I wrote of in my fifth notebook, who claimed (accurately) that in 1905 I had described her husband as an "impotent old fool" — everything, in short, that might convince the judge we needed hanging. Samuels never produced any evidence that showed us violating the neutrality laws, nor did he need to do so; it was sufficient to show that we were plotters and skulkers and all-around bad citizens, and therefore guilty.

The only bright moment in the trial came when Job Harriman was cross-examining a felon called Trinidad Vázquez, who had been in jail with us in Los Angeles, and who testified that we were socialists.

"How did you know they were socialists?" Harriman asked Vázquez.

"Pues, por su manera de andar," said Vázquez. By the way they walked.

The judge waited until the ensuing commotion had died down, then, drying his eyes with his handkerchief, asked Vázquez just how socialists walked. Vázquez climbed down from the witness box and waddled across the room in a manner that, I am told, looked exactly like my own manera de andar. The judge had to retire to his chambers at this.

The judgment of course went against us. We were convicted of "conspiring to commit an offense against the United States of America," sentenced to eighteen months in prison, and fined $100 each — money with which to pay Samuels for his testimony, we supposed.

We were taken in a bus to the old penitentiary in Yuma, one of America's worst. It had been a fortress during the Apache wars of a few decades earlier, and then was converted into a prison for the Southwest's worse offenders. The prisoners lived in long adobe wards within a walled enclosure. The guards patrolled the tops of the walls, but seldom dared come all the way into the enclosure. For once I longed for a cell of my own, because the dormitory life at Yuma was not only overintimate, but downright dangerous: most of the prisoners were either Negros or Mexicans, and they roamed about the galleries in savage little packs, fighting one another and terrorizing those of us who were mere "politicals." Discipline, such as it was, came from a squadron of brutal trustees who carried thick clubs which they used on us for the slightest infraction of whatever rules they chose to invent.

We all had to rise at four each morning. After breakfast — a mug of tea, a bowl of watery oats, and a slice of bread — we were sent to spend the day at our respective jobs. Librado, less hardy than Villarreal and I, was allowed to work in the infirmary. We went to the tailor shop, where we were required to turn out eighteen pairs of pants a day, or a dozen undershirts and drawers.

Please know that I do not complain about this sort of manual labor. On the contrary, my years in various prisons have taught me that physical work, even the most mindless sort, can be the best possible stimulus to intellectual activity. The clearest thinking I have ever done was in the tailor shop at Yuma, shearing trousers out of bolts of denim. The most dangerous thing about prison life is not the guards, or one's fellow prisoners, or the forced labor, but solitude, time spent sitting on one's bunk, staring at one's shoes, the mind as torpid as the body.

When the hands are busy, the mind can range; the time passes. If time were not passing so swiftly for me now here in Leavenworth, if I thought these notebooks could go on and on, I would argue for you now that the working classes are far more intellectual than the bourgeoisie, because of the freedom that labor gives the mind. But I feel more certain each morning that within a very few days one of two things will happen: either I shall be freed; or I shall be dead. However it goes, my time for writing is growing short. I must press on.

The authorities moved us in January 1910 to the new prison in Florence, where living conditions were somewhat better. This transfer presumably suggested itself to the Arizona authorities because of our growing celebrity in America. In Chicago, a man named John Murray persuaded the League for the Defense of Political Prisoners to look into our case. Fifty suffragettes stood one freezing day in the Loop and hawked copies of magazines containing articles about our plight written by Samuel Gompers, president of the American Federation of Labor. The women collected sixty-two dollars, which Murray forwarded to us. In May, Gompers, working through the League for Defense, launched a protest against our mistreatment by the courts. Mother Jones and Eugene V. Debs joined him in this, and by June we were famous.

By August we were free. John Kenneth Turner, whose muckraking articles had Americans aware for the first time of Porfirio Díaz's barbarities, met us at the prison gates with a delegation of men from the Western Federation of Miners. They were there not only to honor and greet us, but also to make sure that we were indeed set free, and allowed to leave Arizona.

They escorted us back to Los Angeles, where a triumphant reception awaited us. People at the depot threw flower petals in our path, and cheered as we were taken to the Labor Temple, where a huge crowd of well-wishers went wild as we were carried in on the shoulders of Turner, Job Harriman, and our escort of miners. They seated us on the podium. When the noise subsided, an orchestra played the Mexican national hymn, after which Harriman read a manifesto provided for the occasion by the writer Jack London. It went, in part:

> We socialists, anarchists, hoboes, chicken thieves, outlaws, and undesirable citizens of the U.S. are with you heart and soul. You will notice that we are not respectable. Neither are you. No revolutionary can possibly be respectable in these days of the reign of property. All the names you are being called, we have been called.

London's manifesto went on to praise what he called our "gallant band," and to subscribe himself a chicken thief and revolutionist, like us. ("Who does this man call a chicken thief?" Librado whispered to me. "I never stole a chicken in my life.")

I found all this a little lacking in dignity, but I appreciated London's kind intentions — until a couple of days later, when I read his comment that he was "first of all a white man, and only secondly a socialist." This was my first evidence that novelists are not to be trusted, especially when you give them a chance to appear in public, even by proxy. And I suppose this is partly the source of the animus I directed against poor Mariano Azuela in the first of these notebooks.

The rally continued, with Antonio Villarreal being invited to speak. He made a solemn promise, in the name of our Junta, that we would continue the struggle. John Turner spoke about our persecution. Then they turned to me. This was my first chance to orate since that original rally in San Luis Potosí, nine years earlier, and I made the most of it.

"My arm is raised until death," I said to the crowd, "in favor of the weak and against the despot. I bear on my flesh the scars of the chains, and I am proud of them. I believe in a future of happiness, and as we march to that future, let us cry out, 'Viva la revolución social!' "

The vivas rang out. A collection was taken, and we gained $414. Not much to Mr. Hearst, perhaps (he laughed at us in his paper the following day), but a considerable amount to come from an audience of poor people — and enough to allow us to resume publication of *Regeneración*.

We rented an office in the heart of the slums, in an old building on the corner of Fourth and Towne streets. I sat down at my new desk, took the cover off the big old Royal typewriter Librado had dragged up the three flights of stairs from the street, and by September 3 the first issue was out. After so many months of silence, I could not help fairly shouting at my readers. I began with "Mexicans: A la Guerra!" and went on to say that the Revolution must come, as the sun comes to banish the anguish of the night. I told them it would not be enough for them to change their masters. I said they must learn that all riches — houses, palaces, railroads, ships, factories, plowed fields, everything, absolutely everything — have been made by them, and must belong to them. I told them there was no political freedom without economic freedom. I told them they would have to fight for this. And I concluded by hurling at them the battle cry of the Narodniki in the 1860s, as taken up by the Catalan anarchists and passed on to me by Florencio Bazora in a St. Louis café: "Tierra y Libertad!"

A year later, Emiliano Zapata would take up this cry in Morelos. It was perhaps my major contribution to his campaign.

My postimprisonment enthusiasm was not so great that I failed to keep track of what Francisco Madero was up to, those days. In January 1909, his parents had given him permission to publish his book, *The Presidential Succession*. In this powder-puff polemic, Madero continued his argument that Porfirio Díaz could be persuaded for once to obey the Constitution, which called for a four-year term, and no reelection. He put himself forward as the No-Reelection candidate for the election scheduled in 1910, and asked for all Mexican progressives to join him.

The elections were held in November. Don Porfirio's men stuffed ballot boxes, terrorized polling booths, and threw out the tallies of entire states; and the old president was reelected illegally but resoundingly. Díaz tossed Madero in jail for the inconvenience he had caused. The little man escaped and fled to San Antonio, where he wrote his Plan de San Luis Potosí (it wouldn't do to have one's Plan issue from a gringo city, would it?). This called for a revolution, to commence in November 1910.

I sent a circular to all members of the Liberal party, telling them that they might take part in Madero's revolution, but they were on no account to confuse it with the real one. I pointed out that Madero wanted to provide Mexico with a new government, but that governments have to protect the right of property above all rights. I told them not to expect that Madero would attack the right of property in favor of the proletariat. He would never emancipate them, I said: they would have to do this themselves.

Madero remained in Texas until February 1911, when Pancho Villa and Pascual Orozco and the other rebel generals made it safe for him to stick his feet back onto Mexican soil. In the meantime, columns of my Liberals fought alongside his troops, often bravely and with distinction. Many of our people died.

But Madero had sent secret word to his commanders that the Partido Liberal Mexicano was potentially very dangerous to the progressive government he hoped to form. One way or another, we must be suppressed. We should be persuaded to cease being Magonistas, and become Maderistas. If we refused, we should be disarmed. Or extirpated. (Historians who write so fetchingly about Madero's benevolence and altruism should look at this corner of the war, and learn that their man had perhaps just a touch of ruthlessness in him, too.)

I watched all this unfold, but only out of the corner of my eye. From our new office I ran the magazine as zealously as ever, while simultaneously I set in motion my own military campaign against Porfirio Díaz. Being a journalist and polemicist was suddenly not enough: now I had to get into the fight, myself. (That the press was writing these days about *General* Madero had something to do with this, I admit.) I was too fat to run or ride, and too blind to fire a rifle, but I could still lead troops. "Yes, lead them from his Los Angeles office," say my detractors; but surely I had by now given ample evidence of my physical courage in other ways, in matters requiring endurance and tenacity. Surely I could be the sort of general who leads by administering: aren't there many of those?

Unfortunately, I turned out to be an absolutely rotten military administrator. My initial strategy was, I must say, brilliant. Our chief battleground at this time was in the state of Sonora. I reasoned that, if we suffered reverses there, we could retreat to the long, nearly empty peninsula of Baja California, where there were few Federal garrisons, where it would be easy to run contraband from the United States, and where we could marshal our resources until we were strong enough to take the offensive in Sonora, then move on to Sinaloa and Chihuahua, and finally down across all Mexico. It was scarcely a modest plan, but it seemed reasonable and promising to me. All we needed was matériel, which would presumably come from the United States; some experienced soldiers to lead the troops; and — of course — some troops to be led.

We scoured Baja California for volunteers, pulled as many of our men out of Sonora as we dared, and held recruiting drives in Los Angeles and San Diego. Within a month, we had 600 men enlisted and ready to fight. Of these, 400 were Mexican, and the rest American or international — Jack London's hoboes and chicken thieves, mainly, pulled from flophouses, mission homes, and drying-out establishments. Perhaps forty of these were real workers, members of the strongly anarcho-syndicalist International Workers of the World, or "Wobblies," as they were called.

These Wobblies were our best hope as leaders, but they were dangerously volatile: if they felt like fighting, they fought with abandon and something like joy; but if their orders were not sufficiently quixotic or dangerous, they grew bored and disputatious, given to protest meetings in the midst of battle. They would give counterorders to "down tools" when asked to defend a position they found unsuitable. Nevertheless, from the Wobblies came men like Jim Edwards, Joe Hill, William Stanley, and Simon Berthold, who were not only brave but skillful as well. Stanley and Berthold died fighting for the Junta, and Hill only just escaped death in our last battle; but while they lived they gave me real hope that the movement against Díaz could become, more than just a Mexican war, an international event, one that would perhaps cause reverberations even in Europe.

On January 29, 1911, led by a British soldier of fortune called Caryl Rhys Davis, we moved against Mexicali, and we won. A month later troops under Stanley took Algodones. In April, Berthold was killed as we took Tecate. We were advancing so rapidly that Díaz became alarmed, and ordered his General Mayol to land his Eighth Battalion at Ensenada to reinforce what garrisons remained on the peninsula. Rhys Davis led our troops against Ensenada to fight Mayol, taking Tijuana along the way. I began to think we were invincible.

We were not, of course. We were a little pickup army of fugitives and drifters, and anyone should have been able to predict that we'd never win more than small, temporary victories. When we were defeated, though, what brought us down was not failure in battle, but my inability to foresee the avalanche of chicanery sweeping down on us.

I neglected to take into account that large sections of the peninsula were on permanent loan to William Randolph Hearst and several other West Coast capitalists, like Harry Chandler and Harrison Gray Otis. Hearst had no intention of losing any of his southern fiefdom to a pack of mad anarchists. He wrote to his President Taft, demanding that troops be dispatched to protect the border against the Red Menace. Taft obliged by sending a regiment of cavalry to patrol the strip of land between Tijuana and San Diego, thus effectively interdicting our lines of supply and reinforcement.

Then Hearst used his editorial power to convince America that I was fighting not to free Mexico from tyranny, but to establish a socialist state of my own in Baja California — that I was nothing but a "filibustero," a soldier of fortune myself, full of grandiose and selfish schemes.

In case this campaign of slander and libel did not succeed (which it did: many people in the United States immediately began calling me a bandit, and demanding my arrest), Hearst to confuse things further sent down an absolute clown named Dick Ferris, an itinerant actor, promoter, charlatan, and all-around mountebank. Before I knew what was happening, Ferris had driven his enormous blue limousine down through the army's blockade to Tijuana, where he began holding court and promising great rewards to those who were willing to accept him as the new leader of the Junta. He sent a long wire to Porfirio Díaz, offering to set up a new state in Baja California, which he proposed to call the Republic of Díaz. (Díaz, to do the old villain credit, refused indignantly.) Ferris told all my leaders that I planned to betray them, and many of them believed him. Having sown the seeds of our defeat, he drove back to Los Angeles and reported to Hearst. A day later Ferris announced in Hearst's paper that he intended to turn Baja California into a "republic for whites"; and he and Hearst retired to San Simeon to see what would happen.

They did not have long to wait. Within four days they were joined by Rhys Davis, our leader in the field. The American recruits — all except the Wobblies — dwindled away, leaving us with a sad band of unemployed braceros for an army. We had almost no ammunition for our obsolete weapons. There was no artillery. For cavalry we had forty mules. Food was scarce, and fresh water was almost nonexistent on the barren peninsula.

But, even before we could retreat, we came under attack from another enemy: Francisco I. Madero. The new jefecito was gaining ground every day — or, rather, Villa and Orozco were, while the jefecito waited in the North, sporting a pair of bright yellow boots, riding about on his charger, and looking as bellicose as he could. In February he had condescended to announce that, when he became president, I should become his vice president. I rushed to print a denial of this in *Regeneración*, and announced that henceforth the Partido Liberal Mexicano would oppose Madero. On February 25, I wrote that he was "a traitor to the cause of liberty."

On the morning of February 26, as the staff of the magazine sat with me in my office, drinking coffee and eating our usual breakfast of enchiladas and garbanzos, Antonio Villarreal entered, looking pale and anxious. He held his hat in one hand; in the other was his revolver, which he quickly placed before me on the desk.

"Bueno, Ricardo," he said, "that's it. I'm sorry, I must leave. Good-bye." As he spoke he was already turning toward the door.

"What's this, compañero?" I asked, laughing. "Who has hurt your feelings?"

Villarreal stopped, looked back at the men and women who had been his friends and allies for so many years, and said, "Everything hurts me, Ricardo. It's been too long. I'm tired. I'm not a rebel anymore. I want some peace. From today, I'm a Maderista. No more revolution. Now, please, Ricardo, let me go."

He began to cry. So did we all, a little: this was our first defection. And Villarreal was no traitor, but a good man worn down by the years of flight and imprisonment. Not everyone can make a career of anarchism. I told him I did not regard him as a traitor, but as a fallen comrade. We embraced, and he gravely settled his hat upon his head and walked out the door and down the stairs, leaving the revolver with me.

On May 2 Díaz resigned. Just like that. The Porfiriato was over, and Madero was the man of the hour. He could have — should have — marched into the Capital, thrown all the pachorrudos out of the Chamber of Deputies, disbanded the army, turned the haciendas and factories over to the people, and got away with it. But he sat where he was, temporized, sought everyone's advice, and forgave all his enemies (who laughed at him for his foolish innocence).

Even me, apparently. After ordering a troop of his soldiers across American soil (so much for those famous neutrality laws, which apparently applied to some Mexicans, but not others) to Tijuana, where they dispersed the remnants of my army, he sent a "Commission of Peace" to me in Los Angeles.

This arrived one day in the middle of June, and consisted of two delegates whose appearance filled me with consternation: Juan Sarabia, just freed from San Juan de Ulúa, and apparently a fervent new convert to Maderismo; and that most bourgeois of revolutionaries, my very respectable older brother, Jesús. Madero, who must have thought I would welcome them, could not have chosen worse delegates. I was so enraged to see these two as representatives of my enemy that I shouted down their sorry attempt to reason with me.

Juan was soothing, placatory. "Old friend," he said, "you must come to Mexico City and join us. Don Francisco holds you in the highest esteem. You can guide him along the paths

you want him to follow if you abandon your long and fruit-
less struggle and come with us."

I told him that I would not abandon a revolution that
was barely begun. I said that, as far as I was concerned,
Madero and all who followed him were only a fresh set of
jackals, moving in to take up where the old jackals left off.
I called Juan a coward. I tossed his old self-applied nickname in his face. "Ravachol!" I shouted, brandishing Villarreal's revolver at him. Juan Sarabia cowered, and moved
behind the comfortable bulk of my brother, who stood before me looking both prosperous and lugubrious, already
dressed in the morning coat he would wear as Madero's
Minister of State.

This was my own brother, this respectable Jesús. This
was the man who had spent a year beside me in Belén Prison.
I did not wait for him to speak, but simply pointed at the
door. The two left, silently and (I thought) sorrowfully. Later
that day, I learned, Juan and Jesús called on little Librado
and his wife, who had come west to join him a month earlier.
Juan was furious, and said to Librado, "If you don't cooperate with us, I will do all the evil that is in my hands to do
to you."

The next morning as I sat in my office with Enrique and
Librado, another delegation called: a phalanx of police, bearing
with them a warrant for our arrest, charging us with "conspiring to raise an armed expedition against a potential friend."
We were taken to court, arraigned, and then released on
$2,500 bail — put up, I learned later, by Jesús Flores Ma-
gón. Since I assumed that Jesús had been one of those behind my arrest, I felt no gratitude.

This temporary freedom had nothing of pleasure in it for
me. The Maderistas — those who were my old enemies, and

those who had been my old friends — now began a program
of slander against me that was to have a devastating effect.
Rumors began circulating that I had been motivated by greed
as well as megalomania in my Baja California offensive, and
had pocketed all the money sent to the cause by progressive
groups across the United States. Juan Sarabia wrote an open
letter to me in the *New York Call*, pointing out that Mexico
had no need of either socialism or anarchism. Antonio Villarreal wrote that article I mentioned in my second notebook, calling me a scoundrel and philanderer. Essays appeared
criticizing me for not taking the field personally, for not
maintaining an efficient chain of command, and for allowing
buffoons and adventurers like Dick Ferris to take over the
campaign.

I fought back blindly, clumsily, with mounting disgust
and despair. When Samuel Gompers wrote that he had decided to drop me in favor of Madero, I issued a denunciation
of Gompers's union, the American Federation of Labor.
Mother Jones visited me, and came away convinced I was
too unstable to lead the Liberals any longer. She went around
to the city's various labor unions, making them promise to
give us no more aid. I wrote that she was a well-meaning
old woman who had gone senile. Job Harriman wrote to say
that he could not continue to be my lawyer, or to have anything more to do with me. I wrote to Juan Sarabia, calling
him a Judas, and telling him that if he came near me again
I would kill him. When Eugene Debs wrote that he was
withdrawing support from me because I had hidden my anarchism from the public, professing only socialism, I answered him in *Regeneración*, saying that he was obviously in
the pay of Madero. The attacks came even from Europe,
where Jean Grave, in *Les Temps Nouveaux*, said I was not a

true anarchist, and that the Mexican social revolution existed only in my own mind. Kropotkin himself wrote a rebuttal to Grave, but the damage was done. I was a pariah.

I was bitter, yes, perhaps even a little berserk after all these attacks and betrayals. But, hurt as I was, I was still capable of performing the only worthwhile act to come out of the whole sordid affair. I might be ruined, but I could still write. On August 23, 1911, I published in the magazine a new Manifesto, one which I intended to replace the old one of 1906. In this new version, the content was uncompromisingly anarchist. I urged the campesinos to expropriate the land and the workers to take over the factories and mines and work them themselves. I told Mexicans they must choose between a new governor — a new tyrant, that is — and freedom. I told them to refuse government of any kind, and to fight to the death. Tierra y Libertad was the battle cry thrown at them once again.

And then I went to prison. Once again, with Enrique and Librado, I sat through a farcical trial; but I had lost my capacity to laugh at my misfortunes. The only difference between this trial and the others was that the courtroom was full of Mexicans, working people who still loved us. When the verdict — guilty, of course — was announced, and sentence passed — twenty-three months' imprisonment — a riot broke out in which many were injured, including poor María Talavera de Brousse, who had stayed by my side through all the recent humiliations, and who now was rewarded for her constancy by being beaten and arrested.

María was free and healthy in a matter of weeks. Not so Librado's wife, who died of cancer while we were serving our sentence in the penitentiary on McNeil Island, in the state of Washington. We appealed to the new president, Woodrow Wilson, for a parole so that Librado could attend the funeral in Los Angeles. Wilson agreed, but we had no money for Librado's trainfare, so his wife was buried without mourners. Shortly after this, Enrique's wife Teresa wrote him that she'd had enough, and wanted a divorce.

We were let out of McNeil early, for good behavior, in January 1914. Our colleagues, those who had stayed with us, had kept the magazine going. We returned to Los Angeles and tried to fit ourselves into the goings-on at the new Casa del Obrero Mundial, which had been founded simultaneously in Mexico City and Los Angeles. But we felt old, superannuated. My energy had carried us all for years, but now I was exhausted. I could not meet the looks from the smiling young faces of those we saw each day, speaking so easily about the happy future of the workers.

Madero had died while we were in prison, assassinated by the old Porfirista general Huerta. It was bound to happen one way or another: Madero was too innocent to survive for long. I confess to a certain jealousy that this little man, and not I, should have become the first real martyr of the Revolution.

I moved us all, the original old gang, out to an abandoned farm in Edendale, in the hills east of the city. We brought *Regeneración* with us, but no one much cared to work on it. I told myself we were simply taking a needed rest, that we needed to lie about and listen to the birds and cows and grow our own food, and treat one another with great kindness. But the air of grief lay on us too heavily for us to see any future for ourselves. Librado became our mailman and courier, and Enrique our farmhand and hunter. I became our brooder, good only for sitting on the veranda of the farmhouse and listening to María talk cheerfully of that dead thing, the Revolution.

General Huerta was now the enemy of the old rebels,

who were at war once again. Villa and Obregón were rampaging in the North, heading once more for the Capital. From Edendale, I paid scant attention to any of this. I was a bitter sort of Candide, telling myself to concentrate only on the garden we should have been growing.

But then, in September 1914, a letter came from Antonio Díaz Soto y Gama, that mad young teacher-cum-disciple from my days in San Luis Potosí and Belén at the turn of the century. He had left the capital and gone to Morelos, to the camp of General Emiliano Zapata; and he wrote to say that he had just banished a delegation sent to Zapata by Venustiano Carranza, who was taking up, after Huerta's interregnum, where Madero had left off. This delegation, hoping to enlist Zapata's support, consisted of Juan Sarabia and Antonio Villarreal.

"I called them traitors and counterrevolutionaries, Ricardo," Díaz Soto y Gama wrote. "I told Zapata to purge his camp of such weaklings, and what do you think he did? He went up to Villarreal, grabbed him by the throat, and said, 'You say you are a revolutionary, you hijo de puta? You go back to Carranza and tell him revolutionaries are men, not maricones!' What do you think of *that*, Ricardo?"

I didn't need to think. I scarcely even finished the letter, beyond reading that this Zapata had used my Manifesto as the model for his Plan de Ayala. I splashed some water in my face, found my old black jacket (too tight, as always, across my shoulders), said good-bye to María, told Librado and Enrique to keep things going, grabbed up a few dollars and five hundred copies of *Regeneración*, and was off to Mexico and Emiliano Zapata. And the Revolution.

Notebook 9

November 19, 1922

Be patient. There is only a little more, and it will not, I think, take long to write. I realize just now that I have been hiding from what I must tell you, because it means writing of events I dread to recall (but recall hourly, even four years later), and of thoughts that frighten me badly. I hope they reward your patience, poor old reader. I hope they frighten you, too. I suspect you need a little frightening. Remember that I promised you blood aplenty in this tale? Well, here it comes.

After the meeting with Emiliano and the Zapatistas in Xochimilco (the one around which I have circled throughout these notebooks), and the relatively calm winter and spring of 1915 in Morelos, I could almost say I was a Zapatista myself. I carried a pistol, a great clumsy Colt .44 revolver which I would have been terrified to fire; I wore the white blouse, calzones, and huaraches of a campesino. But my black fedora — I could never keep one of those preposterously floppy sombreros on my great head — and my spectacles, still cracked and now pitted badly from all the sand I had ridden through as we ran from our attackers, marked me as an outsider, one of los que tienen ideas.

From time to time I could argue a little ideology with

Antonio Díaz Soto y Gama or Gildardo Magaña, and listen with something like nostalgia as Soto y Gama continued as feverently anarchistic as ever, hurling Bakunin and Kropotkin at Gildardo who, as always serious and responsible, leaned now toward an almost submissive form of socialism based on the old Indian communism our father had shouted at me, Enrique, and Jesús so long ago in Teotitlán. I seldom intervened in their arguments, though, perhaps because I had come to realize that Soto y Gama was a truer anarchist than I, now; and that my own confused views shared much with Gildardo's. I lived from day to day almost without thinking, as one might behave when newly awakened from dreaming into a daylight that held little promise.

Venustiano Carranza, unwilling to leave us alone, had of course sent Pablo González down into Morelos after us, having proclaimed to all the world that he intended to extirpate Zapata and his bandits once and for all. Emiliano sent almost daily messages of defiance to Carranza; and we watched from our caves, or from the edges of pine forests high in the sierras, as González's troops rode through the state, shooting any campesino who looked as though he might know us (and, of course, everyone in Morelos did know us), rounding up hostages for deportation to the fever-ridden plantations in the Yucatán and Quintana Roo, torching towns and crops, and tearing apart the sugar refineries, so their metal tracks and machines could be hauled back to the Capital for sale. Emiliano had needed those refineries: they gave work to many of his people, and they continued to bring money into the state long after the crops had died and the mines shut down. But González, like almost everyone else in this war, was happy to tear down anything he could to enrich himself; so more people starved, and Mexico's sugar crop died.

Eufemio had been right in what he told me during that

long night's conversation in the winter of 1915: the people of Morelos loved us, and would never betray us; but they were tired of the tribulations that our presence brought them. They wished us well, but they wished us gone.

We fought back, of course. And, because Pablo González was no better general than he'd ever been, we knew that we'd drive him, like Huerta and Robles before him, from Morelos. But it was obvious to all of us by the beginning of 1917 that the rest of Mexico would never leave us alone. Emiliano thought of autonomy, and sent appeals to the United States, England, and even Cuba, asking them to help him secede, to make a separate nation of Morelos — one small piece of land where there could be tierra y libertad, where his agrarian reforms could be carried out, where the elders could lead the pueblos, and the land be owned communally, and all things belong to all. And where Amparo's schools could make it possible for every child and adult to read and write, and learn to value his freedom. And even where the Church, unencumbered by the rapacious curia of Mexico City, could exist in peace, bringing the sacraments to all the workers, not just the rich few who could afford two months' wages for a baptism or marriage.

This was all a pretty vision, of course, and many good men and women had died for it. (And I had rushed down from Edendale to help it along, half believing that in Emiliano Zapata's rebellion lay the last, best hope for the establishment of a pure anarchist state, one created and guided not by governments, but by the laws of nature, as Kropotkin and the others had preached.) But entropy, or something like it, had set in. I watched as Emiliano made his daily rounds through whatever village we happened to be in, his huge dark eyes taking in the torpor that was falling over his people.

He had still never truly lost a battle. González, wiring back news of resounding victories to Carranza, was defeated almost daily, retreating as fast as he could toward the Capital. We had as many horses and weapons as we could use. But Emiliano's men looked at their ruined fields as we rode through them, and the poisoned wells, and the smoking piles of lath and adobe that had been their homes. They were no longer resentful or mutinous; only sad.

Trouble came, of course — and, of course, from the top. The despicable Manuel Palafox fought with Soto y Gama, and accused him of communicating secretly with Carrancistas in the Capital. Soto y Gama denounced Palafox publicly as a thief and a sodomite (which he was, blatantly so). We awoke one morning in January to find Palafox gone, along with most of the silver coins that had been entrusted to him — very nearly all of our small treasury. Within a month he was on González's staff in Puebla, writing lurid denunciations of Emiliano: attacking him for his illiteracy, his poor generalship, his gaudy horsemanship, his tight trousers, his many philanderings, and above all for the way he had enriched himself in his campaigns.

We laughed at these ridiculous defamations, but Emiliano did not. For reasons none of us understood, he had always trusted Palafox, valued his counsel, and kept him close by his side. He would hear nothing ill of Palafox, not even when some of the troops came upon him one evening deep in an arroyo, pants around his ankles, about to mount one of the pack of young boys he kept as his "couriers." The rest of us were overjoyed to see Palafox go. But Emiliano muttered darkly about "treason," and withdrew even further into himself.

One did well to listen to Emiliano when he spoke of treason. He was not, after all, a man of many ideas. But he had a few words that he carried with him almost as talismans. He lived by them — or by the special meaning he gave them — and it was necessary to know precisely what he meant by each word, and what actions his meanings would lead him to.

For Emiliano, traición carried almost its full biblical weight. It was the greatest sin a man could commit, and the word had connotations known only to him. When victories were stolen from him by the machinations of politicians, Emiliano spoke of "those triumphs in which the defeated are those who win"; and the men he had defeated became traitors. The last time Madero broke a promise to him, Emiliano sent him a wire calling him a traitor, and announcing his intention of marching on Chapultepec Castle with 20,000 men, so as to hang him from the highest tree in the forest there. "I can forgive the man who kills or steals," he often said, "because he may do it from need. But I can never forgive the traitor."

Treason was his obsession, in fact. One day in Tlaltizapán, as I was drafting a lesson in political history for Amparo to use in her classes, Emiliano sauntered up to me, and stood before me as he always did, slouching, contemplative, as if only half aware of why he was there.

"Listen, Tío Ricardo," he drawled. "Think of how to put this in your lessons. It's a kind of parable I just made up: A worker from around Anenecuilco had a dog that guarded his ranch. He was a yellow mutt, with long shaggy ears. Whenever this animal heard the coyotes yapping he'd run out to chase them. And when the animal returned, the good man told the cook to throw it some tortillas, because it had earned them protecting the chickens. One time the coyotes came so near that, when the yellow dog ran out to chase them, the man ran after it to see if it caught one. And he discovered, under a huizache tree, the dog and the coyotes eating a hen together, like old friends. The coyotes fled, while the guardian continued eating. The rancher, seeing that the dog was a traitor, took out his machete and cut off the dog's head with one blow.

"That's the way traitors behave, Ricardito, and that is how to deal with them. They may be as familiar to you as that yellow dog was to the rancher, but you must kill them quickly and without remorse. Am I right?"

"I'm sure you are, Emiliano," I replied. "But if it's a man and not a dog, do you give him a trial before killing him?"

"Perhaps as a formality, or if you've known him well for a long time," he answered. "But you still must kill him. Treason cannot be forgiven."

I knew what would happen to the invert Palafox if he ever fell into Emiliano's hands, and I must confess that this knowledge gave me some pleasure.

This business of treason took an ugly turn in May of 1917, when the Zapatista general Lorenzo Vázquez found himself outvoted on some trivial matter by the intellectual officers of our headquarters. He discussed the matter with old Otilio Montaño, who had been Emiliano's teacher and confidant since the early days of the Revolution; and Otilio was sympathetic. Vázquez then tried to start a revolt at Buena Vista, only four kilometers up the road from Anenecuilco. Emiliano ordered an attack and, backed by reinforcements led by Genovevo de la O, stormed the Buena Vista hacienda and put down this first mutiny against him in a matter of hours.

On May 7 Vázquez was hanged for treason, and no one was surprised. But a week later Emiliano walked into the hut we intellectuals used for an office, came up to Otilio, put his hand on his shoulder, and said, "Viejo, you've got to die. You know that, don't you?"

The old man, who thought of Emiliano as his son, stared up into his general's eyes, ready to cry. "I never spoke against you, 'Miliano. I only told Vázquez I thought he had a point. Must I die for that?"

"You acted as a traitor, Otilio my father. You must die."

"A sus órdenes, my general. Will it at least be you who shoots me?"

"I love you, Otilio, but you are a traitor, and hanging is what we do to traitors. As a mark of honor, I will let them shoot you first. But then you must hang." He drew Otilio to him, and the old man wept for a moment on Emiliano's shoulder. That afternoon Emiliano rode off in the direction of Ayala, and did not return until Otilio was shot, hanged, and buried. I suppose he could not bear to stay and see his oldest, most devoted lieutenant put to death. But I was there. I saw the stout old man who had taught Emiliano Zapata almost all he was ever to know about how to fight against oppression forced to his knees, then shot through the base of his skull as he threw out his arms and cried his innocence. And then I saw him hanging from the limb of a cazahuate tree, with a sign on his chest that read, This Is the Fate of Traitors to Their Country. His bandy legs barely twitched as he slowly revolved in the grip of the noose.

You can see that, when Emiliano spoke of treason, we all trembled. And he did so often in the days to come, as we lay idle waiting for González's next offensive. Our brain trust, such as it was, was now reduced to myself, Soto y Gama, and Gildardo — and little Serafín Robles, "Robledo," whose presence almost no one ever noticed, but who was always quietly there to anticipate his jefe's orders. Officers quarreled. Men deserted. Friends fought, drunk, over women they had earlier shared without rancor. We seldom saw Emiliano, but when we did he looked darker, heavier, more given to brooding than he had ever been before. I think now that he was beginning to realize he was ceasing to be Morelos's savior, and was becoming its destroyer; and that this realization weighed heavily on him.

I had my own heavy realization to deal with, too: that I was no bringer of the Peaceable Kingdom to these people. With my ideas, and my capability of setting them in motion, I was a destroyer myself. Were not, then, the three of us — Emiliano, Eufemio, and I — destroyers?

For a time I was able to divert my attention from this grim development. Emiliano had Josefa Espejo, his snub-nosed little wife of six years, with him then, and spent whole weeks with her in her family's home in Ayala. Amparo thus had more time to spend her days with me and her nights with Eufemio.

She, at least, was happy these days, presiding over her escuelas racionales, finding teachers, rounding up the few books that had survived the war in Morelos, getting idle soldiers to help her pile thatched roofs over the open frames of caña brava she called her schoolhouses. She looked like a typical Tehuana at this time: tall, authoritative, even a little imperious. The women, soldaderas and guachas alike, all loved her, and so did most of the men — those who could get their minds around the idea of being bossed around by a woman.

I followed her about like a fat puppy, cavorting shamelessly to catch her attention. (So much for the man who was the Conscience of the Revolution, the mastermind of the war in Baja California, the courageous, prison-defying journalist: I was only a fool, now — passion's plaything, you call it? — and content to be one. When I could catch her resting, or about to set off on a walk to the next village, I would come up beside her, touch her arm diffidently, and ask shyly if I could keep her company.

"Of course, Florecito," she would laugh. "You honor me. What lesson can you give me today? Do I get to hear about the Narodniki some more? Or have we quite done them?" She knew all this history just as well as I did, perhaps better. Perhaps she wanted me to discuss these things a little less pedantically — which, old hack that I was, I could not.

I had never learned how to talk to a beautiful woman. With Emma Goldman and María Talavera, it had always been politics. With whores or guachas, there had been no need to talk. To listen to one's attempts to speak lightly, and know that one is sounding like a bore, is a hard thing, truly. But I had no vocabulary for trees and flowers. I could see how the sun lit the tiny golden hairs on her arms and shoulders. I could mark in my memory for all time the way the tip of her long, straight nose would bob just perceptibly whenever she said "no" or "nada." I could recognize the trick she had of peering quickly at me through the strands of black, straight hair that fell over her forehead when she inclined her head downward, and take delight in knowing that this must have been a trick learned in childhood. I could watch her strong, smooth calf muscles flex as, barefooted, she side-stepped sharp rocks as we walked across the sandy hills behind Anenecuilco. But I could not speak of these things, not to my Amparo. I could only store them in my memory for the long hours in prison that were to come, and to pass on to you now, who doubtless know the language of flirtation well, and are laughing at my painful clumsiness.

No, faint with desire I would breathe in Amparo's smell of sun and sand and warm, moist skin — and tell her how Álvaro Obregón, in Mexico City, had organized the workers into Red Battalions, which he had proposed to send down upon us; and how this was Obregón's canny way of subverting the natural union of agrarian and urban workers. And Amparo would listen, and understand everything I said, and agree with me — and still make me feel like a dunce.

She, in turn, would talk of her childhood down in Tehuantepec, of the heat and fragrance of the selva, and of how strong the women had been, how compliant the men. The society she described for me, wholly free of the disease of machismo, seemed idyllic and impossible. How could there be a single place in Mexico free of the terrible customary barbarism of the brutal male, the cringing woman? Look at Morelos, our putative paradise: here there might be women who fought, perhaps commanded; but even those women cooked the meals of their men, and behaved toward them with that docile acquiescence it would take centuries of education to eradicate.

Once I took Amparo's arm almost roughly as we sat on the rail of a corral outside Ayala, where we were watching Eufemio and three or four of his men breaking a wild pony.

"Isn't any of this important to you, Amparo? Why do you behave as though all of this we're doing is *easy?* Doesn't any of this *worry* you?" I wanted to sound angry, but my words came out only as petulant, the complaint of a spoiled child not getting his way.

Without taking her eyes from the graceful Eufemio, who seemed to be dominating the pony with insolence alone, Amparo murmured in my direction, "Ah, Florecito, none of this is really hard; it's all only inevitable. Carranza does this, 'Miliano does that; everyone fights, somebody dies. It's all just the great dance. You dance when you hear the music, you smile at your partner, and you stop when the dance ends. Though perhaps you keep humming for a little while afterward. The trouble with you is that you haven't heard the music yet. Or you've heard it, like that night long ago in Tepoztlán, when Quetzalcóatl was watching you, and you were so sad. You still don't know about the dance."

Eufemio grinned over at us, his hand on the tether of the bridled, exhausted pony. His jacket and charro's trousers were covered with dust. With his free hand he reached for the flask one of his vaqueros was holding out to him.

"Hey!" he cried. "Cagatintas! You old ink-shitter! Want to ride this one for me while I mess around with that novia of yours?"

"Does *he* know about the dance?" I hissed at Amparo, who was waving amiably enough to Eufemio. "Can you drink, and kill, and behave like a complete sinvergüenza, and still hear the music?"

"Come on over here, Florecito!" called Eufemio. "You can look right up her skirt from where I'm standing!"

Amparo turned her amazing black eyes full on Eufemio for an instant. "Oh, Florecito," she said, "he hears the music louder than any of us. For me it's only a song, but for him it's a mad banging that crashes in his ears day and night. That's why he behaves as he does: to try to drown out the banging for a bit."

Eufemio had turned away from us, busy with his flask.

"Is that why you love him, Amparo? Is that why you go from Emiliano's bed to his?"

"How could I love a man like Eufemio, Florecito?" Amparo smiled sadly at me. "I go because he needs me. I'm all he has of peace. I'm the only woman he doesn't despise. I keep him sane — or something like sane. 'Miliano needs him. He's frightened that he's losing him. I keep Eufemio whole for his brother's sake."

I understood none of this, then or now.

"But you love Emiliano, then?" I asked her.

"Of course I do, Florecito," she replied. "I told you before: it's easy for a woman to love a symbol. And 'Miliano's the best symbol there is: he's the best of the best part of the Revolution. He's the man every man would want to be. Whatever he does, he does better than anyone else. I can't take my eyes off him. Who wouldn't love such a man?"

"And he doesn't mind your sleeping with his brother?"

"He's never said so. In fact, I think he's grateful, a little."

"But you love Emiliano?"

"As I have said."

"And he loves you?"

"Insofar as a symbol can love."

"Madre mía, this is all too much for me, Amparo. Is this the way men are meant to treat women?"

"I don't know, Florecito. Perhaps it's the way women are meant to treat men, no?" She smiled and flicked my earlobe lightly with her fingertip.

"Two more questions then, Amparo, and then I'll go back to the world I know."

"Muy bien, my little anarquista furioso. Two questions only. Let's hear them."

"Does Eufemio love you?"

"Eufemio loves me the way he loves a full bottle or a good horse. That's more than most men love a woman."

"All right, then: do you love Eufemio?"

As she almost never did, Amparo looked straight at me, swinging down from the railing onto the sand of the corral to do so.

"Listen to me, Florecito." She gripped my knees with her strong hands. "What I say now is not poetry, so don't give me that soulful expression you put on when you think that's what you're hearing. I love peace, and harmony, and the little gestures, and the small kindnesses. I love to laugh. I love to see the way you look at me, you sweet, sad man, and I wish the world were such that you and I could love one another and treat one another gently. But my world is bounded on one side by 'Miliano and the other by Eufemio. There is no freedom for me from either of them. You want to talk of love? Here it is: I love them both. I hate them both. In their totally different ways they are the best we have. And they are not enough. Ya basta. Leave me in peace, now."

Amparo turned from me and strode across the corral, in the direction Eufemio had taken. I saw her only once more — in that same corral, a week later.

With Manuel Palafox and Otilio Montaño both gone, now, there were only three of us to talk politics and strategy to Emiliano: myself, Soto y Gama, and Gildardo Magaña. I was still an outsider, perhaps not yet fully trusted. Soto y Gama was sound doctrinally, but unsound in every other way that counted. So the intellectual leadership of the campaign in Morelos fell to the good, sturdy, phlegmatic Gildardo, a man more at home with conciliation than confrontation.

Gildardo knew already what Soto y Gama and I could still not bring ourselves to admit: that our peaceable little realm, our home for the New Millennium, was after all only Morelos, a tiny, green island in the midst of a harsh and brutal land. If Mexico and the rest of the world left us alone (which they would not), then we might just be able to pretend that our little arcadia was real and permanent, that the true anarchist spirit could prevail in this one small corner of the world, at least. But Gildardo had already come to terms with the unhappy fact I had fought all my life not to face: that a world given over to anarchism might or might not be beautiful, but that in either case it was an impossibility. Man did not want it, except in his speeches and manifestos. If it tried to create itself, man would destroy it.

It was all too simple: a world of happy people, just and kind and bold and free (as I've twice described it: remember?), with no government and no army, with all belonging to all — just the land, the people, and freedom. It was all, as Amparo said, a pretty dance — but a dance that could — that always did — become macabre, a cacophonous, maddening clatter in one's ears.

We sat together through the next few nights in Anenecuilco, Soto y Gama and Gildardo and I, and thought of what we could say to Emiliano that would convince him the time had come to cease the struggle. Or at least to try something else, a union with Obregón, perhaps. But none of us dared approach him, and he made no attempt to come near us. Either he was with his wife, or he was riding alone at night in the sierra, perhaps grieving for Otilio Montaño, perhaps making his own plans, for all we knew.

I do know now what Emiliano was doing these days and nights in early June of 1917. He was waiting for his brother to die.

For some months Eufemio had been looking for trouble. Drunk almost constantly, he had threatened with his machete a Zapatista general of almost mystical cruelty, Francisco Pacheco. Out of respect for Emiliano, Pacheco let Eufemio live.

Then Eufemio began writing a series of sarcastic letters to Emiliano, suggesting that he had become afraid of a number of bullies who were enriching themselves at the expense of the Zapata family. Eufemio knew, of course, that it was *his* duty, as the elder brother, to defend the family's honor; but this did not stop him from taunting Emiliano — who paid no attention at all to Eufemio's drunken ranting. Except, that is, to humiliate him by removing him from his position as Chief of Staff of the army.

This left Eufemio with nothing to do but break ponies and drink. In the madness of his inebriation he came to feel it his duty to call a halt to public drunkenness in the towns of Morelos. He took to lurching through the streets of Cuautla and Yautepec, pulling drinkers from cantinas, and beating them with a whip he'd made from a membrillo tree.

A week after Amparo and I had seen him in the corral at Anenecuilco, Eufemio went into a cantina in Cuautla and found an old campesino huddled over the bar. Enraged, Eufemio pulled the old man into the street, beat him senseless, and screamed at him: "Aren't you ashamed, at your age, of drinking till you fall down? *This* ought to cure you of that vice!"

The old man's son was one Colonel Sidronio Camacho, well known as "el loco Sidronio." This Camacho, when he heard what Eufemio had done to his father, tracked Eufemio back to Ayala, walked up to him in the street, and emptied his carbine into Eufemio's belly. Then he tied Eufemio's feet to his saddle and dragged him through the dirt of the road all the way back to Anenecuilco, where he left him at the door of his family's house. Camacho fled north that night, and offered his services to Pablo González.

I was dozing in the hut I shared with Soto y Gama and Gildardo Magaña when the shouting began. I ran out into the rainy street (the others slept on) to see Eufemio — still, incredibly, alive — on his knees in the doorway of his parents' house, trying to get to his feet. Someone, a woman, was helping him, her arms around his shoulders, her face next to his. It was, of course, Amparo.

I ran back into my hut for a lantern. When I came out

the street was empty. I called, but no one answered. For perhaps a quarter of an hour I stumbled over cobblestones and into bushes, putting out the light half a dozen times.

Finally I came to the corral, now a circle of dark sand turned to mud by the rain. At the center of the circle sat Amparo, holding in her crossed legs the head and shoulders of Eufemio. He was staring up at her face. As I came up to them with the lantern I could see that Camacho's bullets and the dragging from Ayala had not left very much of Eufemio's body together. It was not a messy scene: most of the man's blood had poured out during the long ride; and the carbine had done away with his entrails. What Amparo was holding of Eufemio was pretty much all there was of him, except for the improbably long legs that stretched out flat across the sand.

I do not know how long I stood holding the lantern above them. There was nothing to say. Amparo said nothing. She did not look at Eufemio, or at me, but at a point over my shoulder.

I heard a faint noise behind me, that of a boot scraping across the sand. I turned and saw Emiliano, wearing only his trousers and boots, and carrying his Winchester carbine in his hand, its muzzle pointed downward.

He walked past me, and stood over the two for a long moment. Then he bent and took Amparo's arm. He lifted her to her feet, so that Eufemio dropped onto the sand. He lay there, looking up at his brother. I believe he was grinning.

Still holding Amparo by the arm, Emiliano lifted his carbine and pointed it at Eufemio's forehead.

"Adiosito, 'mano mío," he said. And pulled the trigger.

Amparo broke free at this, and ran (the way the pony had run from Eufemio the week before, I thought for some idiotic reason) for the railing of the corral. The lantern light barely reached her as she climbed over the fence where we had sat and talked; and then she was gone in the darkness.

Somewhat to my surprise, Emiliano made the Sign of the Cross over Eufemio; then he turned to me and said, in his slow, grave way: "She loved him, you know. She won't be back. Now we must see to burying him. Get men with shovels. We will bury him here, in this corral."

And that is what we did, that night. And two weeks later Emiliano Zapata ambushed Sidronio Camacho and shot him to death, along with two hundred of the men who had defected with him.

There was no more life for me in Morelos. Emiliano never spoke of Eufemio or Amparo, but it was useless to pretend that things could go on as they had. His men had always revered him, but now they feared him. His normal taciturnity became darker and more crabbed. Perhaps he was thinking that Eufemio had foretold his own death down almost to the very month, and that he had given Emiliano only a little over a year beyond that. But I don't think so; I think Emiliano knew he had to die, and was thinking of how it might best be accomplished. He had to have a hero's death, a symbol's death — a death that was a nondeath, even.

To be sure, there was the business of governance to be taken care of, and Emiliano did not neglect that, sick at heart though he must have been. Pablo González made one more drive into Morelos, and for a change scored some victories. In November he massed his artillery against Cuautla, and took the town. Then he moved on to Jonacatepec, and won again. Next Zacualpan fell. Finally, though, he overextended his lines once again, and had to withdraw back across the Sierra de Chichinautzín.

Our generals commenced fighting one another again, and Emiliano's army began to look more like a loose confederation of bandit gangs. Emiliano must have seen that he could not hope to keep them all together for many more campaigns. By the end of 1918 he was listening to the advice of Gildardo, who wanted him to form an alliance with Álvaro Obregón against Carranza. Even Soto y Gama was for this, and I am sure it would have been a wise move. In any event, Obregón was too shrewd to betray Carranza just now. (Later he would, of course, and have the old goat murdered as he tried to escape to Veracruz like so many tyrants before him.)

Emiliano made one last appeal to Pancho Villa for support, but that old rogue was hiding deep in the mountains of Chihuahua, under serious sentence of death by Carranza and with no army to protect him, and he couldn't even chance a reply to Emiliano.

But by this time I was long gone from Morelos, and back in the United States, where I really belonged. Enrique and Librado Rivera had been begging me for months to come back to Los Angeles and help them keep *Regeneración* from sinking again. "Come away from there," they wrote. "The Revolution is not in Morelos: that is only an obstinate, doomed insurrection. Come back to us, and see where the *real* Revolution is: where it always was, in the hearts of men and women who seek not to free just one little state, but states everywhere. You are not a guerrillero. You are a man of Revolution, a *voice*. Come home to the real struggle."

I wish I could say that it was such exhortations that made me leave, but no. I left because I was hurt, more so than I had ever been in all my years in prison. I wanted to run, as Amparo had run.

I had a driver take me down to Tlaltizapán, where Emiliano had reestablished his headquarters after González's last offensive. I was taken in at once to meet him. He had gained weight in the couple of months that had passed since that night in the corral, and the dark circles under his eyes were darker than ever. But he smiled, rose from his makeshift desk, and embraced me.

"Do you know why we always embrace a friend when we meet him, Tío Ricardo?" he asked. I shook my head.

"Because it's a good way to tell if your friend is carrying a gun or knife." He laughed. We sat, and he offered me a cigar, which I accepted, and a bottle of aguardiente, which I declined. (There were three things I never learned from the Zapata boys: to ride, to shoot, and to drink.)

He gave me one of his long looks. "They say you want to leave. Is this so?"

I nodded.

"They will surely arrest you if you return to the United States, no?"

I shrugged. This seemed more than probable. I was not exactly a fugitive when I left Edendale for Mexico in the fall of 1914; but they had never needed much of an excuse to arrest me, and I didn't suppose they would need one now.

"Look, then," Emiliano said. "You have become valuable to us. I trust you. Since Otilio's unfortunate death" — he frowned for a piece of a second — "I have few advisers who are at the same time men of principle."

"You have Gildardo Magaña, who is very much an hombre de confianza. And you have Antonio Díaz Soto y Gama, whose ideology is identical with mine." This was all mere politeness on my part: I knew I would not stay, even if I were the last sane man in Morelos.

"They are good men, yes," said Emiliano. "Even Soto y Gama, when I can shut him up. But you have forgotten one thing which makes you valuable to me: you are the voice of *Regeneración*. It was you, Flores Magón, who set us all in motion so long ago. We all knew how they silenced you and jailed you, and how you came back time and again to speak out. It was you who gave us our battle cry of Tierra y Libertad. You taught us to say no to everything but complete freedom for the people. Even when we laughed at you down here, we remembered who you were: maybe we were even laughing a little at ourselves at the same time, because we thought we were so big, while a great man like you saw us for the little campesinos that we were. No?"

"No, my general. I came here because I thought that the struggle of the newspapers and the trials and the prisons was going nowhere. I thought that the real class war was winnable down here — or I tried to make myself think so. So I came running down like a vaudeville clown to join the circus, and found myself among real people, all right; and in a real place, realer than any place I'd ever seen. And it was all too much for me."

I was thinking, as I rattled this off to Emiliano, that Eufemio had called it all just an opera, and Amparo had said it was just a dance. But what it all was, was reality; and I'd had enough of it.

"Bueno, I'll make you an offer," Emiliano said. "Have your friends bring your *Regeneración* down here, by way of Cuba if they have to; and you can publish it from Morelos under my full protection, as often as you want, with no interference from me. How's that?"

I shook my head.

"Hijo de la gran puta, tío mío. What the fuck more do you want? Can't you still be the fucking Voice of the Revolution from here? Do you have to have gringos to beat you up before you can write?"

His anger was not in a class with that of Eufemio: I knew he would never be violent with me. So I simply stood up, held out my hand, and said, "A thousand thanks, my general. I have to go back. We martyrs have to go where they want to martyr us, no?"

Emiliano kept my hand, and looked closely at me through our cigar smoke. Then he smiled one more time, dropped my hand, and said, "Right, old compañero. And we have to be there on time too, no?"

He saw me to my auto, handed me aboard it, and took off his black sombrero as we rolled down the hill away from Tlaltizapán. He didn't move as the dust from the car's tires rolled up over him. He looked good: he was still el charro entre charros, el Plateado, the silvery one.

Notebook 10

November 20, 1922

I do not think there will be many more days for me to write these notebooks. For all they think of me here as a hypochondriac, the truth is that my chest hurts, often severely; the cough that has plagued me since my return to the United States grows worse, untreated as it is; and my eyes smart and burn so that writing for even a few minutes is almost more than I can bear.

I have always told you as much of the truth as I could (as much as I could bring myself to face), invisible reader, so perhaps the time has come for a few credos. Perhaps I'll even conclude today with a good act of contrition, just in case. But for now, let me say that I do not believe in the State; that I support the abolition of frontiers; that I fight for the universal brotherhood of man; and that I consider the State as an institution created by capitalism in order to guarantee the exploitation and subjugation of the masses.

There, that's it; that's what I hold to. As though to ratify this statement, H. M. Daugherty, the Attorney General, has just written to my lawyer Weinberger that I should not be freed, regardless of my poor health, because I am still a dangerous man, "because of the seditious and revolutionary doctrines which he asserts and practices, and his determination not to abide by the laws of this country." Never mind that this country is Daugherty's, not mine; and that my own Mexicans are eager to have me back: here is where I am in prison, and here is where I shall stay. Of course, they are all hoping that my illnesses will carry me off before I embarrass my captors further, but I may be taking too long to die. They may have to urge me along. And soon, I think.

What Emiliano Zapata warned me would happen if I returned to the United States did happen, and quickly. Worn out by the events in Morelos, hurt and confused by the flight of Amparo (I shall always see those long legs swinging over the corral fence and racing into the darkness beyond the reach of my lantern), I was almost too ill to greet Enrique and Librado when they met me at the depot in San Diego, and drove me back to our farm east of Los Angeles. To poor María Talavera, who had heard no word from me during all my months in Mexico, I had nothing to say.

Regeneración still existed. There was nothing for me to do but write. Enrique had printed two articles some months before, attacking the Texas Rangers for their mistreatment of Mexican migrant workers, and signed my name as well as his to these. No one has ever attacked these bravos with impunity, and we were no exception. Two weeks after my return, an automobile full of men followed us back to Edendale from the Los Angeles Post Office. Before we could call out a warning to the other members of the commune, they jumped us, and beat us both senseless. They roughed up the women, destroyed what little furniture we had accumulated, looked around for Librado (who was hiding in the woods behind the house), and then tossed me and Enrique into their auto and took us to jail.

At the trial, which took place a week later, I had to be carried to the courtroom on a stretcher. Enrique had to speak for us both. In spite of this, the judge refused to allow him to read a defense statement, saying that it was a "political document." Because of my health, I was sentenced to only a twelve-month term, and fined $1,000; but Enrique got three years, and a fine of $3,000. Serving of the sentence was delayed until my health improved.

I was so ill that the judge almost begged for someone to put up bail for me. He wanted only $3,000, which I took to be almost an insult. But the money came, and with it a note, which a bailiff brought to me in the prisoners' ward of the local hospital. It read: "Bless you, Speedy-Boy. You're the bravest of us all." And it was signed by Emma Goldman and Sasha Berkman. I never knew where the note or the money came from, nor how they knew of my latest plight; but it was a wonderful gesture, and it gave me the first lift out of my despair after Morelos.

Throughout the remainder of 1918 I attempted to recuperate, but improvement was slow. I spoke at rallies in Los Angeles, often supported by Enrique, and having to pause frequently to rest my throat. When my friends asked for something lively for *Regeneración*, I gave them one last essay, which I called "Carranza se Despoja de la Piel de Oveja," Carranza Takes Off His Sheep's Clothing. When first inaugurated, this pompous ass had proclaimed himself the friend of the workers, and had actually allowed labor unions to form. But as soon as one of them, the Electrical Workers, tried to strike for higher wages, Carranza shut down the union and arrested its members. Then he revived an 1862 law dealing with public disorder, according to which he could threaten striking workers with the death penalty. Finally, he disbanded the "Red Battalions," which he had allowed Obregón to organize to fight against the Zapatistas.

I took Carranza to task for all this in my article, but

saved some of my scorn for the Red Battalions, for being the dupes of the capitalists, for failing to realize that their allegiance lay not with the bosses, but with the campesinos in Morelos. I said that, in part because of their failure to join Zapata's struggle, the Revolution had degenerated into a mere political rebellion of the lowest kind.

Well, Carranza had been recognized by the United States by the time I wrote my last essay, and this was, after all, wartime for you gringos, and so I had attacked not just another Mexican scoundrel but a valuable ally of America. This was bad enough, but we concluded the issue with a "Manifesto to the Anarchists of the World and the Workers in General," in which we incited the people to rebel against the oppressors and launch the Final War, the Social Revolution, that would end for all time "a criminal and rotten society."

You will not be surprised to learn that our bail was revoked immediately, and that Librado was pulled into jail with Enrique and me. Enrique was sent straight to Leavenworth, but Librado and I were tried anew, this time for violation of the espionage laws. We were, it seems, abetting the enemies of the United States in the Great War. For me, no me daba la puta gana — which doesn't translate well. Let's just say, I couldn't have given less of a shit.

On August 25, 1918, Librado and I were sentenced to fifteen and twenty-one years respectively. During the trial, which was held in camera for fear of rioting by the hundreds of supporters who filled the streets around the courthouse, the judge told the jury that our activity had been a constant violation of the law, of all the laws. We had, he said, "violated the law of God and the law of man." On Wednesday, April 9, 1919, we were taken by train once again to the penitentiary on McNeil Island in the state of Washington.

On Thursday, April 10, Emiliano Zapata was assassinated at the hacienda of Chinameca, nineteen kilometers south of the village of Anenecuilco, in the state of Morelos. The American newspapers went wild with joy that this unspeakable bandit, this modern Attila, had finally been put to death. But there was only silence in the penitentiary, where there were many prisoners, both Mexican and American, who knew what they had lost.

In early 1919, because McNeil Island was too damp and drafty for one of my weak constitution, I was sent to Leavenworth Prison. Librado followed me nine months later; and there you find us today.

I will not bore you with more accounts of my appeals, or of how we passed our days before they removed Librado from my cell, presumably so that we two dangerous men could not plot the overthrow of the United States. The days passed; they pass now, with three letters a week my warders allow to my lawyers and the tender ladies who shower me from New York and Boston with their encouragements, their cough lozenges, their embroidered handkerchiefs.

The guards take from me after I have read them the letters that arrive from Mexico, because we are not supposed to receive any communication not written in English. A letter came in early 1920 from Antonio Díaz Soto y Gama, telling me of Emiliano's death. If I still had it, I might quote from it for you. But perhaps it is better this way, for Soto y Gama always took one thousand words to say what needed only a hundred. (He was a good madrina de guerra to me, a good soldier's correspondent; but he was always an enemy of brevity.)

Emiliano's death was quick and uncomplicated, and I can myself write it far more quickly for you than Soto y Gama could. Here it is. If my manner is a little dry, reflect that I write this over three years after the event. And I have so many deaths to remember, here; what is one more?

Venustiano Carranza knew that Emiliano had sent word to Carranza's chief general, Álvaro Obregón, that they ought to join forces. Carranza could not permit this to happen, for such an alliance would exclude him, and mean the end of his authority in Mexico. Obregón was too powerful to touch; therefore Zapata had to be got rid of, immediately.

The hapless Pablo González was still Carranza's commander in Morelos, with his headquarters in Cuautla. Carranza sent an addition to González's staff: a Colonel Jesús María Guajardo, a vain young chulo with upswept mustaches and a reputation for ruthlessness. This Guajardo was to pretend to pick a fight with González, and then to sulk about, allowing rumors to spread that he was thinking seriously of defecting to the Zapatistas.

These rumors quickly reached Emiliano in Tlaltizapán, and he fell for them. He wrote to Guajardo, offering a commission in his army; and Guajardo of course wrote back to accept — and to offer to bring along with him a troop of Federal cavalry, with plenty of munitions and weapons. To convince Emiliano of his sincerity, he staged an "attack" on Jonacatepec. The Carrancista commander there had been warned by both González and Guajardo what to expect. The result was a quick and bloodless raid on Jonacatepec. Three days later, in case there were still any doubts in Emiliano's mind about this new ally, Guajardo executed fifty-nine Zapatistas who had defected from the Liberator Army of the South, and who were hoping for preferred treatment from Carranza's people. Emiliano was convinced that in Guajardo he had a new friend; and arrangements were made for Guajardo to offer a fiesta to his new commander on April 10 at the hacienda of Chinameca, where Guajardo and his cavalry troop had fled after their supposed desertion from the Carrancistas.

Emiliano spent the night of April 9 in Tepalcingo. He had with him a troop of only two hundred men, really nothing more than a guard of honor. According to Soto y Gama's letter to me, a "woman" came to Emiliano's tent that night to warn him of the treachery, and spent the night with the general. ("*What* woman?" I wanted to ask him. What, in the name of God, was her name? But names and faces were never very important to Soto y Gama, and I'll never know if it was she.)

Emiliano rose at dawn, and Serafín Robles helped him dress in his white collarless shirt, black waistcoat, frayed black jacket, and charro's trousers with silver coins stitched down the outside seams. He mounted his new stallion, a sturdy and spirited sorrel, and waited as his men kicked sand over their breakfast fires, saddled their own mounts, and formed up behind him. He seemed quite cheerful, not at all the sour and silent man he had been for the past few months. There were those who attempted to tell him that this could be a trap; that it was too soon to trust someone like Guajardo. Feliciano Palacios, his aide, reminded him of the caution that had served him so well for so many years of combat. Emiliano only laughed.

"They told me that he rode," Soto y Gama wrote me, "like a man who had made his mind up about something, and was happy with his decision."

It was of course to Chinameca that the boy Emiliano had brought bricks on his mules; and it was Chinameca that had been the scene of his first attack against the Porfiristas in 1911. I do not suppose the significance of these facts was

lost on Emiliano, who was as superstitious as any other campesino in Mexico. This was a kind of homecoming for him.

When he arrived at the broad gates of the hacienda,
Guajardo's men threw them open for him; and Emiliano and
ten companions entered to greet their host. Guajardo's troops
were lined up at attention around the central patio. As Emiliano raised his sombrero to Guajardo, a bugle sounded three
notes. On the third note Guajardo's men raised their rifles
and fired at Emiliano and his men. Emiliano swung his horse
around, stood in his stirrups, flung his arms out from his
body, and fell to the ground, dead.

His attackers continued to fire for several seconds, so
that his body, crouched in the sand of the patio, knees drawn
up under his chest, jerked from the force of the impact. Finally, the firing stopped, and the body fell over. The Zapatistas outside the gate were fired upon by the remainder of
Guajardo's soldiers, who had been hiding on the roof of the
hacienda. They had to retreat, leaving their chief to Guajardo's mercies.

Guajardo tossed the body across the rump of a horse,
tied it down as though it were a slaughtered pig, and carried
it to Cuautla, where it was thrown upon the floor of the
Municipal Palace. González turned the body over to see the
face, and was satisfied that this was in truth Emiliano Zapata. He notified Carranza in Mexico City, who promoted
Guajardo on the spot and sent him an award of 50,000 pesos.

The people of Morelos poured into Cuautla by the thousands to view the body, which by the next day was dressed
in a gray charro's outfit and laid in an open wooden coffin.
Emiliano's face was badly swollen, but his campesinos recognized him by the mole under his right eye, and by the tiny
crescent scar over the left. There were more than a few, of

course, who denied that this body was that of Emiliano Zapata. This could not be their 'Miliano, for who could ever
kill him? This had to be someone else's cadaver: the real
'Miliano was off in the sierras somewhere, playing a trick on
everyone, gathering another bunch of the boys around him,
preparing to swoop down yet again on his enemies.

But the body was genuine enough, Soto y Gama assured
me. The rest of his letter was concerned with what could be
done now in Morelos. Gildardo Magaña was in charge, and
the Zapatista generals were still holding their columns together; but Gildardo was a bargainer, a conciliator, not a
warrior, and it was clear that some sort of peace would have
to be made with Carranza — at least until Obregón should
emerge from his chief's shadow and begin really to govern
the country.

Soto y Gama closed his letter by pledging to remain an
anarchist and continue to work for the dissolution of the State.
But as I write you today (today? It is already almost dark
in my cell, and there is not much more time for writing),
Gildardo governs Morelos as a good Liberal, and the zealot
Antonio Díaz Soto y Gama is a senator in the Chamber of
Deputies. Now that Carranza has himself been assassinated
by Obregón, there is some sort of peace in Mexico.

Enrique, released months ago from Leavenworth, has been
deported to Mexico. There is some little estrangement between us, about which I can say little, since we do not com-
municate. Yesterday I was allowed to take my lunch in the
mess hall with the less dangerous prisoners, and there was a
brief moment when Librado and I passed in the hall. He
whispered, "Take cheer, Ricardito. María is well, as are the
others. Many work for our freedom. Have hope."

But as I sit here now, I think of what Theodore Roosevelt said in 1908: "The anarchist is the enemy of humanity,

the enemy of all mankind." And I think that this is what the world believes of us, and Librado is wrong: there is no need to have hope.

I think also of what, in braver times, I wrote to a friend: "We know that we are destined to absorb a dagger in our flesh or to die of consumption in some prison. We accept our destiny with pleasure, satisfied with having accomplished something on behalf of the slaves."

I know what my destiny is; I know damn well what it is. But do I accept it with pleasure? Well, I can accept the inevitability of it, just as Eufemio Zapata knew he would die, and just as Emiliano Zapata knew he would die. If I think of the two of them, now, and of the manner of their living and dying, I can almost see a place for myself between them.

Eufemio was no anarchist. He gave no thought to throwing over government so that freedom could grow in its place. He appeared to relish life, but I believe that he feared and hated it, because all he saw around him, beneath all the shouting and killing and drinking and whoring, was oblivion, blackness. If he was anything at all, Eufemio was that most pitiful of creatures, a nihilist.

And Emiliano? He was no anarchist, either, although for a long time he looked awfully good to those of us who were — or thought we were. He was the purest of us all. His ideas were simple, his methods of pursuing them direct and open. He wanted one thing only: freedom and land for his people — the people of Morelos, of Anenecuilco. And he fought for this one thing, until it became clear to him that his sort of revolution would do better without him. All his people required of him, finally, was to become a martyr. And so he became one, happily so, at Chinameca. Eufemio and Emiliano Zapata: two suicides.

And between them, Amparo, moving from one to the other.

You know by now that you cannot trust me on the subject of women; but I will tell you anyway that she loved them both, and that she did so out of pity. All right, let us also suppose that she lusted after Eufemio, and rejoiced in what you, gringo, might call his carnality and I, his brutality. And let us suppose as well that she loved Emiliano as a woman indulges a little boy, one who is being brave, doing good. And maybe she felt a little proud to be the woman of the great Emiliano Zapata. Or maybe, just maybe, she did not much distinguish between them, or saw them as incompletely separated parts of a whole. Who knows what the hell women think about men, or to what lengths women will go to get themselves into trouble about men?

And what of that place for myself that I mentioned a moment ago? I have sometimes presented myself to you as a buffoon, but you have surely not failed to notice that Ricardo Flores Magón is also a man much burdened with the sin of Pride. I know as I sit here on this sagging cot in my darkening cell that my life has been as full of rage and passion as that of Eufemio. And that I am just as much a martyr, a martyr conscious of his martyrdom, as Emiliano. Eufemio never had any belief; Emiliano had his simple belief, and never lost it. I had my belief, once, and dedicated my life to it. Once the belief was gone, dissipated by too many arrests, beatings, trials, imprisonments, defeats, and betrayals, I still clung to one little hope: that by attaching myself to that warrior chieftain from Morelos, I could absorb some of his faith, and thereby rekindle my own.

But I was wrong. My original faith, that given me by my father, had really been fatally weakened by books, by theories, by abstractions. It was a beautiful faith, theoretical anarchism, lovely and romantic and idealistic. But it could not hope to stand up against reality, the world of men and things. Challenged, it became either timid or cruel.

Placing myself in Morelos, between Eufemio and Emiliano, I could only be torn apart. I learned that ideas are no match for reality. Or that there are many ideas, some of them having nothing to do with the betterment of Man.

I have enough light and enough vision — my bad eyes, you know — to give you only two more thoughts.

The first of these has been with me ever since the days of my bawdy Spanish mentor, Florencio Bazora, whose favorite dicho was the old business from the Golden Age: *La Vida es Sueño*, Life Is a Dream. If I think of this, then all of us, Eufemio and Emiliano and I, swirl away in a cloud of smoke, or in an evanescent dance, the one of which Amparo spoke. And, since we're being mystical here at the end of things, why can I not think of her as something ineffably Mexican, something about which she tried to tell me, but which I was too deracinated to hear? (But which both Eufemio and Emiliano could hear, in their different ways.) So we're all fantasmas, ghosts that exist only on the flimsy pages of these notebooks; and you needn't take us all that seriously, poor tired reader.

And the last thought? That Life is no Dream at all, but real, and palpable, and terrible — and terribly funny, in the sense in which old Posada's calaveras were funny. There is nothing realer than the body of Eufemio as I saw it, or the body of Emiliano as described to me. Amparo is a beautiful woman who comes to me almost nightly in my dreams, lightly stroking me, exciting me, soothing me. Seen and felt thus, she is a fantasma. But she also lay beneath two brothers, and rode with them, and took part in the Revolution, and ran one night away from the horror of what had happened to one of her lovers. And perhaps it was she who appeared in Emiliano's tent that night outside Chinameca, to try to prevent another horror. But fantasmas do not serve in the real world.

This last thought is what tells me that I am Ricardo Flores Magón, and that is all: these are my knees on which I place these, my hands. My buttocks rest upon my mattress. My head, with its thick crop of dark hair, leans against the concrete wall of my cell. High on the wall to my left is a small, barred window, which lets almost no light down on me, now. The right hand, on the right knee, holds a pen and from time to time makes a mark — this mark — on the small pad of paper my guards have given me. My feet are quite numb; but I know that if I stamp one of them on the floor of my cell there will be a noise, and perhaps the guard will come to bring me my supper. All this is real. I have no illusions.

But that's tonight. Maybe tomorrow morning I shall have more for you, escapades and scandals and sorrows and farces. There's always another notebook.

Afterword

Ricardo Flores Magón was discovered dead in his cell at Leavenworth Prison early on the morning of November 22, 1922. According to Warden Biddle and Doctor Yohe, the prison physician, his death occurred at approximately 5:00 A.M., and was caused by cardiac arrest. The prisoner Librado Rivera, known to be a friend of Flores Magón, was brought to view the body, and was asked to write a telegram to be sent to any friends and relatives of the deceased. Librado saw that Flores Magón's head was "black down to his neck," and that "there were what seemed to be bruises around his neck that must have been made by strangling." Flores Magón's head, as he lay on a stretcher, was twisted backward in so violent a posture that Rivera was sure his friend had been murdered in his sleep. At first he declined to write the telegram as it had been dictated to him. But, under threat himself, he eventually complied, and the world learned that "Ricardo died this morning from a heart attack."

When the news reached Mexico City, the Presidium of the Chamber of Deputies was draped in black to signify its mourning; the members of the Chamber passed a resolution offering homage to "the great Mexican revolutionary Ricardo Flores Magón, martyr and apostle of libertarian ideas";

and Deputy Antonio Díaz Soto y Gama delivered a long and impassioned eulogy to the martyr. The Chamber then voted to have the remains returned to Mexico, at the expense of the government.

This his comrades refused. Instead, the workers of the Confederation of Railway Societies insisted on bringing Flores Magón home. In early 1923 the long trip commenced, with dozens of stops along the way. At each of these the funeral train was met by thousands of workers carrying red and black flags, crying out to the man they called "La Voz de la Revolución." In Mexico City 10,000 workers followed the coffin past the Palacio Nacional to the Panteón Francés, where it lay in state for twenty-four hours before being placed in a mausoleum.

In 1944 Ricardo Flores Magón's body was exhumed and reburied in the Rotunda de los Hombres Ilustres, where it lies not far from the remains of Emiliano Zapata and Francisco "Pancho" Villa.